ALMOST FLYING

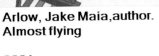

ALMOST FLYING

Jake Maia Arlow

Dial Books for Young Readers

DIAL BOOKS FOR YOUNG READERS
An imprint of Penguin Random House LLC, New York

First published in the United States of America by Dial Books for Young Readers,
an imprint of Penguin Random House LLC, 2021

Copyright © 2021 by Jake Arlow

Visit us online at penguinrandomhouse.com.

Library of Congress Control Number: 2021936275

Book manufactured in Canada

ISBN 9780593112939

10 9 8 7 6 5 4 3 2 1

FRE

Design by Cerise Steel
Text set in Agmena

To Jina, my squirrel.
If our friendship survived middle school,
it can survive anything.

CHAPTER ONE

MY heart starts thumping before the video even loads. And then it pounds even harder as Mega Drop Unhinged ("If You Don't Puke, We're Not Doing Our Job!") comes into view. I can't believe I haven't watched a POV video for this roller coaster before.

The opening shot is a sweeping look at the whole ride. It's taller than every other coaster in the park by a mile, its steel track stretching up into the sky. Human beings shouldn't be able to hurtle through its giant loops and twists and (mega) drops and come out unharmed.

But somehow, we can. And somehow, it's the most amazing thing in the world.

Well, okay, fine. I don't actually know how amazing it is in real life. The truth is, I've never been on a roller coaster. But I've watched pretty much every roller coaster point of view video in existence, and that has to count for something.

So, there's that opening shot of the ride, and then the

perspective switches so that it's like I'm sitting in the front row of the roller coaster. That's what the camera position's like in all POV videos. There's excited chatter behind me, which dies down as a voice crackles over the loudspeaker. "Keep your arms and legs inside the coaster at all times." The ride groans, releasing a burst of air. "Now, sit back, relax, and try not to think about that Mega Drop!"

The roller coaster rumbles and creaks, and we start climbing. I keep my head as close to the screen as possible, so it's almost like I'm actually on the ride. In the video, it's a cloudless day and the way we're tilted back makes it feel like we're just going to keep riding up into the sky forever.

But then we get to the top. There are a few seconds where I can't see the track in front of me and I can't see anything below me and it's just blue going on and on and on and there's no horizon and maybe no one else in the whole universe.

I want to stay here, in this moment before the drop, a little while longer. So I pause the video.

It really does feel like I'm in another world when I'm watching roller coaster POVs. It's a world where the sky is always blue and cloudless. Where you're safely flung through the air on a set track with a group of happily screaming riders sitting right behind you.

Most of all, it's like another world because of the whole never-been-on-a-roller-coaster thing.

I know that's super weird, that I watch these videos when I've never been on one. I first found POVs when I was trying to convince my dad to take me to an amusement park, but that was like a year ago and we still haven't gone. I thought I could use the videos when I presented the idea to him, but I never even made it that far.

I felt guilty about wanting to ask him to take me somewhere so expensive, and somewhere where he couldn't just hop on his computer and send a spreadsheet over to his boss if he needed to, because he always needs to.

I don't want to sound like I'm not happy watching POVs, though. Like, they're the best.

But that doesn't matter. Because this'll finally be the summer where I ride an *actual* roller coaster. I know my dad's saved up a bit of money since last year, and I just need to convince him that it's worth it, even if it is expensive.

And now it's crunch time: There are only three weeks left of the whole summer. Three weeks to make this happen.

I just need a good plan.

The problem is, I'm completely terrible at coming up with ideas. Abby was the one who always came up with our schemes, so this is new for me. And if Abby hadn't ditched me, I bet I'd already have been to, like, every amusement park in the country.

And there it is again.

That feeling I get when I think about Abby. It's how I imagine I'd feel if I was riding a roller coaster with a drop that went on forever: close to puking, too weighed down by gravity to move. Miserable.

I take a deep breath and press the space bar on my dad's laptop to start the video back up, which immediately makes me feel a thousand times better. The person holding the camera angles it down so you can see the drop, and my heart is pounding because it feels like *I'm* about to drop.

In the distance, there's this parking lot with all these tiny cars and trees. But the coaster is so high up that it's barely visible. It's like the only things that exist are the roller coaster and the sky.

Suddenly the train can't hold still any longer and we're zooming down the track and I can almost feel my stomach flip and then the camera is upside down and the person filming is screaming and the sound of the wind is so loud and I know I should lower the volume but I don't because you can't lower the volume in real life. And I hear something that sounds like knocking at a door, but I figure it must just be the car rattling on the turquoise tracks so I keep twisting my body along with the video—left and right and left and right and—

"DALIA!"

Oh.

I pull out my earbuds and slam the computer shut.

"Can I come in?" my dad asks.

"Uh, one sec!"

I grab the nearest book and open it to a random page so that when he comes in, it'll look like I was reading.

I don't even really know why I hide the videos from him. It's the only thing in my whole life that my dad doesn't know about. We're close like that. Which makes sense, because all we have is each other.

We spend a ton of time together, so sometimes it's tough to hide the POVs from him. We even have a shared weekly schedule. Like on Sundays, we'll ride our bikes down to the bay and spend the mornings there, and if it's low tide we'll look for horseshoe crabs. They're usually dead, which is kind of sad, but my dad does this thing where he'll pick them up by their tail and pretend they're talking to me. He'll make them say things like "Helloooo Dalia, would you like to play?" in a creepy voice that makes me laugh so hard.

They're super weird looking, the horseshoe crabs, with a hard brown shell on top and ten wriggly legs underneath. My dad likes to tell me about how they've been the same for millions of years, since before dinosaurs even existed. It's pretty amazing that they figured out their *thing* and now they don't need to change, ever. They're always, always gonna look the same—like weird giant shells with eyes and a spikey tail. I like that about them.

So anyway, I'm sitting on my bed pretending to read, and I try to make it look like I'm concentrating really hard. "Come in," I tell my dad. I nod at the book a little bit, like my dad does when he reads the newspaper. I'm going for *Ooh, look how interesting and sophisticated I am,* but it must just look like I'm a bobblehead, because when my dad comes in he asks, "What's wrong?"

"Nothing."

"You're reading? In the summer?" He clutches his chest like he's about to faint. "Who are you and what have you done with my daughter?" I laugh a little and roll my eyes. "Well, I don't want to stop you from reading about . . ." He examines the front of my book. "*1001 Tax Breaks and Deductions*?"

And there goes my cover. I guess I should've checked to see which book I grabbed before I let my dad come in. But that's just the sort of stuff that happens when your bedroom is also your dad's office.

When we first moved into this apartment over a year ago, he told me we could decorate the room however I wanted. He even got me a sparkly blue pillow that kind of looks like the ocean on a sunny day, to try to convince me that it would be okay that we were moving out of the only home I've ever known. As if to say "Who needs two parents living in the same house when you have a sparkly blue pillow?!" I told him that I was too old for a sparkly pillow, but it's secretly my favorite thing in the room.

My bed is an island in a sea of boring dad business. We never got around to decorating the rest of it.

So, he's looking at me, waiting for an answer as to why I'm reading his tax book.

I tell him, "It's never too early to start thinking about taxes." That's something he's told me before, so I hope it'll work now that I'm basically just repeating it back to him. "And I'm a teen now, so I'm gonna need to know these things."

"You're thirteen, Dalia. Why don't I worry about the taxes?" He walks over to my bed and sticks out his hand. I give him the book.

"Were you just looking for a book, or . . ." I trail off. I want to get back to watching my POV videos.

"Oh, right, right. I knew there was a reason I came in here." He sits on the edge of my bed, looking nervous, which is weird. "Want to get bagels?"

Why is he nervous about getting bagels? Is there some sort of bagel shortage?

Before I say yes, I have to ask the most important question when it comes to getting bagels with my dad: "Where?" There are like a gazillon bagel stores in our town, but there's only one good one. I'm kind of a bagel connoisseur, so I keep track of these things.

"I was thinking . . ." He rubs his hand on his chin, like this is a huge decision. But we both know what he's going to say. "Bagel Boys?"

Ding ding ding! That's the right answer. I mean, it makes sense. My dad's passed everything he knows about bagels down to me. And he knows *a lot* about bagels. Partly because we're Polish Jews, so our people basically invented them, and partly because we live on Long Island, which is like the bagel capital of the world.

So obviously I tell him I'm in, because how can you not be in when there's Bagel Boys involved? Plus, maybe this is the opening I've been waiting for to finally ask him to take me to an amusement park.

There's no harm in asking. I just have to do it.

We ride our bikes to the shop, and my dad locks them up on the bike rack outside while I order our usual (an untoasted fresh-out-of-the-oven sesame bagel with cream cheese for me and a toasted everything bagel with butter for dad).

"You got it," Tony says. Tony works every Sunday morning, so he pretty much knows our order by heart. He even gets us coffee without me having to ask.

"Now, don't go bouncing off the walls on account of me," he says with a wink. It's a little inside joke that Tony and I have, because he only ever gives me decaf.

Bagel Boys is always crowded on Sundays, but the table my dad and I like to sit at is empty. It's tucked into a back corner, squeezed between a window and a mural. The mural's of a giant sesame bagel that has eyes and a face eating a faceless poppy-seed bagel and giving a thumbs-up. My dad likes to comment on it every time we sit here.

"Does the bagel know he's eating himself?"

"Daaad." I say it like it's two different words, but I can't help smiling. He's so predictable.

Once we're settled, I immediately press the outside of the bagel to my face.

"Bagel facial?" he asks.

"Of course."

I know it's weird, but when a bagel is fresh out of the oven it feels like a warm hug on my face. My dad discovered it one morning and decided to call it a bagel facial, because when you put it on your cheek it makes your skin feel all steamy and fresh. And now I like to give myself a bagel facial whenever we come to Bagel Boys early enough for fresh bagels.

I split my bagel into four quarters and take a big bite of the quarter that has the least cream cheese on it. I always save the most cream-cheesy part for last.

"Hey, so, I've been meaning to talk to you about something." My dad lifts the lid off his coffee, blows on it, and takes a sip.

Of course my dad chooses the moment right after I take a huge bite of my bagel to tell me that he's been "meaning to talk." I swallow and then ask, "What is it?"

My heart starts pounding. My dad's never "meaning to talk," because "meaning to talk" is code for something's wrong. The last time my dad was "meaning to talk" he told me that he and my mom were getting divorced. He was crying when he told me, which was scary and horrible. It was only the second time I'd ever seen him cry. (The first was back when I was in third grade when my mom left for three weeks without telling us where she was going.)

When my dad told me that he and my mom were getting divorced and she was moving to New Jersey, it didn't surprise me. Not really. My mom may have only moved out about a year ago, but she was mostly gone before then, leaving me and my dad alone for days at a time. And even when she *was* home she would just sleep on the pull-out couch in the basement and watch old DVDs all day.

But it was still awful.

And now I definitely can't ask him to take me to an amusement park. Because whatever he's about to say is probably gonna be scary and horrible and there will be no room in my brain for roller coasters or fun ever again.

I know it's bad, but my brain always gets super focused on the worst possible thing that could happen. And since I know my parents can't be getting divorced *again*, I think that it has to be something worse. Like, not even "I lost my job" worse. More like "There's a mob boss looking for me and I gambled away my life savings" worse.

See, I told you. My brain makes everything seem ten times worse than it actually is. It's probably not even that bad.

My dad puts his coffee down. "I have a girlfriend."

CHAPTER TWO

OR maybe it really is That Bad.

I'm sure I misheard him, so I ask, "What?"

"I have, you know, a girlfriend."

"A what?" I can't be hearing this right. Dads don't have girlfriends.

I really want to ask him what the heck he's saying, but I can't seem to form words. Maybe it's all the cream cheese stuck to the roof of my mouth.

"A girlfriend, Dalia," he says. "A girlfriend. A woman I'm dating. In a romantic way."

"Oh." I swallow. It's definitely not the cream cheese.

This is bad. This is really, really bad.

"How do you feel about this?"

"Fine," I mumble, because what else am I supposed to say?

"Are you sure?"

No. "Yeah."

He lets out a big breath and rubs his palms together, then

takes a bite of his bagel. Of course he can still eat, he didn't just find out that *his* dad has a girlfriend. Meanwhile, I can't even look at my bagel. And at this point I'm really regretting agreeing to go to Bagel Boys. Why couldn't he have told me at a bad bagel store? You don't tell your daughter about your new girlfriend at the good bagel store. I'm sorry, but you just don't.

This is way worse than finding out about the divorce, because at least I saw that one coming.

My mom leaving felt logical. There were signs. This, on the other hand, my dad having a girlfriend, feels completely wrong. I mean, I never even saw my mom and dad kiss. The only thing I ever really saw them do was fight.

I must be quiet for a pretty long time, because he asks me what I'm thinking.

I want to tell him that I'm thinking that he shouldn't be allowed to have a girlfriend. That he's a dad, and more importantly he's *my* dad, and dads don't have girlfriends.

I want to tell him that I'm thinking that he and mom only got divorced a year ago. One year's not even close to enough time, even if things weren't great for a while before then. I want to tell him that maybe he should put this off for a year or five or ten.

That's what I *want* to tell him.

But I don't. Because if I tell him all that it'll just make him upset. And even though I'm upset he just told me he has a girlfriend, I still don't want to stress him out.

And I *can't* stress him out, because he's the only family I have. But apparently I'm not the only one he has.

Because he has a *girlfriend*.

He takes a few more sips of coffee, then opens his mouth like he's about to say something. And then he stops. And then he takes another sip of coffee. And then he opens his mouth again. And then he stops again.

He probably wants me to chime in, but I don't say anything.

After a minute, he says, "We've been dating for about six months now, and I think you two would get along really well."

Pause.

Rewind.

Six months?

He's been dating someone for six months and he didn't even tell me until *now*?

And, okay, I always wondered what my dad does when I'm at school or swim practice or wherever. I thought he was just doing his work, but I guess he's been sneaking around, going on dates. Maybe he's even brought her to Bagel Boys.

The thought makes me push my bagel away.

My dad folds the last quarter of his bagel in half, then eats it in one bite. Usually when he does this, he makes a really silly face, like he's a monster and the bagel is an unsuspecting victim. It always makes me laugh. But this time it just looks like he's in pain. And I'm sure I don't look any better.

He chews for a long time. "I'd really love for you to meet her."

My heart falls into my stomach. I feel like the riders of Mega Drop Unhinged after they get back into the station: like I just got spun upside down at sixty miles per hour.

First my dad tells me he has a girlfriend. Then he tells me they've been dating for six months. And now he wants me to *meet* her.

My brain hurts.

I just sit here, not eating my bagel, not saying anything. My dad's watching me, and I know he's waiting for a response.

I can't say no. First of all, it would make my dad mad, and second of all, I'm going to have to meet her eventually.

That's the worst part—I don't actually have any control over what happens. It's like when Great Adventure closed Rolling Thunder, which was this amazing dueling wooden roller coaster. It had two tracks and the trains would race over huge, bumpy hills. The ride opened in 1979, and according to all the YouTube comments and stuff it was basically everyone's favorite.

Then they decided to shut it down in 2013 to make room for a line for another ride. I mean, come on. You don't shut down a classic to make room for a *line*. And obviously everyone was super mad about the ride closing, but it still closed.

That's sort of like what's happening now. I'm mad that my dad wants me to meet his girlfriend, but I'm going to have to meet her anyway. He's not looking for my input—the coaster's closing. I'm going to meet her because they've been dating for six months, because my parents got divorced, because sometimes life is a dueling roller coaster and you're on the losing train.

"Can I tell you about her?" he asks. He sounds hesitant but also really excited. And his eyes are all mushy. It's gross.

This can't be happening. This. Can't. Be. Happening.

"Sure," I say, looking down at my bagel. The word comes out of my mouth before I can ask my brain politely to please say *no*.

But unfortunately, my brain and I aren't always on the best of terms.

He looks so relieved that I almost feel okay for a second.

I try to tell myself that whatever he says, it doesn't matter. He could be talking about a made-up person, really. Someone from a story who I'll never have to meet.

"She's a high school chemistry teacher," he says, "and she loves everything bagels, just like me. We bonded over that, actually." He chuckles, like this is the most romantic thing in the entire world.

Somehow, it's the worst thing he could say. I don't want

to know that she loves everything bagels. I don't want to know anything about her.

I nod, and he must think that means I want to hear more about his girlfriend, which it definitely does not. It's just all I can force myself to do right now.

So then he says, "All right, what else can I tell you about her?" He rubs his chin. "Well, she was born in Colombia, and she grew up in Minnesota. But she's been living in New York since college."

My ears perk up a little at the Minnesota thing, because that's where my new swim-team friend Rani's from, and she's really cool. Before this moment, I was pretty sure everyone from Minnesota was fun and nice and maybe a good swimmer, but now that I know that my dad's *girlfriend* is from there, I think Rani's probably cool *despite* being from Minnesota.

"So, would you be up for meeting her?" Before I can say anything, my dad clears his throat. "Um, actually, I should probably mention that when you meet her you might also meet—no, uh, maybe that's not the best idea." I look up at him, but I don't ask what that was all about, because I know if it has anything to do with this situation, I'm not gonna like the answer. "So, would you want to meet her?"

I would not. "Um, I guess."

"Great," my dad says. "That's great. I'll let Vanessa know."

Vanessa. Of course she has a cool name like Vanessa. Why can't she have a silly old-fashioned name like Fannie? Fannie would be the perfect name for Dad's new girlfriend. But no, her name's Vanessa.

And now that I know her name, there's no going back.

CHAPTER THREE

"**HAPPY** Monday," Coach Leah says. "Let's get started with ten laps of freestyle."

Cue the groans.

It's the second to last week of swim practice, but Leah's still being ridiculously hard on us.

"Well, now it's twelve laps."

Groans times two.

I pretend like I'm mad about having to do twelve laps for warm-up, but after the whole dad-having-a-girlfriend debacle on Sunday, I'm ready to hop into the water and start swimming. Maybe it'll help clear my brain.

Everyone's standing by the side of the pool with their arms wrapped around themselves. I dip my goggles in the water, suction them to my face, and sit so my calves are submerged, the jagged concrete digging into the back of my thighs.

But before I can work up the nerve to slide in, there's a *splash*, and I'm soaked.

I scramble backward onto the pool deck and throw my arms over my face. "Hey!"

The splasher jumps up from under the water and drags a long finger over the surface. "Is it just me, or is there less pee in here than usual today?"

I giggle, and look up at Leah, who rolls her eyes. But she doesn't say anything, because the splasher—Rani—is the best swimmer on the team by a mile. So she can pretty much get away with anything.

And now that Rani's in the pool, I have to get in too. It's not that I want to impress her, but, like, I guess I kind of do.

Plus, maybe the freezing cold water will knock some of the thoughts about my dad having a girlfriend out of my brain.

I hate that it came completely out of nowhere. My dad isn't the having-a-girlfriend type. He can't be. The only people he ever talks to are me and his coworkers, and, like, people from synagogue. But I know all those people, and he'd never date any of them. Whenever we go to services on High Holidays and stuff, we always laugh about how crotchety everyone is, and how sometimes people even leave the service early so they can get to the rec room and grab the best bagels before everyone else.

My dad will lean over to me and whisper, "There go the Greenfields," or whoever's shuffling out of the service, and I'll have to stifle my laughter so that Rabbi Miriam doesn't give me a funny look.

I just can't imagine that version of my dad—the one who gossips with me at synagogue—having a girlfriend. I can't imagine *any* version of my dad having a girlfriend.

I shimmy myself into the water, and it's so freezing that for a moment it's all I can think about. No thoughts about my dad. No thoughts at all, really. I lift my arms above the surface to keep the cold away from my armpits. I never like to just dive right under, not like Rani. She's way braver than me.

"If you're not in the water in the next ten seconds, it's gonna be twenty laps," Leah says to the kids on the pool deck.

Most of them jump in when she says that. Leah's kind of mean, but she's a pretty good coach. Well, okay, she's the only coach they could find us, so it's not like we had a choice. She's just a lifeguard at the pool.

No real swim coaches wanted to come to our run-down public pool, where the lanes aren't even regulation length and we have to get out every ten minutes because some little kid pooped in the shallow end.

Maybe I'm making it sound worse than it is.

It really isn't that bad, because I have Rani here with me. We're the two oldest people on the team—we're both thirteen, and everyone else is like eight or nine or something.

I met Rani at swim practice at the beginning of the summer, back when I thought I would never have a friend again after what happened with Abby.

And I had sort of accepted that. The never-having-a-friend-again thing. I figured, you know, who needs a friend if they're just going to leave you behind? I definitely didn't need someone who decided she was too cool for swim team, just because she hangs out with Cassie and actually needs a bra now.

Abby and I met on the first day of first grade. We used to go home from school every day to my house and play Puppies.

Puppies is exactly what it sounds like: We were both, well, puppies, and we had to get adopted. She was an Old English sheepdog, and I was a Great Dane/dachshund mix, because it seemed like an unlikely combo. And I always like things that seem a bit unlikely.

We would never tell anyone about the game, especially when we got to middle school, but even then, it was always the best part of my day. We were still playing Puppies when Cassie and her friends started going to dance class.

But then Abby started talking about maybe wanting to do dance too. And she stopped wanting to play Puppies. She just wanted to talk about Cassie, and how Cassie does dance and Cassie has boy-girl parties and *Oh, did you hear who Cassie kissed?* Cassie this and Cassie that.

Then, one day in April, Abby showed up to school in these really short jean shorts, and I honestly couldn't believe it. Only popular girls like Cassie wear The Shorts. Once Abby started dressing like them, it wasn't long before she was part of their friend group.

Abby told me the day before swim team started that she wasn't going to be doing it this summer, probably because she needed more time to hang out with her new boyfriend, and with Cassie.

The whole thing makes me feel like I'm still a little kid. Like somehow she grew up, she's a real teenager, and I'm just stuck. I don't have boobs, I still wanna play Puppies, I watch videos where I pretend to go on roller coasters. Maybe she was right to ditch me. Maybe hanging out with me now would be more like being a babysitter than a best friend.

After Abby told me that she wasn't doing swim team, I didn't want to do it either, but my dad was like, "What else are you going to do this summer?" And I'll admit that he had a point. Because the answer was nothing. Without Abby I thought I would be doing absolutely nothing this summer.

Until Rani came along. It was one of the first days of swim practice for the summer, and I had a lane completely to myself after Abby ditched me. Rani showed up halfway through practice and jumped right into the water, no hesitation (of course).

"Hi!" she said.

"This is Rania," Leah had told me after a minute of me having no idea what to say to this new girl who was around my age and brave enough to jump right into the pool. "She's joining us all the way from Montana."

"Minnesota, actually," the girl said. "And you can call me Rani. So, what's your name?"

"Oh, right," I said quickly. "Um, it's Dalia." And then I added, "Both of our names end with 'uh,' so it sounds like we're confused. Dali-uhhhhh. Rani-uhhhhh."

I knew it was silly the moment I said it, but to my relief she giggled and said, "True. Maybe that's why I go by Rani."

And since then I haven't been alone in my lane.

I hold my breath and duck under the water, then pop up like Rani did. The little kids are slowly but surely making their way into the pool.

Now that I'm used to the temperature, my brain's yelling at me again. And it's saying something I don't expect: *Tell Rani about your dad's girlfriend.*

I have to admit, I *do* want to tell someone about the situation. Like, I might explode if I don't talk about it. Rani and I don't usually talk about serious stuff, but then again, now that I don't have Abby, there's really no one else I *can* tell.

So, while Leah is distracted I say to Rani, "Something kind of weird happened yesterday."

"Weird how?"

"Let's get a move on, people, chop chop!" Leah shouts.

Rani rolls her eyes at Leah and smiles at me.

Even though the water is cold, my face gets hot.

"Tell me when we get to the other end of the pool so Leah can't hear."

And with that, she's off.

Rani's wearing a black two-piece sports bathing suit, like the ones Olympic swimmers wear when they're training. If I wore something like that I'd look like a little kid in a Halloween costume, but on her it seems like the most natural thing in the world.

From where I'm standing by the wall, I can watch her swim from above. She's long and fast, and this might sound weird, but her legs look like fish legs. I know that fish don't have legs, but if they *did*, they'd look like hers. It's like she was made to be in the water. And her shoulders are wide and muscle-y, and she has maybe the world's longest fingers.

Not that I'm staring. It's just that you notice things about a person when you share a lane with them.

I let Rani get a bit ahead of me, then I kick off the concrete wall and glide underwater. Even though it's freezing, it's the best feeling. Once I actually get myself all the way underwater, I always wonder why I was hesitant to do it in the first place. I love the way the water flows over every part of my body, over my hair, my neck, even the tiny space between my nails and the tips of my fingers

I glide for as long as I can hold my breath. Then I angle my head up to the surface, and start swimming freestyle. I'm not as fast as Rani, but my stride is long. I can cross the pool in ten strokes. Seriously. My arms are, like, weirdly long. Honestly, my whole body is weirdly long, so I guess my arms just match.

The thing is, swimming is when I do most of my good thinking, so it's super unfair that the only thing I can think about is the whole dad-having-a-girlfriend situation. There are plenty of other things I could be thinking about, like my summer amusement park plan, or POV videos, or literally anything else.

Rani's waiting for me at the far end of the pool, and when I get there I put my goggles up on my forehead and tell her, "So, okay . . . my dad has a girlfriend."

"A what?" Rani asks.

"That's literally what I said!"

Leah blows her whistle from the other side of the pool. "PICK UP THE PACE," she yells over to us.

"WE'RE THE ONES SETTING THE PACE," Rani yells back, and I laugh.

"Let's talk again when we're back at this wall," Rani says, and takes off.

I follow her, watching her feet flutter and make a storm of bubbles underwater. I'm glad she wants to talk about it, that she doesn't think it's super weird for my dad to have a girlfriend.

Maybe it's only super weird to me, because I know my dad. I know him better than anyone else on the planet.

Well, actually, I guess I don't.

"So, what are you gonna do?" Rani asks when we've gone two lengths of the pool and we're back at the far wall.

Leah blows her whistle and Rani rolls her eyes. But neither of us moves.

I take off my goggles, float on my back, and stare into the bright morning sky. "I have no idea."

CHAPTER FOUR

WE'RE in the locker room after practice, and Rani's putting a T-shirt and shorts on over her swimsuit. I feel a little silly because I always come to practice in just my suit, like the little kids on the team.

This is the only time during practice that I get to talk to Rani completely alone, which is really nice. All the little kids just walk out to the parking lot in their bathing suits, without a towel over their legs or anything. I don't remember ever feeling that comfortable.

I turn and face the wall even though I'm just wrapping my towel over my suit.

"You know how some people are afraid there are sharks in the pool?" Rani asks out of nowhere.

I turn around, and she's combing leave-in conditioner through her hair like she does after every practice. I rarely see it outside of her swim cap, but her hair is thick and black and shiny and goes right past her shoulder blades. I wish my hair looked more like Rani's, but instead it's a tangled bushy mess.

"Wait, what?" I ask, laughing.

"Yeah, they think they sneak in through the drains or something."

We're both laughing now as we head out of the locker room together. I always make sure to time what I'm doing to take just as long as what Rani's doing, so we can talk a little while longer after practice.

"Do *you* think there are sharks in the pool?"

"Well, duh," she says, looking over at me, "but they only come out at night."

"Great, now I'm scared of night sharks," I say as I sit down on the sidewalk to wait for our parents to pick us up.

"If I ever start a band, I'm gonna call it Night Sharks," Rani says, and I grin at the pavement. Rani doesn't sit down, though. Instead she looms over me and says, "I actually wanted to ask you something."

I stop grinning, but just as my brain's about to go into panic mode about what it could be, she says, "I just thought I'd ask if you maybe wanted to come to my house?" She pulls out her phone and tosses it back and forth between her hands. "My dad's at work and my mom made a new friend and she's over at her house, and it's still kind of a new place, so I don't really wanna go back there alone." I don't respond for a second, and she says, "Only if you want to, of course."

"Yes, definitely," I say, too quickly. "I mean . . . sure, sounds good. I just gotta check with my dad."

So far, Rani and I have just been swim-team friends. Like, we snap each other sometimes, and text a little, but only about practice and stuff like that. Not that swim team friends aren't real friends, but we just haven't taken it to the next friendship level. And going over to her house is definitely the next level.

I can't mess this up.

I pull out my phone and send my dad a quick text, and he responds right away, which almost never happens.

> Me: can i go over to my swim friend's house?

> Dad: Of course, Dals. Just txt when you need a pickup.

That's not the answer I'm expecting. He doesn't even ask me if her parents will be there or where she lives or what her name is. I probably could've texted "I'm running away to Siberia" and he'd just be like, "Sounds good, don't forget your winter coat!"

"My dad says it's okay," I tell Rani.

"Awesome, we can walk from here. My house is pretty close."

"Cool, is it in Madison Heights?"

Madison Heights is the area of town where I live, though our apartment is in the part that's kind of far from the pool. It's mostly shared houses, not like the other part of town, Hillcrest, which is filled with huge estates and mansions. That's where Cassie and all the other popular people live.

As a general rule, if you're mega rich, then you live in Hillcrest. And if you're *that* rich, you're popular. That's just how things are.

"Um, I think it's in Hillcrest, actually."

My heart drops. I try to tell myself it's fine. That it doesn't matter where Rani lives. That she'll be different from Cassie and the other popular people. I mean, she's definitely different.

So I smile and say, "Lead the way."

"We should never leave," Rani says, jumping on top of the mountain of pillows we just made in the secret room we found inside of her closet.

Yup, that's right.

As it turns out, Rani lives in a *mansion*. With secret rooms hidden behind trapdoors.

So, Rani's sitting on Pillow Mountain with her eyes closed, and my brain is almost short-circuiting because now it's basically confirmed that if Cassie and her friends found out that Rani lived somewhere with secret closet rooms, they'd definitely want to be her friend, and if they definitely wanted to be her friend, then Rani definitely wouldn't want to be *my* friend.

But before I can think about that too much, Rani says, "You wanna watch something? I can run and grab my computer."

"Sure," I say, feeling relieved.

She crawls out of the closet room and comes back a minute later with a shiny silver laptop, then sits back down on Pillow Mountain.

"Come over here." She pats the pillow next to her and I slide over, leaving a ton of space between us and not quite leaning back. "What do you wanna watch?" She opens up the computer and goes to YouTube. Most of her suggested videos are costume makeup tutorials.

I look over at her. "You like makeup?"

Hanging out with Rani outside of swim practice is kind of terrifying, but it's also amazing because I can ask her questions like this and it won't seem completely random. When you're in the pool you can't just be like, "So what's your favorite fruit?" because that's never going to come up in conversation. But now that we're at her house—mansion—there's so much more to talk about.

"No, my mom doesn't even let me wear any. She says I'm too young. But I love watching other people do their makeup, especially when it's a look I've never seen before. It's super relaxing." She laughs. "It's kind of embarrassing. That I'm not even allowed to wear makeup but I watch other people doing theirs."

"That's not embarrassing at all," I tell her. "I watch these videos where people go on roller coasters and film the ride so that you can see what it's like."

Oh no. *Brain, why did you say that?* I would never have told her about POV videos at swim practice. It's too embarrassing. Or maybe too secret. Or maybe both.

I'm about to crawl out of the closet room and run back to my dad's apartment or maybe move to a shack in the woods when she says, "That's so cool, I love roller coasters. Let's watch one."

"Really?"

"Yeah, it sounds like fun. I haven't been to an amusement park in so long."

Ugh. Obviously she's been to an amusement park. No one who's as cool as her hasn't been to one.

She passes the computer over to me. "Pull up one of the videos! Plus, after we watch it, I'll make you watch a makeup tutorial."

"Um, all right," I say quickly. I think for a second before I type anything into the search bar.

And then I have it. The perfect roller coaster POV video.

"Boulder Dash?" she asks, shifting so she can see the screen.

"Yeah, it's the best," I say, starting to feel the pre–roller coaster—or roller coaster POV—jitters. "It's this wooden roller coaster that goes through the side of a mountain and into a forest."

"Whoa."

"And it's really bumpy and fast and it's like . . ." I try to think of a word. "I don't even know. It's just the best. And the video is really smooth, like it's not shaky at all."

"Have you ever been on it? On Boulder Dash?"

"Um, well, no," I say, "but I really want to." I don't add that I've never been on any roller coaster, ever.

"All right, let's do this," Rani says. She moves to sit next to me in a certain way so that the computer's resting on our legs. Which are touching. My whole body tenses up because I don't know if she meant for our legs to touch or not.

I don't usually like sitting that close to other people, but the way she's looking at me like we're really about to go on a roller coaster makes it feel less weird.

I press the space bar, and for the first time ever, I'm not entirely focused on the video. I sneak glances at Rani, who has her face up super close to the screen, which is a good sign because that's exactly what I do when I want to feel like I'm actually on the roller coaster.

So, the volume is all the way up and the wheels are clanking over the track, the wood rumbling and creaking. We're on this steep angle, where all you can see are tall trees lining the whole track, because the ride's, like, in the woods. The train climbs up the slope, and my heart thumps along with each mechanical *click, click, click.*

And with the video on full screen and both of us close to the computer it's really like we're there, and I can tell Rani's totally into it because her face is as close as it can possibly get to the laptop, and her skin's glowing green from the trees. And in that moment, I feel really protective over her.

I know, it sounds weird. But I guess I'm just imagining what it would be like to be with Rani on an actual roller coaster, to be able to tell her about how big the drop is and how many miles per hour it goes and to hold her hand through the whole situation.

Not, like, literally.

Just to tell her about it. To show her how it's done, to help her feel brave.

I turn back to the video.

The roller coaster reaches the top of its climb, and it's about to drop and I can tell Rani's really excited. Her leg is bouncing and I get that feeling in my stomach, the one I think she's feeling too, where it's almost like you're the one who's about to fall off the edge of the world, even though it's just a video.

So the coaster drops and the people on the ride are screaming and then Rani starts screaming too, and she looks over at me and bumps my shoulder until suddenly I'm screaming right along with Rani and the video people. And then she puts her hands up, so I put my hands up too and we're both shouting and pretending to twist and turn along with the roller coaster and my heart is beating weirdly fast.

"THIS IS AWESOME!" Rani shouts as the roller coaster

passes over a bunch of quick bumps that make the person filming fly up in their seat.

And then we're almost at the part where they take the ride picture, so I tell her, "That's the part where they take the ride picture."

Rani pauses the video and says, "Then we need to take our own ride picture." She pulls out her phone. "Put your hands up so it looks like we're on the roller coaster."

I do, and we both open our mouths really wide, like we're screaming.

Then she unpauses the video.

The end of the ride comes too quickly. The roller coaster slows down, and then it stops in the covered station house. I want the video to go on forever.

"Let's get a snack," Rani says, bouncing up from where we're sitting. "Are you hungry?"

I reach for the part of my leg that was just touching hers. It's cold now.

"Sure," I say, my heart still pounding.

I try to tell it to stop, that the ride's over. But for some reason I'm super jittery, like it hasn't even started.

I sit there in a daze for another moment, but Rani's already crawling out of the secret hideout, so I follow her.

We head down to the kitchen, which takes like five minutes because Rani makes a wrong turn. That's how big her house is. I try not to gawk at the beautiful golden-framed portraits and domed ceilings. But when I look over at Rani, she seems to be gawking too. So I gawk away. I guess the mansion's new for both of us.

When we get to the kitchen we eat lavashak, which Rani tells me is Persian fruit leather, and it tastes super good and we have a ton of it. Then she pulls up a makeup tutorial on her phone and we watch it while we peel and chew the sticky plum-flavored snack.

In the video, a girl tells us how to get a lizard-inspired look. It sounds weird, but it's actually pretty cool. She uses a ripped piece of fishnet stockings for the scales, and she really does look like a lizard by the end of it.

When the video's done, Rani puts her phone facedown on the marble counter.

"What if I showed up with lizard makeup on the first day of school?"

"Oh, you totally should," I tell her, playing along. "And wear all green."

"I'll camouflage perfectly."

I laugh a little too loudly, imagining Rani with bulging eyes and her tongue sticking out, a lizard at Madison Middle. Abby would be too embarrassed to even joke about wearing something like that to school. It wouldn't be Cassie-approved.

But Rani's not Abby.

We're both quiet for a minute after that, and I'm not

really sure what to say now that there's no video playing and no lavashak left to shove in my mouth. But then I think of something. "How come you moved from Minneapolis?" I've been wondering about this for a while, but now that I'm at her house it feels okay to ask.

"My dad got a job at the hospital in town," Rani says.

And, okay, I have to admit that what I really wanted to know when I asked that question was how her family can afford this house, but my dad always says it's impolite to ask about other people's finances, so I just say, "Cool."

"Yeah, it's whatever." She opens the fridge and looks inside for a second but closes it without getting anything. "Did you know that your dad was starting to date people?"

It takes me a second to realize she's talking about my dad's girlfriend situation, and to remember that I told her about it in the first place. For some reason, I don't actually mind that she brought it up. "No," I say. "He kept it a secret, I guess."

"My dad can't keep a secret at all," Rani says. "One time he told my mom about her surprise birthday party because he was too excited about it."

"Was your mom mad?"

"No, she hates surprises, so it actually worked out really well." Rani uses her arms to hoist herself up onto the marble countertop, and she wraps her long fingers around the edge. "I'm much better than my dad at keeping secrets, though."

"Oh yeah?"

"Yeah, I'm practically like a secret agent."

"I'll keep that in mind." She smiles at me and I look down at my lap. "My dad wants me to meet his . . . yeah."

She doesn't respond for a second, like she's thinking hard. "Do you think *she's* a secret agent? I mean, she's managed to hide from you for, like, six months, right?"

"No, she's a chemistry teacher."

"That's pretty cool, though."

"Not as cool as being a secret agent."

"Well, not everyone can be *that* cool."

We smile really big at each other. The fact that I'll have to meet my dad's girlfriend feels far away. It's like the only thing in the world right now is talking to Rani.

But that feeling is ruined by a text from my dad.

Dad: Do you need a ride home yet?

I tell him sure, because I feel kind of bad that I've been gone for so long. Even if he does have a girlfriend now who could probably keep him company whenever he wants.

"I think my dad's gonna pick me up in a few minutes," I say.

"Already?" Rani asks, frowning. "But I'm having funnnnnnnnn." She turns the last word into a whine, which makes me feel kind of nice because I can tell she really means it.

"Me too," I say quickly. I don't want her to think I'm

leaving because I'm not having fun. "I'm having so much fun." Maybe that was overkill. "I mean, I just need to get back to my dad's apartment."

"Oh, I get it," she says. "If my parents weren't out of the house right now they would totally want me to be hanging out with them." She opens the fridge and pours herself some water. "But I'm glad you came over today."

She smiles at me and I smile back and if I was feeling awkward at all before, I'm definitely not now. Because it's official: Rani's more than just a swim-team friend. She's a *friend* friend. Maybe even a best friend.

But I know that's not quite right, either. Because things feel completely different with Rani than they did with Abby. Not bad, just different. And that might be really nice.

CHAPTER FIVE

COACH Leah's making us swim twenty laps for warm-up today. One of the little kids literally burst out crying when she told us, but Rani and I are in the zone. I think we've done ten laps so far, but who knows. The only thing I'm keeping track of are my arm's long strokes. One, two, three, then a breath. One, two, three, then a breath. Over and over again.

This is probably going to sound terrible, but as my arms cut through the water, I'm thinking about how I'm happy Abby didn't do swim team this summer. Because if she had, it might've just been me hanging out with Abby, following her around, swimming and goofing off in our own little best friend bubble. I might never have gotten the chance to really meet Rani. And now I don't have to share her with anyone.

Maybe that's weird.

But it's amazing to hang out with Rani at swim practice because when I'm talking to her I don't have to think about anything else if I don't want to.

Like, for example, I don't have to think about how I'm going to be meeting my dad's girlfriend tonight.

Yup.

Tonight.

I've been dreading this day since my dad told me about . . . *her* . . . in Bagel Boys on Sunday. It's been in the back of my brain for the past three days, since I've been distracted by trying to salvage my going-to-an-amusement-park plan. But when I woke up this morning it was at the very front, screaming, "PAY ATTENTION TO ME, DON'T THINK ABOUT ANYTHING ELSE! MEETING DAD'S GIRLFRIEND ALERT!"

But I *refuse* to think about my dad's girlfriend right now. Because I'm at swim practice. I'm with Rani.

Things are fine, *brain.*

Plus, Leah's finally letting me and Rani race each other. The little kids are always begging us to race, since Rani's, like, super fast, and I'm her closest competition (but only because I'm taller and older than everyone else).

Racing Rani is pointless, because I always lose. But I love trying to catch up. I push my arms to cut through the water like propellers, and my chest hurts when I'm done, but it's the good kind of hurt, where I feel unstoppable.

"So close," Rani says when I touch the wall way after she's already finished. She's leaning against the side of the pool, elbows out of the water and a huge grin on her face.

And there's another amazing thing about swim practice now: It means there's a possibility that I'll get to spend more time with Rani afterward. Like, going over to her house wasn't just a one-time thing. I went over yesterday too, and we hung out in her secret closet and her mom brought us sliced fruit and it was amazing.

But the thing is, today I *really* need to make sure we hang out. I can't be alone with my thoughts, because my thoughts are just going to be chanting the words "Dad's girlfriend! Dad's girlfriend!" over and over.

But asking her if we can hang out feels kind of weird. The other two times we hung out after practice, Rani asked. Now *I'm* going to have to make it happen. I can't just wait for her to suggest it.

"Hey, so . . ." I scuff one of my flip-flops on the sidewalk by the pool parking lot.

"Yeah?"

"Can we, like, hang out today or whatever?" I hold my breath and don't look up.

"Obviously," Rani says, and I meet her eye and instantly feel better. "But actually, can we go over to your house? My mom's having some people over and she always makes me talk to them for like an hour."

Uh . . .

Okay, so, here's the thing. I thought maybe we'd just always hang out at Rani's place.

"Well, it's not really a house, it's more of an apartment," I say, stalling a bit. I want to hang out with Rani so badly, but my whole body tenses up thinking about her seeing my bedroom that's mostly an office.

"Okay, let's hang out at your apartment, then!"

And the way Rani's smiling at me makes me think she really *wants* to come over, so I have no choice but to say "Sounds good."

And that's when my dad ruins any good feelings I might've been having.

This is what happens: He picks us up from the pool and he's all like, "Hi, Abby!"

When he says Abby's name instead of Rani's, my head literally hurts from embarrassment. I feel like I just rode the Mind Eraser, which is apparently the most painful roller coaster in the whole country. Your head bangs against the back of the seat over and over again. That might be better than this.

Even after he apologizes for saying the wrong name— "Rani, Abby, lots of *E*'s, don't you think?" (I get my terrible sense of humor from my dad)—I still feel weird. Because Rani *isn't* Abby. I've only had one real friend my whole life, one friend who knew everything about me. And I don't have her anymore.

Now that we're walking up to my apartment, I hate the way it looks through Rani's eyes. I want to make excuses, like, *The apartment's barely my home, really. I mean, I lived in a* house *most of my life up until now.*

But I don't, because this is where I live, and there's a part of me that *does* want Rani to see it.

"We're going to *my* room," I tell my dad as we walk through the door. I try to send him a signal with my eyes to not say anything about how it's also his office.

I don't think he gets the message (our telepathy's been off lately), but he just says, "Okay, girls, have fun."

I feel better when we get to my room, though, because Rani hops onto my bed and pats the space next to her like it's her room and I'm just visiting. She fits in so naturally, and I like that.

We pass our phones back and forth, picking makeup tutorials and roller coaster POVs for each other to watch. We even try to match the makeup looks to roller coasters, which is super fun.

"We should do, like, a roller coaster makeup tutorial," Rani says after she shows me a video where someone turns themselves into a phoenix with flaming red feathers, and I show her the POV for a coaster called Firebird that has like a thousand red-and-yellow loops.

"I thought your mom doesn't let you do makeup."

"She does on Halloween," Rani says. "Last year I was a zombie mermaid." She scrolls back through her phone and shows me a picture.

"You did that?" It looks amazing. I mean, it's super gross—there's blood dripping down her face and lifelike scales made to look like they're peeling off and decaying—but amazing.

Rani seems sort of embarrassed, but she smiles as she looks down at her phone. "Well, I watched a tutorial, but yeah."

"It's incredible."

She smiles, and we're both quiet for a minute.

In the silence, my brain starts wandering, which is never a good thing because it always wanders down a dark, scary hallway, even when I try to stop it. Right now, it's wandering off to thoughts about how I'm meeting my *dad's girlfriend* later.

The good feeling I usually have when I'm hanging out with Rani goes away, and my stomach flips inside out.

Rani reaches out and taps one of my shins where it crosses over the other and I almost jump out of my skin. "You okay?"

I take a deep breath, but my whole body's shaking like I just rode the Hydro Racer (a mixed log flume/roller coaster—it's *so* cool) in the dead of winter.

"So, remember how I was saying that I have to meet my dad's girlfriend?" She nods. "That's supposed to be happening, like, tonight."

Her eyes go wide. "Are you nervous? I didn't think you were gonna meet her so soon."

I almost laugh. "Same. And yeah, like, super nervous." It comes out all shaky. "I don't think I can do it."

I expect Rani to change the subject or not say anything, but instead she asks, "How come?"

I want to say *Because she's my DAD'S GIRLFRIEND.* But then I really think about it for a moment. "I guess because she's this person who my dad's been spending, like, a ton of time with for the past six months, and he *hid* her from me." I say the next part quietly because my dad's just in the other room. "I thought my dad and I were super close."

Rani smiles at me like she's letting me in on a huge secret. "But now you have someone who you're spending way more time with too."

My heart starts thumping. I'm pretty sure I know what she means, but I still ask, "Who?"

She laughs. "Me, of course. So it's almost like you and your dad are even."

I want to tell her that it doesn't count because she's not my girlfriend, but that would be so weird, so instead I just groan and say, "I can't meet her. I literally feel sick."

"Just tell your dad that!"

"That I'm sick?"

"Yeah, tell him you feel bad. Because he can't make you go if you're not feeling well, right?"

I laugh a little, but then it's right back to worrying. "But wouldn't I be lying? If I told him I was sick?"

"I mean, if you *feel* sick, isn't that pretty much the same thing?"

I don't say anything. What it *feels* like is a lie. But then I think about how my dad has a girlfriend he didn't tell me about for six months and I shiver a little, the way I do before a race. I want to try this, to try getting out of meeting Vanessa.

"Maybe it is," I tell Rani. "I mean, it can't hurt to try."

"You totally should," she says. "And then you can report back."

My stomach flips again, but this time it's not in a bad way. Rani wants me to report back, like I'm a spy in her secret agent agency and she's sending me on a mission.

I nod. "Sounds like a plan."

Later that afternoon, once Rani's been gone for a while, I knock on my bedroom door, which is sort of weird because it's *my* bedroom. But I don't wanna just storm in on my dad while he's doing his tax things or whatever. Sometimes he works from the table in the living room, but if he has to use his desktop, then I need to clear out of my room.

"Yeah, Dals?"

I open the door just a bit. The excitement from before has worn off, and now I'm nervous about what I'm going to do on top of being nervous about meeting my dad's girl-friend. But I think about what Rani said, that she wanted me to report back.

I open the door the rest of the way.

"Um, I don't feel so good," I say, hugging my stomach and trying to contort my face into the most miserable version of itself.

It's not that hard.

My dad gets up from his spinny chair and puts the back of his hand on my forehead. "You don't feel hot." He moves his hand and tucks a piece of hair behind my ear. "What's wrong, hon?"

"I don't know," I say, making my voice sound small. "I feel like I'm gonna throw up or something."

"Well, why don't you lie down? I'll get out of your way." He picks up his laptop from the desk. "You need to feel better for Vanessa!"

My heart drops. "I don't think I feel good enough to meet her today."

"I think you'll be fine," my dad says, dropping the gentle tone.

"I'm *really* not feeling well." I climb into bed, more desperate than I was a minute ago. This has to work. And even though I feel horrible about not being completely honest with my dad, I feel worse when I think about meeting his girlfriend. "Can't we just do it another day?"

I wrap the blankets around myself and curl into a ball, trying my best to look like a sick little kid and not like my too-tall thirteen-year-old self.

"Please, Dad?"

He sits next to me on the bed and rubs my hair. He's quiet for what feels like a long time.

"Fine, Dals." He sighs. "I'll text Vanessa and tell her we need to push it." He moves to stand by the door. "But you're staying in bed for the rest of the day. We need you getting better soon so the two of you can meet!"

I nod as he shuts the door, and try to act as sick as possible as he gets one last look at me.

I can tell he's mad at me. He's probably going to text his girlfriend about how I'm so dramatic and silly and she'll laugh and tell him not to worry about it and their relationship will get so much stronger and it'll all be because of me in the worst way.

I feel like I'm gonna throw up.

But instead of doing that, I pull out my phone.

Me: i did it
i don't have to meet her today

Rani: omg congrats
our master plan worked
:)

Even though I got the meeting postponed, the knot in

my stomach doesn't go away. I still have to meet her. It might not be today, but I can't put it off forever.

I reread the text Rani sent and notice how she called it "our" plan. The knot loosens. Just a bit.

CHAPTER SIX

DESPITE my best efforts, it's happening. I'm in the car, riding toward my doom: my dad's girlfriend.

I don't wanna go. I don't wanna go. I don't wanna go. I don't wanna go.

"I don't wanna go," I tell my dad.

Did I mention that I don't wanna go?

"I'm sorry, hon," he says, turning his head from the road to look over at me, "but you made a promise."

After that first time I got out of meeting my dad's girlfriend, I just kept telling him I didn't feel well.

But after a few days that strategy stopped working.

We pull off the highway, and I need to open the window. I'm gonna vomit. I'm gonna vomit right out the window. But maybe that wouldn't be so bad, because it would be evidence that I really am too sick to meet my dad's girlfriend. Like, ever.

"I think I'm gonna puke," I tell my dad.

"You're not going to throw up," he says, and there's an edge to his voice.

"I might," I mutter.

He sighs, and his tone is gentler when he speaks again. "I know this is hard, but the longer we put this off, the worse it's going to get."

That doesn't make me feel better, but I don't say anything. I don't talk at all for the rest of the drive.

Which turns out to be way shorter than I thought, because now we're pulling into the restaurant parking lot.

The poster in the window says this place is "Fun for the Whole Family!" I wonder if it's also "Fun for a Single Dad and His Daughter and His New Girlfriend." That might be a bit long for the poster.

My dad turns the car off, and takes a deep breath.

"Listen," he says, not quite looking at me and tapping the steering wheel with his index fingers. "There's something else I need to tell you."

I literally can't imagine what the something else might be. Even my brain (*my* brain!), the organ that can make the worst of any situation, can't think of a way this could possibly get worse.

"I should've told you before, but I thought it might be a lot of information at once," he says. "But she's back from college, and Vanessa and I thought it would be a good idea for you two to meet." I have no idea what he's talking about. He keeps rambling as he says, "I didn't want to pile all this on you when I first told you about Vanessa, but I don't know. I should've mentioned her." He puts his face in his hands. "What if we both take a deep breath?" That last part sounds like he's talking more to himself than me.

"What?" My chest is tight. "Who are you talking about?"

"Alexa," he says. "Vanessa's daughter."

Oh no. No, no, no.

Vanessa has a daughter? Vanessa has a daughter who's in *college* and my dad thought it would be too much to tell me about her. That I couldn't handle it.

Great.

"Why didn't you tell me?" I ask, because it's the only thing I can think to say. Tears blur the edges of my vision. "I'm not a little kid," I add under my breath. Even though I sort of feel like one right now.

"I know, I know," he says. "I should've told you." He sighs and rubs his forehead, then looks up at me. "I'm sorry if this is tough for you. I'm trying my best."

"It's fine." *It's not.*

"I've only met Alexa once, so I don't know her that well. But she seems . . ." He pauses for a moment. "Interesting."

I don't ask him what that means. I guess I'll find out in a minute when I walk into the restaurant and meet two complete strangers who my dad already knows.

He gets out of the car, and I wait a moment before I follow him. I don't even know why I'm nervous. It's not like I need to impress Vanessa. If anything, she needs to impress me, because if I don't like her, then it's over. My dad can't date someone I don't like.

Right?

"They're waiting for a table inside," he says.

He holds the door open for me, and a perky waitress greets us. "Will it just be the two of you?" she asks.

I wish.

"Our party's already inside," my dad says, looking past the waitress.

I don't think *party* is really the right word. It's not a party when you're miserable.

My dad spots them, and his face lights up. I don't think I ever saw him that happy to see my mom. And I hate it, because that's not how it's supposed to go. If you have a kid with someone, you're supposed to love them. You're supposed to work it out. My dad shouldn't even *need* a girl-friend.

He walks up to a woman who I guess is Vanessa. Well, I hope it's Vanessa, because my dad kisses her. Ew. Ew, ew, ew, ew. And there's a girl next to her looking down at her phone who seems just as excited to be here as I am.

That must be Alexa.

I walk toward the three of them, looking at my shoes, the wall, the ceiling, anything but Vanessa and Alexa. Because this is it. After this moment, Vanessa won't be my dad's imaginary girlfriend. She'll be someone I know. It's the point of no return, the moment when the roller coaster reaches the top of the hill and starts to fall.

"Dalia!"

And there it is. We're flying downhill.

Vanessa says my name like she's all excited about meeting me. "I've heard so much about you." She reaches out, like she's about to give me a hug.

I back away, which, like, probably isn't the most polite thing to do. But I've never liked giving people hugs, and I especially don't want to hug Vanessa.

"Say hi, Dalia," my dad says, and he doesn't sound happy. He pushes me toward her a little, but I scramble away. I don't want to hug a stranger. And maybe if I don't hug Vanessa, she'll keep being a stranger.

"Um, hi," I say, looking down at my feet.

"Alexa, say hi to Dalia," Vanessa says, sounding just as unhappy as my dad did. I guess parents don't stop getting angry at you even when you're in college and basically an adult. I don't know if that's sad or comforting.

"Hey," she says after a while. Alexa's wearing jean shorts, but they're not The Shorts. They go down to her knees and they're frayed at the end. They're pretty cool, but I wouldn't say that to her. I *also* wouldn't tell her that she has the most amazing hair I've ever seen. It's black and super curly and chopped right at her chin, and she's got half of it tied up in a high ponytail with a velvet scrunchie.

I wouldn't say any of that.

I'm staring down at my feet, but I look up long enough to see my dad and Vanessa giving each other a Look. A long time ago, before things got really bad and my mom was gone all the time, my parents used to give each other that Look. Somehow it hurts the most that my dad is sharing this with Vanessa.

"All right," he says, "now we're all acquainted."

Things are sort of awkward after that, because no one's saying anything. But that's the good thing about this restaurant: You don't have to talk. Because the star attractions are the Ping-Pong tables.

That's why my dad chose it, I guess, because you can play Ping-Pong while you're waiting for your food. I bet he thought we would all play Ping-Pong and laugh and bond and automatically become one big happy family.

Yeah, that's not gonna happen.

"Wanna ping some pong?" my dad asks.

"That sounds like a blast!" Vanessa says with way too much enthusiasm.

I don't say anything, and neither does Alexa, who's busy typing out something really quickly on her phone.

We walk over to the Ping-Pong area, but all the tables are full. There's a family at one of them—a dad, a mom, and two daughters.

I stop short. What if all the people here think my dad, Vanessa, Alexa, and I are a family?

They might. It would be the most logical conclusion, even though Alexa's, like, way older than me and none of us look anything like each other.

I know that families don't need to look alike. But even

if we were all exact copies of each other we wouldn't be a family. We'd just be four awkward clones, waiting silently for our turn to play Ping-Pong.

I take a few steps away from my dad and Vanessa and Alexa, because I really, really, really don't want anyone mistaking Vanessa for my mom or Alexa for my sister. I just don't.

"Looks like those people are almost done," Vanessa says as a waitress walks over to a group of girls around my age to tell them their table is ready.

They're all wearing The Shorts, so I try to hide behind my dad. I can't deal with popular girls and meeting my dad's girlfriend at the same time.

Oh no.

These aren't just any popular girls. It's Cassie . . . and there's Abby, standing right next to her. Laughing at something Cassie said, throwing her head back like Cassie's some sort of comedic genius.

I look down so that Abby won't see me. Please, please don't let Abby see me.

But, then I look up, because I have to sneak a peek.

She sees me.

Abby freezes, and one of the other Shorts-wearing girls bumps into her. She stares at me for what feels like a long time, and I stare back.

"It's Abby!" my dad says, turning to me, as if I can't see that it's Abby.

My whole face goes red. Why is my dad totally and completely oblivious? How has he not noticed that Abby hasn't been over to our apartment in months? It was never this bad before he met Vanessa.

He waves to her, and I bury my face in my hands.

"Dad, stop," I half whisper, half whine.

"Should we invite her to play Ping-Pong with us for a minute?" he asks as he points to where Abby's standing.

I start to feel panicked. "Please, *stop*," I say, pulling on his outstretched arm.

"What, you don't want Abby to sit with us?"

But then he finally looks over at me, like, really looks.

Maybe he can see the pleading in my eyes. Or maybe it's the fact that I yanked his arm so hard I might've dislocated his shoulder. Either way, he gets the message. Or at least he doesn't push it.

The waitress walks Cassie and Abby and the others to their table, and Cassie grabs onto Abby's arm as they rush off. Abby looks back at me, but as she does I turn away. I don't want our eyes to meet again. I'm worried that all the years of being best friends with Abby will mean that I'll know exactly what she's thinking. And I'm worried that what she'd be thinking is this: *I'm so relieved.* Like, maybe I'd see a look in her eyes and I'd know it meant that she's glad she doesn't have to deal with me anymore.

This is the worst day of my entire life.

"Ping-Pong time!" my dad says, as if he's already forgotten that he just completely embarrassed me in front of the most popular girls in my grade. As if he's already over it.

Only my dad and Vanessa head toward the Ping-Pong table. They both grab paddles and start playing so badly that it would be embarrassing if I weren't already at maximum embarrassment. Alexa stays off to the side, leaning against the wall with her arms crossed.

I walk over to her. I don't know what she is to me, or what she's gonna be. Right now she's just someone I don't know who hasn't said anything but "hey." So I try to strike up a conversation. "This is pretty weird, right?"

"I guess," Alexa says, "but I don't really care."

"Um, yeah," I say quietly, "neither do I." I try to make it sound like I really *don't* care, even though this is the biggest thing that's happened in my life since my parents got divorced.

Right after I say that, though, I need to take it back. "Wait, really?"

"Well, yeah," she says. "I mean, I don't really even live at home anymore. My mom can do whatever she wants."

"So you're in college?"

"Yup," she says. "Gonna be a sophomore."

"That's cool."

"It's fine," she says. "But once you're there for a while it's the same as everything else."

"But it's college!"

She looks at me with her eyebrows raised. "You're what, like twelve?"

"I'm thirteen."

"All right, well I was thirteen once too. And let me tell you, things are a lot easier when you don't get your hopes up. Middle school sucks. High school sucks. College is cool, but then you'll get used to it and it sucks too." She puts her phone into her back pocket. "And it's not just school. I didn't want my mom to go on dates all the time, but she did anyway, with tons of horrible men. But now it's whatever, because I stopped getting my hopes up."

"What do you mean?"

She laughs a little, but not in a happy way. "Do you ever want something to happen so badly, and instead the exact opposite happens?" I don't say anything, but, like, obviously. "Well, I definitely didn't want my mom to start seriously dating anyone, but then she met the 'love of her life' and wouldn't stop talking about it. All. The. Time." Alexa rolls her eyes. "So, yeah. It's a lot easier to deal with life if you don't get your hopes up in the first place."

I don't know how to respond to this, to Alexa. So I don't say anything.

"Vanessa?" the perky waitress asks. "Table for four?"

"That's us!" Vanessa says, putting her paddle down. She turns to my dad. "Good game."

"I'll win next time." He puts his arm around her waist. "I'm a little rusty."

"Sure," Vanessa says skeptically.

Alexa looks over at me and rolls her eyes. I'm pretty sure we're thinking the same thing: *This is gross.*

Things don't improve when we sit down. My dad and Vanessa decide we should get a pie for the table, but they can't choose between plain cheese or mushrooms or olives. I don't weigh in.

Alexa pulls her phone back out, so I check my phone too to try to make it look like I have places to be and people to talk to, like Alexa clearly does.

There's a text from Rani.

"Uh, I'm gonna go to the bathroom," I say, not waiting for anyone to give me permission to leave the table. Because if you gotta go, you gotta go. Even if I don't really gotta go.

When I'm in a stall, I open my phone.

> Rani: i hope ur dads girlfriend isnt terrible!!
> i watched the boulder dash vid again
> i rlly wanna go on it
> which other POVs should i watch???????

I decide not to respond to Rani's first text. Because even if Vanessa turns out to not be completely terrible, this whole experience is.

I read the texts again and have a *whoa* moment: Rani's watching the POV videos I've shown her even when I'm not there. That must mean she actually likes them.

Me: boulder dash is the best!!
but you should watch this one called outlaw
run
it's really cool

I can stay in the stall for a bit longer. No one's going to ask any questions about what I was doing in the bathroom. So I add:

Me: any makeup tutorial recommendations?

Rani: omg
ill watch it rn
and YES
one of my fave youtubers just posted this

She sends a link to a video of a "toxic unicorn." The person's face is all covered in rainbow glitter and green slime and it's super cool and gross and it totally seems like something Rani would love.

Texting Rani isn't like texting Abby. It's more like a game, or a challenge. I want to impress her more than I ever wanted to impress Abby. Maybe it's just because Rani's a fairly new friend. I guess I don't really know. But I know I like talking to her, and watching the videos she likes and having her watch the ones I like.

Me: yay!!!!!!!!!!!!
lmk what u think
and i'm literally gonna watch this one rn
too!!!!

I play the beginning of the toxic unicorn video, and I can't stop smiling. Watching a video that someone sends you is like looking into their brain. Like, the good part of their brain. Because roller coaster POV videos definitely live in the best part of mine.

I walk out of the bathroom and the smile on my face from texting Rani and watching the video she sent is still there. I'm lighter and happier and somehow far away from everything I was worried about.

But as I make my way back to the table, trying to avoid staring at Abby and her new friends across the room, and my dad and Vanessa and Alexa in the center of it, I feel heavier and heavier. It's like I'm on the Tower of Terror roller coaster in South Africa. It's this coaster where you go up on an elevator lift and then plummet straight into the ground through an abandoned mine shaft. It broke the record for the highest g-force of any roller coaster ever. So when you go on it you feel like you're being pushed back into your seat by an anvil, like there's no escape.

But at least the ride ends.

While I was gone the pizza came. They decided on plain cheese. Figures. Everyone starts to eat, and we're all pretty much silent except for the occasional "Yum" or "This is great!" from my dad and Vanessa.

The waitress barely comes by to check on us, even though she's been checking in on all the other tables. Maybe she can sense that if she asked "Everything good here?" the answer would be a resounding *no*.

The whole time we're eating, I alternate between sneaking quick glances at Abby and trying as hard as I can not to look at her. From what I can tell, she's having a blast with Cassie and the popular girls. They're all sitting in a clump on one side of the table, looking at Cassie's phone and laughing. Abby's slightly removed from the other girls, but when she catches my eye during one of my quick glances, she scoots her chair closer to Cassie and laughs along with everyone else.

When the waitress clears our plates, Vanessa says, "So, Dalia, what are your favorite subjects in school?"

"Vanessa's a chemistry teacher," my dad chimes in before I can answer, even though he's already told me this.

"We don't take chemistry in middle school," I mumble.

"Well, when you do, you know where to find me!" Vanessa says, laughing awkwardly.

Alexa sinks down in her seat.

"That's a nice offer, isn't it, Dalia?" my dad asks.

The waitress comes over with the check then, and I almost cry with relief. My dad and Vanessa split it, both putting down their credit cards, and then we all say our goodbyes (they kiss again . . . ew).

"I thought that went well," my dad says as he pulls out of the restaurant parking lot and onto the highway.

I can't tell if he's being serious or not, because whatever happened in there went just about as far from well as something could possibly go.

And I don't know if it's the kind of thing where he's looking for a response, or if he just said that hoping it would make it true.

I don't say anything.

CHAPTER SEVEN

OF course I can't just meet Vanessa and Alexa once and leave it at that. I should've known.

"My dad wants me to hang out with them *again*," I tell Rani the next day at swim practice. "He's making us all go bowling." I make a face like *bowling* is code for taking a bath in dog poop or something.

Which might actually be better than bowling if I could do it *alone*.

Rani convinced Leah to let us do kicking drills, where we keep our heads out of the water and hold on to a kickboard, because you can talk and kick at the same time. I would never have thought of asking Leah to change her practice schedule, but I don't think she had anything planned in the first place.

So now Rani and I are holding kickboards and swimming next to each other with our heads above the water.

"That sucks," she says as we touch the wall and turn to swim back in the other direction. "I mean, not the bowling part so much. But it sucks that you have to see them again. Could you pretend to be sick this time too?"

"I don't think so," I say. Because I really don't. I think I'm just gonna have to see them again. And I hate it. "That barely worked the first time. Plus, my dad's been acting super weird. But like I honestly don't even know what else he has to act weird about."

"Sometimes dads are just weird," Rani says thoughtfully. "My dad's weird all the time. Like, he's way quieter than my mom, but then he'll say something like how he thinks birds actually watch *us* and we're always like, 'What did you just say?' and he pretends like he never said anything."

I giggle. "That *is* weird."

We kick in silence for a minute. I wish Rani would give me another secret mission. Maybe that could be our game, Secret Agent. Like Puppies was with Abby. But it's silly to think like that, because it wasn't even a game when she gave me a mission before. It was just part of my real, depressing life.

"Okay," Rani says after a minute, "I actually have a strategy for when I have to do something I really don't wanna do, if you wanna hear it."

Of course I want to hear it. I want to hear whatever Rani has to say. And "strategy" is sort of like a mission, really. "What is it?"

"You have to go to your happy place. Imagine you're on a beach or something."

"Is that where you imagine you are?"

"No, I imagine I'm in Sephora, and I'm the only one in the whole store and I can pick out any makeup I want and my mom just lets me." I laugh at that. "Or you could imagine the other people are wearing really weird makeup, like the look from that tutorial where the guy pretended he was poison ivy and he made his face all green and then he did his friend's makeup and made it super blotchy."

I stop kicking to laugh, and Leah yells at us to keep it moving. "Oh yeah, that one was so good."

"*Or* you could imagine that I'm there with you and I'm making this face." Rani ducks underwater. When she comes back up, her eyes are crossed and her tongue is sticking out and her goggles are squishing her nose.

I laugh and splash her with the arm not holding my kickboard. "Do your parents ever tell you your face is gonna get stuck like that?"

"All the time."

"If it does, that would *really* make me laugh."

"I mean, then it would be totally worth it," she says. "But seriously, whatever happens tonight, will you tell me about it?"

Even with all of Rani's advice, I still want to throw up on the drive over to the bowling alley.

"When was the last time we went bowling?" my dad asks, stretching his arms above his head as he gets out of the car.

He's acting so casual, like it's a completely normal night. I hate it.

"I don't remember." I wrap my arms around my waist.

"We should go more often!"

I have a feeling I'll never want to go bowling again after this, but I say, "Yeah."

Vanessa and Alexa meet me and my dad by the door. I want to scream. I want to run away.

I hate that I'm seeing them again after only one day. I hate that my dad thinks this is normal, that he's treating it like a regular night. And I hate that *I* have to treat it like a regular night too, or else he'll be mad.

When we walk in, the bowling alley is loud and dark, with like ten TVs going at once and music blasting. I don't usually like places that are this loud, but maybe that means I won't actually have to talk to Vanessa or Alexa.

And I don't, for a while at least. When we start bowling we keep the bumpers down, and we all keep getting gutter balls. Vanessa tries to high-five me when I somehow get like two pins down, but I pretend I don't see her hand. I don't want her sympathy high five.

As the game goes on, I start thinking that this isn't even so bad. Maybe we'll just bowl for a while, and then I'll go home and watch POV videos and text Rani and everything will be okay.

Then the game ends.

"Anyone else hungry?" my dad shouts over the music and the rolling balls and crashing pins.

"I could eat!" Vanessa shouts back.

And because the universe is out to get me, the bowling alley has a quiet-ish food court. So that's where we go. We sit down at a bright red and very dirty table. My dad gets me fries but I don't touch them, and I don't even complain when he starts eating them all himself.

Then, he clears his throat. It's never good when my dad clears his throat. "So, Alexa, I hear you like roller coasters."

I freeze.

It seems impossible that Alexa and I could have anything in common. Especially something that big.

"What? Oh, yeah," Alexa says, ripping chunks off a doughnut Vanessa got her, but not eating it.

"I told Steve all about the road trip you had planned," Vanessa says. It's weird to hear her call my dad Steve. I know that's his name, but it's still weird.

"Five amusement parks in one week?" my dad says. "Pretty ambitious."

And, okay, I have to admit that I perk up at this. Talking about amusement parks is a guaranteed way to get my attention, especially because of my failed summer roller coaster plan. I never even came close to asking my dad to take me to an amusement park, and there's no point now.

"Yeah, my friend and I have been planning it for a while,"

Alexa says, sounding slightly suspicious. I don't blame her. There's something off.

"About that," Vanessa says. She grabs my dad's hand. "Steve and I have been talking about it, and it would mean a lot to us if you postponed it. Or canceled."

"I'm sorry, *what*?" Alexa crushes an innocent piece of doughnut in her hand.

"We just want you two to spend some time together," my dad adds, gesturing between me and Alexa. "And with you heading back to school soon"—he says this to Alexa—"this might be your only chance to really bond."

"We're bonding right now," Alexa says. "Why do we have to bond more?"

I want to say that we're not actually bonding at all. That she didn't even speak to me at the pizza place beyond telling me that the rest of my life's gonna suck, and she hasn't spoken to me at all at the bowling alley.

But I don't say this, because Alexa and I are clearly on the same page about not wanting to bond.

"Yes, and I'm so glad you two are getting the chance to spend some time together," Vanessa says. "But—" She exchanges The Look again with my dad, the one she gave him when we went for pizza.

"Mom, this is literally not fair at all," Alexa says, interrupting Vanessa before she can finish. "I've been planning this for months."

"I get that, I really—"

"I don't think you do!" Alexa says, butting in again. "Dhruv and I have been planning this since *October*. Don't pretend to be all understanding just because your boyfriend's here." She pushes her hair back with both hands. "I'm eighteen now. You can't just tell me what to do."

"You might be eighteen, but you're living under my roof this summer. And eating my food. And driving my car." Vanessa takes a piece of Alexa's doughnut and uses it to emphasize her point. "So I don't think you can really make that argument." Then Vanessa eats the doughnut, as if to say "That's that."

Alexa sits back and crosses her arms.

"It's okay. Alexa and I don't need to hang out or anything," I say quietly, trying to make this conversation stop.

"Actually, Dalia," my dad says. "You do. I didn't think we'd be having this discussion tonight, but we need to tell you kids something."

Vanessa gives my dad a stern look and says, "I think what your dad is trying to say—"

"Don't tell me what my dad is trying to say," I mumble to Vanessa. And then, because I've pretty much had it, I'm like, "He's my dad. I know what he's trying to say. I've known him for thirteen years. You've only known him for six months."

"Dalia," my dad says. A warning.

"I don't think you *do* know what he's trying to say, sweet-heart," Vanessa says.

"Vanessa and I are engaged," my dad blurts out. Vanessa puts her head in her hands.

"What?" Alexa and I say together.

This can't be happening. I'm going to wake up and this will all be a dream.

"We didn't want to tell you like this." Vanessa looks at my dad.

I want to scream, but I hold it in even though my blood feels like lava and my brain is on fire. Seriously, though, were they *ever* gonna tell us?

I guess this explains why he's been acting weird. Because he actually *did* have another secret after the girlfriend one. A fiancée secret. Ew times a million.

"Why are you trying to ruin my life?" Alexa asks. "I just wanna go on this road trip with my friend. I can't believe I have to deal with this right now."

Vanessa shakes her head. "I'm not trying to ruin your life, Ale," she says quietly.

"I know it's a lot to ask, and a lot to find out," my dad says. "But you two are going to be family. You need to get to know each other. And that can't happen if one of you is off on a week-long road trip."

But then, just like that, I have an idea. Things might not be going well, but I think I have a way to make them better.

And if it works, I could actually accomplish my summer plan.

"What if I went with her?" I say. "Like, on the trip."

Everyone at the table looks at me. If I weren't stuck inside my own body, *I* would probably look at me.

But I want to go to an amusement park. I want to ride roller coasters. And, okay, Alexa isn't my first choice of company, or my second or third or fourth or fifth or . . . you get it. But I don't really care. All I've wanted for years is to go on a roller coaster, and this is my chance.

"I'm sorry, what?" Alexa asks.

"I, um, really love roller coasters," I say. "And you won't have to cancel if you . . ." I look down, the boldness seeping out of me. "If you take me with you."

"Look kid, that's not happening." Alexa somehow crosses her arms even more than they were already crossed.

"No, wait," Vanessa says. "That's a great idea!"

"It is?" I ask, sounding hopeful.

"It is?" Alexa asks, sounding angry.

I didn't think anyone would actually agree to this.

"This way you wouldn't have to change any of your plans," Vanessa says to Alexa, "and the two of you could still bond."

"I don't know," my dad says slowly. "Dalia's never really been away from home."

I look down, embarrassed. I want to say that that's not

true, but other than sleeping over at Abby's house, I've never been away from my dad for more than a night.

"She won't be by herself," Vanessa says. "Alexa will be there."

"Are you gonna pay me?" Alexa asks.

Vanessa looks at her. "What are you talking about?"

"I mean, this is clearly a babysitting gig. So you're paying me, right?"

"I don't need a babysitter." I've been babysitting for like two years now. If I can babysit other kids, I clearly don't need a babysitter of my own.

My dad makes his fingers into a steeple and rests his chin on top of them. It's something he does when he's thinking.

After a minute he says, "We'll pay for all of Dalia's expenses, of course." Wait. Is he agreeing?

"And we can pay for an extra room in any of the motels you stay at," Vanessa adds, reaching out for my dad's hand again.

"So cool that you're figuring my whole life out for me," Alexa says. "That's great. Super great. Letting a twelve-year-old come with me when you wouldn't even let me take Sara." Alexa says that last part to her mom, and there's something even stronger than anger there. "Really cool."

"I never said—I just—can we not have this conversation here?" Vanessa asks finally.

I don't correct Alexa and say that I'm actually thirteen, and I don't ask who Sara is. I don't want to push my luck.

Everyone's quiet for a minute. We're surrounded by the distant sound of bowling pins clattering and people laughing. I don't understand how anyone is having fun when there's a huge black cloud hanging over our table.

"I'm still bringing Dhruv," Alexa says after what feels like forever.

Wait. Is *she* agreeing? Is she really agreeing to take me on this road trip?

"Of course," Vanessa says. "We wouldn't want to completely change your plans. We just want you to have some future-stepsister bonding."

And that's when it hits me. Alexa's going to be my stepsister.

I used to wish I had a sister when I was younger. Or a dog. Now I think I'd much rather have a dog than a sister, especially a sister who calls me "kid" and who's gonna resent me for the rest of my life after I go on this road trip with her.

But honestly, Alexa's probably going to hate me whether or not we go on this trip together. And that gives me *another* idea.

"Since Alexa's bringing someone, can I take someone too?" I ask my dad. I mean, if Alexa's going to be mad at me, she might as well be mad at me *and* someone else.

"Oh, sweetie, I don't know," he says. That's Dad-speak for "absolutely not." I can actually *feel* my heart sink. "Alexa's already being nice enough to let you tag along."

I don't know if I'd call what Alexa agreed to "nice," but I guess he kind of has a point.

But then Vanessa says, "I don't see why not."

My dad tries to catch her eye, but Vanessa's looking at me and sort of smiling. I sort of smile back.

"No," Alexa says. "I'm sorry, but no. Are you serious? No."

"Think of it this way," Vanessa tells Alexa. "If Dalia brings a friend, you and Dhruv can go on the big roller coasters and they can do something else. You won't have to keep track of her all the time."

That stings.

"I can go on the big roller coasters too," I say, but it comes out way more babyish than I meant for it to.

My dad ignores my comment. "They're not leaving Dalia and her friend alone." Then to me he says, "You're not wandering around an amusement park by yourself."

"Let's all just take a deep breath," Vanessa says. "I think Dalia's old enough to have a bit of freedom, don't you?"

Why is Vanessa being so nice? I narrow my eyes and look away from the table.

Alexa must be wondering the same thing, because she says, "Cool how you can be so 'selfless' and 'understanding' in front of your boyfriend or fiancé or whatever. You're a saint."

She says the words *selfless* and *understanding* in a mean, high-pitched voice.

"Alexa." Vanessa's warning tone is back again.

Everyone's silent for a minute, and then my dad covers his face with both of his hands and pulls down, like he's trying to peel off his skin so that he's only muscle and bone. "I just want you to be safe," he says to me. "And to spend time with Alexa."

After this, we all calm down a little and hammer out some of the details of the trip. We'll be gone for a whole week, and Alexa will make sure to drive incredibly safely and watch out for me at the amusement park (my dad's request).

"And you two have to FaceTime us every night," my dad says, "to check in."

"Fine." I cross my arms in my best Alexa impression.

But actually, it's more than fine. Because the someone I'm bringing? It's Rani.

Well, if she says yes.

CHAPTER EIGHT

"WHAT do you say we take a ride down to the bay?"

It's been a couple of days since the bowling alley, and my dad's trying too hard to pretend everything's normal.

"Sounds good."

That's not to say I'm not pretending too.

He closes out a few tabs on his computer, and we grab our bikes to ride the few blocks down to the water. It's almost sunset, so there are tons of people standing on the dock and taking pictures. My dad and I walk past them and climb a rusty ladder down onto the actual beach, but there's barely anywhere to stand because it's high tide and the sand is covered with trash.

I follow behind my dad as he moves away from the dock and sits on a big piece of driftwood.

"Do you have anything you want to ask me?"

My heart thumps in my chest. "What do you mean?"

"Just about Vanessa, or anything, really." He picks up a beer bottle and walks it to the nearest trash can.

When he comes back I say, "Uh, no, I don't think so."

It never used to be this hard to talk to my dad.

"Okay," he says, nodding. "If you do . . ."

"Yeah."

I want whatever this conversation is to be over right now. But then I remember that I actually *do* have something to ask him. "You know the trip?" I say. He nods. "I was wondering if I can bring Rani, you know, from swim team? Could she be the friend I take?"

My dad looks over at me then. "Not Abby? She's your best friend."

She's really not, I think.

This is all Vanessa's fault. She's clearly the reason my dad has no idea what's going on in my life.

"I just want Rani to come, okay?"

He looks at me for another moment and then turns to face the water. "Okay, whatever you want, Dals."

I'm kind of surprised he's not pushing it, but maybe he feels bad about everything that's happening. Or maybe he just doesn't know what else to say.

After that I look around for horseshoe crabs for a few minutes, but there aren't any.

The next day, Rani and I are sitting on the sidewalk at the edge of the pool parking lot; she's got a T-shirt and shorts on over her damp bathing suit, and I just have a towel wrapped around my waist because I can never remember to bring a change of clothes. She's sitting with me while I wait for my dad to pick me up.

"So, can you come?" I ask.

It took me all of practice to work up the courage to tell Rani about the amusement park road trip and to ask her to come with me, and I finally told her just now. I explained the whole thing in one breath so she couldn't interrupt me and say no.

"That sounds amazing," she says, but she doesn't look all that excited. I get a panicky feeling in my chest, like how I imagine it would feel to get stuck at the top of a roller coaster just before the drop.

"So, is that a yes?" I need it to be a yes. Why is she acting like this?

"It's a . . ."—she looks down at the sparkly beige sidewalk—"I have to check with my parents. And I *really* don't know if they're gonna say yes."

"Oh." I should've known something like this was going to happen. I don't know why I even got my hopes up in the first place. She's probably just too nice to say no, so she's blaming it on her parents.

"But Dalia." She turns her head toward me. Our eyes meet, and she smiles and bumps my knee a little. I smile back at her so big because I can't help it. "I *really* wanna go.

Like, really, really. I'm gonna beg my mom. But I still don't know if she'll let me."

"But you're gonna try?"

She nods, hard. "I promise."

But my heart sinks again, because I know what it's like to want something so badly that it feels impossible to ask. Like when I couldn't work up the courage to even *ask* my dad to take me to an amusement park.

And then I have an idea: "You can report back to me. You know, about asking her."

Rani grins. "Like when you tried to get out of meeting your dad's girlfriend?"

I beam at her. "Yeah, exactly." I wasn't sure if she would remember. If maybe it was something that was just exciting for me and for her it was like, "Oh yeah, I send my friends on missions all the time."

But no. She remembered. And now she's going on a mission for me.

Later that afternoon, Rani texts me:

> ok reporting back
> i spent like the whole day trying to convince
> my mom to let me go
> but she rlly wants you and ur dad to come for
> dinner before she says yes

So it's decided that my dad and I will go over to Rani's house—well, mansion—for dinner the next day. When it comes time for us to leave, my stomach's in knots. I mean, I'm really excited, because I'll get to see Rani, but I'm worried that it'll be awkward, or that my dad will embarrass me, or that even after this meal, Rani's parents will still say no.

When we get to Rani's giant front door, my dad is holding a babka that we got from our favorite kosher bakery, and I'm trying my best not to bolt in the opposite direction.

But then Rani answers the door, and her parents are standing next to her, smiling at us and beckoning us in. Rani's taller than both of her parents, but she's shaped more like her mom. Where Rani is long and lean and built for slicing through the water, her dad is shorter and more compressed. And even though his smile isn't much like Rani's and her mom's, it's warm and welcoming too.

I think about what Rani told me about him, that he can't keep secrets and ruins surprise parties. I smile a little, remembering the day Rani told me about that, and I try to look away so no one sees, but before I can do that, Rani catches my eye. And she's smiling too, and then I sort of feel like I have a secret with Rani, a secret from our parents.

My dad and I take off our shoes and leave them by the rug next to the front door, and before we're all the way inside the grand foyer I'm hit with the most wonderful smell in the entire world. It's a mix of citrus and onion and spices, and my mouth is watering. My dad doesn't cook that much, and my mom never did, so I'm already excited to eat.

We go into one of their living rooms and have nuts and sliced fruit with tea and talk for a while before dinner. If my dad is shocked by the size of Rani's house, he doesn't let on. He's on his best dad behavior, which I'm happy to see.

Rani and I let our parents do most of the talking. They discuss their work, but they also talk about us. They say things like "I can tell Dalia just thinks the world of Rani," and "I'm so glad Rania made a friend in town."

While they're chatting, Rani moves to sit next to me. She whispers, "This is where my secret agent training will really come in handy."

I laugh, from the ticklish feeling of Rani's mouth near my ear and the giddiness of being in on a joke with her. She puts a finger to her lips to shush me and I put my hand over my mouth to stop myself from laughing too hard and distracting our parents.

"What are you gonna do?" I ask, speaking softly but not getting as close to Rani as she did to me. "What's the mission?"

She brings her mouth near my ear again. "I was thinking truth serum, or maybe sleeping potion."

"How would that help?"

"I don't know, but it sounds cool."

"Very secret agent–ish," I agree.

We listen to our parents talk for a few more minutes, but it's not as boring with Rani sitting next to me. It's like we're in it together. Finally, it's time to eat. Rani's mom heads into the kitchen for a few minutes to put the finishing touches on the meal. When she comes back out she ushers us into their giant dining room, which has a table large enough to fit what looks like an entire roller coaster train full of people, but right now it only has five place settings.

The table is beautiful, with a large pot of stew, which Rani's mom tells us is called ghormeh sabzi (I can tell that's where the smell is coming from and I want to eat it, like, yesterday), a pot of rice, a bowl of yogurt, and a salad with cucumbers and tomatoes.

Rani's mom serves me and my dad huge portions, and I'm not even halfway done with my first plate when she tells Rani to offer me seconds. "Rania, why don't you ask your friend if she'd like more food?" She turns to me and adds, "Eat more, eat more."

While we eat, my dad doesn't bring up the road trip, and I start to worry that maybe he never will.

But I don't worry long, because once everyone loses steam on dinner, Rani's mom brings it up herself.

"Rania's been telling us about this little trip," she says after we have a third—or maybe fourth, I can't remember—helping of her ghormeh sabzi. "And we wanted to hear more about it from you." She looks at my dad, who seems like he's been expecting this.

My dad clears his throat and then explains all about the road trip—who'll be there, where we'll be going, how we'll be getting there.

Rani jumps in and says, "And I've been saying how much I miss my old friends, and how I don't really even know anyone else in town—"

"Rania joon, please let him finish," Rani's mom says, giving her a stern look.

My dad looks almost as nervous as I feel as he continues. He talks about how safe we'll be, about how he's already paid for everything (I get sort of embarrassed at that because, you know, *mansion*), and how Alexa will check in all the time, constantly.

Rani's parents give each other The Look, the one I'm pretty sure now that all grown-ups in relationships use to telepathically communicate, and then Rani's mom speaks.

"You'll always have your phone on you," she says to Rani. "And *you* will give me the itinerary and the names of all the motels. And this Alexa girl's phone number." She says this to my dad, who nods vigorously.

Rani looks over at me.

Because I think we did it.

Our parents talk a bit more about the trip and how safe we'll be, then we eat the babka (there's always room for dessert) and head home.

When we're in the car, I get a text from Rani.

> Rani: SHE SAID YES!!!!!!!!!
> im literally so excited
> and ty for bringing the cake
> it was SO GOOD

Me: YESSSSSSSS
my dad is saying to plz thank ur parents again
he wont stop talking about the stew lol

We text for a little while after that, and I can't stop looking down at my phone and smiling. Because it worked.
Rani's coming on the trip.

And the only thing left to do now is hit the road.

CHAPTER NINE

"LET me lay down some ground rules," Alexa says.

We're in the car, heading to the first amusement park on our road trip: Great Adventure in New Jersey. "You two don't talk to me or Dhruv unless you're bleeding. And I don't mean a little scrape. I mean, like, don't talk to me unless you burst an artery or something."

Rani and I are sitting in the back seat of Alexa's car. Alexa and her friend from college, Dhruv, are in the front.

Dhruv's been pretty quiet for most of the ride. And when he hopped into the car, he kissed Alexa on the cheek, so maybe they're dating or something. But then, I don't really know how people in college interact. Maybe everyone kisses on the cheek. It could just be the standard greeting.

"You understand?" Alexa asks after she's finished telling me and Rani not to bother her unless someone, like, chops us in half.

"Mhm," I say.

Rani raises her eyebrows at me, and no one speaks.

"How about some music?" Dhruv asks after a minute. It's the first thing he's really said the whole ride. He sounds nervous, like he's not sure how to talk to me or Rani, which makes sense because we just met him. Plus, he thought this trip would just be him and Alexa. I feel kind of bad.

He takes Alexa's aux cord and plays a song I've never heard, but probably everyone in college knows it. There's this feeling in my stomach, like my clothes are too tight even though they're not.

To me, thirteen feels pretty old. I mean, it even sounds old. Way older than twelve, anyway. But when I'm in the car with these two people who are basically adults, I feel like an overgrown baby.

It's also one of the first times I've been in a car with someone who isn't my dad driving. It already feels weird to be away from him, to know I'm gonna be gone for a whole week.

I remember one time when I was really little, like four or five, I went to visit my bubbe—my dad's mom—in Pennsylvania. Things with my mom weren't bad yet, but she didn't come because she had to work.

When my dad buckled me into my car seat and we pulled out of our driveway, I cried so hard that I almost choked on my own snot. I don't know if it was because I missed my mom already, or because I didn't want her to be away from us. Either way, my dad had to play that Raffi song that's like, "Baby beluga in the deep blue sea" over and over again until I calmed down.

And maybe my little-kid brain was right to be freaked out, because after we got back from that trip, I saw my mom less and less.

But I've never had to drive away from my dad. Especially not in the last weeks of summer before school starts back up, when I get my teacher assignments and my dad and I talk about what they'll be like while we eat too much ice cream and savor the last days of hot August freedom.

I feel, like, super bad for thinking this, but it's also kind of nice to not be stuck in the apartment with him. Because now I don't have to pretend like he didn't just flip my entire life upside down.

Rani taps me on the shoulder, which startles me out of thinking about all of this. About my dad and my mom and being away from home. I must look really surprised, because she stifles a giggle. She motions to her phone, which I think means I should check mine.

> Rani: alexas pretty intense
>
> Me: yeah
> sorry about her
>
> Rani: if she was gonna be my stepsister i'd run away lol

I look up and Rani's smiling at me, and I try to smile

back, but my stomach gets all knotty. I don't want to think about how Alexa's gonna be my stepsister. But I don't want Rani to think I'm mad at her or anything, so I just don't text back.

After a minute, Rani motions down to her phone again.

Rani: well anyway
excited for ROLLER COASTERS?!?!?!?!?!

That's something I can get behind, talking about my number one favorite subject and *not* about Alexa.

Me: YESSSSSSSSSSSS

Rani looks up and smiles at me. I like that we have a secret mode of communication, even if she did use it to tell me that if she had my life she'd run away. It's not like I wasn't thinking it.

I get that same feeling I had in Rani's mansion the other day, when she sat next to me and whispered in my ear. That we're a team; we're united, somehow. And it's not like we're against the Alexa and Dhruv team, but we're not with them, either. We're in our own little bubble, here in the back seat.

As we drive through Long Island traffic, I mostly stare out the window. I'm pretty sure we've been driving for a million years, but when I check the time on my phone it's only been an hour since we left. Rani stares out the window too, but I wish I could see her face. Does she regret coming on the trip now that she has to deal with my almost-stepsister?

I push those thoughts away.

To pass the time, I go over the road trip in my head. Today we're going to Great Adventure, then we're sleeping over at a motel in Connecticut and heading to Lake Compounce tomorrow (that's where Boulder Dash is!). The day after that we're going to Dorney Park in Pennsylvania, and then we're driving all the way to Ohio, where we're going to an amusement park called Cedar Point. It's going to take a long time to drive there, so we're spending a full day driving to the park and a full day driving back. And then the last place we're going is Coney Island, which is the closest amusement park to home, because it's in Brooklyn.

So, basically, minus Alexa, this is going to be the best week ever.

"Dalia, look," Rani whispers, leaning over and pointing to the front of the car.

I must've been in my brain for a long time, because when I look up, there it is, out in the distance.

Great Adventure.

Total Whoa Moment.

I can just make out the tops of roller coasters over a line of trees. And they're actual roller coasters, not just ones on a screen. There are loops and peaks and steep drops in every color.

"I can't wait to ride those," Dhruv says. He looks back at me and smiles.

I'm surprised, but I smile back. Because neither can I.

CHAPTER TEN

I didn't know that amusement parks have a smell. It's a mix of sunscreen and chlorine and metal and excitement. I know it's weird to say that something smells like excitement, but it really does.

It's amazing.

"What do you think a fried Oreo tastes like?" Rani asks me. She's pointing to a stand that has a sign advertising deep-fried Oreos, Twinkies, chocolate bars, and "Anything We Can Fit in the Fryer!"

For some horrible reason, the first thought my brain has about Rani's question is that I should text Abby.

But then I remember I can't.

Because she's not my best friend anymore. She's Cassie's. I've just gotta accept that.

The thing is, I know Abby would *love* to try a deep-fried Oreo. She used to combine the weirdest baking ingredients we had at both of our houses and make "experiments," and I was the guinea pig who had to eat them.

Ugh, brain, no.

I look over at Rani, who's taking a picture of all the stands, framing it so the Oreo sign is in the center, and I feel silly for thinking about Abby in the first place. She's not here with me. Rani is.

I do my best to push Abby out of my brain. "It probably tastes like an Oreo but ten times better."

"Or maybe it's like an Oreo doughnut," she says, her eyes lighting up.

Alexa scoffs and crosses her arms. "Those things'll make you sick before you even get on a roller coaster."

"I thought you weren't talking to us." I cross my arms to match Alexa's.

"No, kid, it's the other way around. *You're* not talking to *us*. We can talk to you all we want."

Dhruv rolls his eyes when Alexa says this, but then he rests an elbow on her shoulder. He doesn't seem mad at her, even though he definitely should be.

I try to ignore them and take in the view, because I'm *finally* at an amusement park. And it's even more incredible than I imagined.

Other than the smell, something I didn't expect is how many rides and stuff there are that *aren't* roller coasters. I mean, of course there are tons of coasters, but there are also carnival games and bumper cars and a teacup ride where you spin around in circles and swings that go really high in the air. I can't wait to try them all.

And the people! I've never seen so many people who

actually look happy to be somewhere. There are kids running around the park from ride to ride, families holding matching ice cream cones, adults who are here by themselves. And they're all having a good time.

"What should we go on first?" Dhruv asks.

He's wearing a loose tank top and these shorts that are pretty short. I guess I didn't notice them before because he was sitting in the front seat and I couldn't see his legs that well. They don't look like shorts any boy in my grade would wear. The boys in my grade all wear long athletic shorts, like the ones I'm wearing now. But Dhruv's are closer to the length of The Shorts, the ones that the popular girls wear.

Now that I'm looking around, a lot of people at the park seem to be wearing The Shorts, which makes me feel like maybe I'm wearing the wrong thing. Maybe there's an amusement-park-going uniform, and I've completely ignored it. I bet Abby would fit right in if she was here. (*No, brain.*)

Then again, Rani's not even wearing shorts at all. She's wearing a flowy polka-dotted skirt that flounces a little when she walks.

"I think we should go on Kingda Ka," Alexa says after a minute, which jolts me out of my shorts thoughts. "Then after that we can split up and ride whatever we want."

"Um, Kingda Ka?" I ask.

She's gotta be kidding.

Because Kingda Ka isn't just any roller coaster. It's the

tallest one in the world (the world!), and the fastest in North America. And I tell her as much.

"Maybe we should save it for later?" I suggest after I give the facts. Because you can't argue with the facts. "I mean, look at it."

Everyone turns to where I'm pointing. It doesn't even look like a roller coaster. It's this huge green tower in the distance. I honestly think it might be bumping into some clouds. That's how tall it is.

"You're not scared, are you?" Alexa asks. "Because if you are, we could always go on that ride." She points to the little kids' section, where some toddlers are rocking back and forth on a gentle swing.

"I'm not scared," I say. "It's just that . . ."

So, yeah, here's the problem: I haven't told them about how I've never actually been on a roller coaster. I should've told them all while we were driving over. But I didn't, and now we're about to go on the biggest, scariest roller coaster in the entire park.

I want to go on Kingda Ka, of course. I just thought I'd be able to ease into the whole Actually Going on a Roller Coaster thing. Maybe start with one that's like beginner level. I didn't expect to start at expert.

"It's, um . . ." Everyone looks over at me. I take a breath and keep talking. "It's my first roller coaster," I say. "I've never been on one before."

"What?" Rani asks, looking confused.

Oh, god. She probably thinks I'm a complete phony for showing her roller coaster POV videos without ever having actually been on one.

"Are you kidding me?" Alexa scoffs. "I knew I was basically going to have to babysit you, but this is next level."

Dhruv and Rani stand awkwardly between me and Alexa. I don't think this is what they thought they'd be getting themselves into when they agreed to go on this trip.

"I'll go on Kingda Ka," I say angrily. "I wanna go on it."

"She doesn't have to," Dhruv says to Alexa. And then he says to me, "It's fine." He looks at the ground, avoiding Alexa's glare. I don't blame him. "I'll go on something else with you."

"No," I say, sounding bolder than I feel. "I wanna go on this one."

"Fine, but if you puke, you're not telling your dad," Alexa says.

"Fine!"

I start walking toward Kingda Ka, ahead of Alexa, ahead of Dhruv—who's being weirdly nice to me—and ahead of Rani.

Ugh. I can't bear to look back at Rani. She thought I was, like, a roller coaster expert, and now she's finding out I've never even been on one. What kind of person watches hours and hours of videos on something they've never actually done? Case in point: I've *seen* Rani's makeup looks. She doesn't just watch the videos, she *does* makeup. And she's amazing at it. Meanwhile I've been pretending to be an expert on something I clearly know nothing about.

Rani runs up to me, so I guess she can't be *that* mad. But it's also possible that she's coming to tell me she never wants to speak to me again.

"Are you mad at me for not telling you that I've never been on a roller coaster?"

"What? No," Rani says. "Why would I be? This is so cool. Now I get to go with you on your first one!"

She smiles at me, and I feel like I could go on a roller coaster that's ten times taller and faster than Kingda Ka.

When we get to the ride, the line is super long, which is good because it means I have more time to prepare before I go on my first roller coaster. My first very tall, very fast, very scary roller coaster.

There are warning signs everywhere. Like, literal warning signs. Some of them say not to go on the roller coaster if you're pregnant or have a heart condition. I'm obviously not pregnant and there's nothing going on with my heart that I know of, so it looks like it's really happening.

The only thing I can think of is something my dad always says, "Oy vey ist mir." That's how I'm feeling right now. It's Yiddish for when you basically can't even.

Oy.

Vey.

Ist.

Mir.

The line snakes around the track, which is really long and flat. I know a long and flat track doesn't sound like it makes for an exciting roller coaster, but the reason the track is built that way is because Kingda Ka works like an airplane. When you're on a plane you have to go down a long runway so that the plane can pick up enough speed so that it can actually fly. That's the same for Kingda Ka: It launches you down the flat part of the track, and then the roller coaster train goes straight up a huge tower, over the crest, and right back down. Like when you're on it you're seriously looking directly into the sky and then you fall directly down to the earth.

And *that's* gonna be my first ever roller coaster.

From here on the ground, the neon-green tower looks way too tall and way too thin to actually be able to hold a roller coaster car on it, yet hundreds or maybe thousands of people go on it every day and so far, no one has died.

I hope.

The four of us get on line, with Alexa standing a bit in front of us, which I'm pretty sure she does so that it doesn't look like she's with me and Rani.

"It'll be over really quickly," Rani says. She must see how

nervous I look. "Like, you just go up and then down and then it's over."

I nod. I can't speak. The closer we get to the front of the line, the more I want to puke.

"I think the scariest part is waiting for the ride to shoot you out of the gate," Rani says.

Why is she saying this? I know it's the scariest part. Whenever I've watched the Kingda Ka POV, I've always skipped ahead past that part because I can't take the anticipation.

So I just say "Yup."

Then, after a minute, Rani adds, "So I was thinking that maybe we should count how long it takes." I look over at her. "That way we'll know how long it'll be when we're on the ride. Like, here, let's start when the next group of people get on."

"Oh, um, right," I say, smiling a little. "Okay."

There's a train coming back into the station, and the riders stumble off. The next batch of people board the roller coaster, looking almost as scared as I feel.

"Once the train gets into position, let's start counting," she says. It takes a minute for everyone to get strapped in, and once they do the coaster rolls to the beginning of the track. "All right, start counting . . . now. One Mississippi, two Mississippi, three Mississippi . . ."

Rani keeps saying her Mississippis, and there are some

mega-sized butterflies in my stomach, even though I'm not the one on the coaster.

And suddenly, just when she reaches eight Mississippi, the train screeches out of the station so fast, it's like there's a rocket engine attached to the back.

"All right, so it's eight Mississippi," Rani says. "We'll just count it out when we get on the ride so it won't be as scary."

I feel better about riding Kingda Ka after that, which is good because the line's moving pretty quickly now. In just a few minutes, we're the next group up.

"Dhruv and I are gonna sit in the front seats," Alexa says. "You two can go wherever. Just don't die."

And with that sweet statement, it's our turn to board. Before this moment I *thought* I knew what it felt like to have pre-ride jitters, because I get them a little when I'm watching POV videos, but it's nothing like this. My mouth is bone dry and I can barely breathe.

Rani hops in first, and somehow, I force myself to get into the seat next to hers. A lot of the other riders are squealing or laughing in anticipation, but I can't make a sound.

"You okay?" Rani asks.

"Mhm," I manage to say, even if it's not true.

The ride attendant straps us in and makes sure the buckles on our harnesses are secure, which doesn't feel like enough. We should each be given a personal parachute or a jet pack or something in case we're flung out at the top and ejected straight into the sun.

The ride seems to exhale, letting out a burst of air. And slowly, slowly, it moves forward. Toward the tower. Toward our doom.

"Remember, eight Mississippi," Rani says. She looks over at me, and I stare back at her, eyes wide. She must see that I look like I've just seen ten thousand ghosts, so she says, "Maybe I'll just do the counting."

And then we're waiting on the track.

"Arms down, head back, hold on," a pre-recorded voice says over the loudspeaker.

Rani starts counting. "One Mississippi."

The tower looks infinitely taller from here on the track.

"Two Mississippi."

There's no way we're gonna build up enough speed to get to the top.

"Three Mississippi."

I can't do this.

"Four Mississippi."

I wanna get off.

"Five Mississippi."

I'm too chicken.

"Six Mississippi."

Oh no.

"Seven Mississippi."

And before we even start moving, I let out the loudest scream I've ever screamed in my entire life, because if I don't let it out now I think I'm gonna explode and now

Rani's screaming too and holy crap I think I'm gonna pass out and I'm almost 100 percent sure this is how I die.

From behind us someone says, "Oh just go alre—"

WHOOSH.

"AHHHHHHHHHHHHHHHHHHHHHHHHHHHH."

That's me. And everyone else.

We're speeding down the track, and I'm suctioned to the back of my seat.

It happens in a blur. We're racing down the bright green track, and suddenly we're angled upward, staring straight into the sun.

Just before we get to the top of the tower, we start to slow down.

"WE'RE GONNA ROLL BACK," I shout at Rani. "WE'RE GONNA ROLL BACK WE'RE GONNA ROLL BACK WE'RE GONNA ROLL BACK."

Everyone on the train is screaming, because it doesn't seem like we're going to make it to the top.

But then we do.

And then there's no more track. Or at least, that's what it looks like. I recognize this moment, from the videos. The moment before the world falls out from underneath you. I look over at Rani, who's looking at me.

Our faces break into the biggest grins, which turn into screams. Because off we go, straight down, into the parking lot. Into the center of the earth.

It's the greatest feeling in the entire world. My stomach lurches, and my butt leaves the seat; we're almost flying. And just before it feels like we're actually going to crash into the ground, the coaster twists and we go up a gentle hill.

I'm laughing hysterically, and maybe crying a little too. I'm more out of breath than I've ever been after a race at a swim meet. Rani's laughing too, and neither of us can stop, even as the roller coaster makes its way back into the station.

And now I know: Roller coaster POV videos could never come close to the actual thing.

I wish I could go back in time and tell past Dalia that POV videos might be a good distraction, but being on an actual roller coaster isn't something you can just play in the background when you're stressed or nervous. Being on a roller coaster is an entirely different world, like being underwater.

Actually, it's not just a new world, it's a new *life*. And I'm never going back. My whole thirteen years of existence can be separated into two distinct times: before Kingda Ka, and after.

"That was amazing," Rani says, hair wispy and eyes wide.

"Totally." But *amazing* doesn't even begin to describe it. I touch my face to make sure it's still there. I'm giddy and shocked and relieved.

We hop off the coaster, and there are Alexa and Dhruv, walking ahead of us. They're both laughing too.

"So, how was your first roller coaster?" Alexa asks, and it doesn't even sound that mean. It sounds like she actually wants to know.

Maybe the roller coaster knocked something out of her. Or maybe it's just hard to be mean after you've almost died.

I look over at Rani. "Incredible."

CHAPTER ELEVEN

AFTER Kingda Ka, I feel like I can do anything—even put up with Alexa.

Right after we get off the ride, I go to my notes app, open a blank note, and write "ROLLER COASTER CREDITS" at the top. I learned about credits from reading the comments of the POV videos. It's basically a list of roller coasters you've been on. And now I get to have a credits list of my own. I'm practically giddy as I type out "Kingda Ka." I mean, my first roller coaster credit is Kingda Friggin' Ka. That's, like . . . epic.

"We have to go on all the roller coasters," I say. I'm pretty confident because this is my area of expertise. Plus, I just went on the tallest roller coaster in all of North America, so I have a whole new level of knowledge.

"The thing about roller coasters is that there are more than just two types. Like, it's not just wooden or steel. And they have most of the types of roller coasters here." Rani, Alexa, and Dhruv look a little confused, so I explain. "Okay, so there are wing coasters, where the seats are next to the track and hanging from it like they're wings and the track is the spine or whatever. And so there's nothing above you or below you, so it's supposed to feel like you're soaring in the air. And there are stand-up coasters where you're on your feet and you stand for the whole ride, which people say is kind of uncomfortable. And there are floorless coasters where the floor goes away after you leave the station and your legs are dangling." I stop because I realize I've been talking for a long time. "Or, like, whatever."

"Sounds like you know a lot about this stuff," Dhruv says, looking impressed. "You can be the trip's roller coaster specialist."

"I guess," I say, but I'm smiling. Maybe it's silly, but this is the thing I know the most about. Some people are experts on dinosaur names or airplanes or plants. My thing is roller coasters.

Alexa gives me a questioning look. "How come you didn't mention all this when we were at the bowling alley?"

"Mention what?" I turn away from her and stare at my shoes.

"That you know all this stuff about roller coasters."

"Oh, well—" I look up at her now, and I can't tell what she's thinking at all, which is kind of scary. "My dad doesn't really know." It sounds silly when I say it. Because it's not like knowing about different types of roller coasters should be some huge secret. But, yeah. He doesn't know.

"Dalia actually knows *so* much about roller coasters," Rani says quickly, before Alexa can respond. "And she showed me all these videos that are filmed on the rides so that you can pretend you're on them."

Alexa snorts. Why did Rani tell them that? I thought maybe it was *our* thing. I look over at her, but she's not looking back at me, which is good, because I can feel my eyes starting to get kind of watery. I wipe them before anyone sees.

Even though Alexa said that she just wanted to hang out with Dhruv after Kingda Ka, we end up going on a bunch of rides all together. My favorite's El Toro, because it's a huge wooden roller coaster and you get so much air time.

"Air time is when your butt flies up from the seat," I tell Alexa, Dhruv, and Rani while we're waiting on line. "That's like the whole point of wooden roller coasters."

"I hate the way my stomach feels when a ride does that," Dhruv says.

And then Alexa's like, "What? It's the best feeling."

It might be a tiny thing, but I guess Alexa and I can agree on air time.

There's this other roller coaster I really like called Nitro, which is technically a hypercoaster. That just means the drop is higher than two hundred feet. We also go on this ride called Bizarro, which is my first upside-down roller coaster. I thought it would be scary going upside down for real, but the loop is over so quickly, I don't even have time to get freaked out.

I add them all to my credits list, feeling unstoppable.

After a while, we take a break to get something to eat.

"I'm in the mood for funnel cake," Dhruv says.

And Alexa says, "I think we can make that happen." She's being sarcastic, because basically every stand on the main boardwalk area has a sign advertising funnel cake.

"Your dad gave me your money to keep track of," Alexa tells me. "Because apparently, I'm not just your babysitter, but also your financial planner."

"I didn't tell him to do that," I say. "I can handle my own money."

"Whatever." She grabs her wallet. "It's fine."

And I guess it is, because she buys us both whole funnel cakes. Which makes me think that maybe Alexa's just a prickly person and she actually tolerates me but doesn't know how to show it.

But probably not.

It turns out that four funnel cakes for four people who just rode a million roller coasters is way too much.

"I'm still sort of nauseous from the rides." I rip funnel cake into chunks and take a few small bites.

"Me too," Dhruv says, but he's digging into his funnel cake like it's the last thing he'll ever eat.

We're sitting on the edge of a fountain on the main boardwalk. It's lined with games where you can win huge stuffed animals like bananas with faces and giant rainbow bouncy balls with googly eyes and things like that.

The four of us are in a post–roller coaster daze, picking at our funnel cakes, when we hear a voice from a bit farther down the boardwalk saying, "Get ready to soar two hundred and twenty-five feet in the air at speeds of over ninety miles per hour in less than two seconds!"

Rani and I look up at the same time to see what's going on. The sound seems to be coming from a ride where there are these two huge metal towers that are weirdly bent outward.

"Let's go look," Rani says.

"Can we?" I ask Alexa, because even though she's definitely *not* my babysitter, I still feel like I should check with her.

"Be my guest," she says, not looking up from her phone. Her thumbs are going at warp speed. She's probably texting her mom to tell her how terrible I am.

I try to shrug this thought off as Rani and I run over to the ride. It's called the Slingshot, and there's already a crowd gathered to watch. Two people are being strapped into seats that are attached to these super long bungee cords. I look up to see what the bungee cords are attached to, and I realize they go all the way up to the top of the giant towers.

The people are strapped in now, and their seats tilt so

they face the sky. Then the operator presses a button that pulls the bungee cords down.

"All clear for takeoff," the operator says, pressing another button.

The bungee cords release, and the two riders shoot straight up into the air. I crane my neck to look into the sky, but when they reach the peak of the Slingshot, they're so high up that I can barely even see them.

"That's so cool," Rani says, using a hand to block out the sun. "We gotta go on it."

"Yeah, but it's like twenty bucks," I say, pointing to the sign. "It doesn't come with park admission."

"Oh, that's fine. I can pay for us. My mom gave me way more money than I need for the trip. Like, I'm definitely not gonna spend it all."

I think about Rani's house, with its secret closets and spiral staircases. And then I think about my cramped apartment, and how I'd be too nervous to ask my dad to pay for something as silly as an extra ride at an amusement park if I knew it cost twenty dollars.

"I don't know," I say.

"Come on, it'll be great."

It feels a little weird to let Rani pay for this. It makes me feel like we're not really a team. It's like she's the captain and I'm just the person dancing around in a giant mascot costume.

But I do really want to go on the Slingshot.

"You should do it," Dhruv says. He and Alexa must've walked up behind us while the riders were being flung into the sky. "We can hold on to your stuff. Right, Alexa?"

Alexa doesn't say yes, but she doesn't say no either. Dhruv looks at her, then gives me a covert thumbs-up.

I still feel weird about Rani paying for me, but I try not to think about it too much. "All right, I'm in."

Despite the crowd, there's no line for the ride itself, so Rani hands the ride operator twenty bucks (I keep thanking her and she keeps saying it's nothing) and we hop into the two seats.

"Do you girls have anything in your pockets?" the person strapping our harnesses asks. We shake our heads. "Good, because if you did it could fly out and hit someone."

Rani and I look at each other and giggle nervously. We're basically about to be two human-sized rocks in a gigantic rubber band slingshot.

"All right, prepare to launch," the ride dude says. "In three, two—"

And before he even gets to one, we're shooting up into the air. We're so high that I think the bungee cords must've ripped and we're gonna rocket straight out of the atmosphere. But then we slow down, and down, and down, and suddenly we're FALLING BACK INTO THE EARTH. Rani and I are both screaming, and my stomach's definitely stuck somewhere up in the sky, but it can stay there if it wants because this is the best feeling.

Before we splatter on the ground, the bungee cords bounce us back up into the air, and I try to spot Alexa and Dhruv on the ground. Dhruv's waving at us with both hands over his head, and Alexa's sitting there, looking at her phone. She's been texting pretty much all day.

I guess those are weird thoughts to be having while I'm free-falling to the ground on a giant slingshot. Maybe it's my brain's way of distracting me from what feels like certain death.

Once the main bounces are over, we hover in the air for a minute, suspended twenty feet above the park.

"That was wild," Rani says. The bungee cords expand and contract and we gently move up and down and up and down. She looks over at me, her face more serious now. "I'm really glad you invited me on this trip."

I'm about to tell her I'm really glad she came, but then a latch clicks somewhere below us and the ride jerks us back toward the ground, stopping right before we crash.

I think this is going to be one of those days I remember for a really, really long time.

The ride operator comes around to unbuckle our harnesses. We tumble out, a bit wobbly, then run over to Alexa and Dhruv.

I grab my phone from the pile of stuff we left with them, and there's a text from my dad. I don't really want to read it, because I'm worried it'll ruin the shiny good feeling I have right now, but I open my phone anyway.

Dad: How's it going?

I look over at Alexa, Dhruv, and Rani. I look up at the Slingshot, and around at all the roller coasters I've been on. I watch the people running by. There are some little kids who are shouting and laughing and drinking slushies that are probably turning their tongues blue.

And even if I don't know how I feel about my dad, I definitely know how I feel about the trip. So, I can honestly say:

Me: it's AMAZING!!!

CHAPTER TWELVE

"THE ride over to Connecticut's gonna be like four hours," Alexa says, glaring at me and Rani in the rearview mirror. "So don't ask how long it'll take."

"We won't," I say. "Because you just told us." I cross my arms and sit back, then turn around as far as my seat belt will allow to watch the sun set over Great Adventure.

We're driving to a motel near Lake Compounce, the next amusement park on our trip, and Rani and I are sitting in the back seat again (duh, because Alexa would never let either of us sit up front). I barely remember being in the car this morning, seeing roller coasters peek over the trees for the first time.

Now the only thing in front of us is a long stretch of highway. I'm a bit nauseous, probably from the combination of roller coasters and the Slingshot and too much funnel cake. That's enough to make anyone nauseous, really.

Rani's leaning against the door on her side with her legs curled under her. She fell asleep almost immediately after the car started moving, and now I'm kind of watching her.

I know it sounds weird, but I just like looking at Rani. I like that her mouth is curved up a bit, almost like she's thinking about something really nice. Maybe she's dreaming about doing gory Halloween makeup, or about swimming or going on roller coasters with me.

I mean, not with me specifically, just going on roller coasters.

I think you can tell a lot about a person based on how they sleep. Well, mostly just if they snore or fidget or things like that. But the best part about watching someone while they're sleeping is that you can think about whatever you want, because they can't see your face and, like, figure out what's going on inside your brain. I don't know why, but I get a little nervous around Rani when she's awake. Or at least I'm worried about what I might say. It's nice to not be nervous right now. It's like being on a roller coaster. You can't mess up what you say while you're riding one, because you can't really say anything. Except, like, "AAAAAAAAAHHHHH!" which doesn't count.

I've felt this way around Rani from the very first day I met her at swim practice.

"So you're, like, new here?" I had asked her.

We were in the locker room after Rani's first practice. She was putting a T-shirt and shorts on over her swimsuit.

"Yup," she said in response to my super obvious question. "My family just moved here from Minneapolis."

"Cool." I wasn't sure what else to say, so I pretended I was really busy wrapping my towel around my waist.

"What grade are you going into?" she asked.

"Eighth. You?"

"Me too!" She said this with so much enthusiasm that I immediately felt a thousand percent less awkward. "At Madison Middle?"

"Yup," I said. And then I felt bad for just saying "yup," so I added, "This is so cool." But then that felt like too much. "I mean, it's nice to have someone else my age on the team."

"Yeah, I'm so relieved. I thought I'd be the oldest one." She slid her flip-flops on. "And it'll be nice to know someone when we go back to school in the fall."

"Totally," I said. But then I realized it sounded like I was agreeing that it would be nice to know someone at school, which made it sound like I didn't know anyone. Or like I didn't have any friends.

Which was technically true. But she didn't know that.

"I can show you the ropes." I meant it to sound all cool, like I knew the ins and outs of Madison Middle, but I think it made me sound like a pirate.

"The ropes?" She looked at me with her eyebrows raised.

"Oh, yeah." And because my mouth wasn't communicating very well with my brain, I kept talking. "Madison Middle is a dangerous place. Ropes everywhere."

"Good thing I'll have someone to guide me." Rani looked at me and smiled.

Even from the first day I knew her, Rani made my face feel too hot.

I keep glancing at Rani while she's sleeping, trying not to make it too obvious in case Dhruv looks back here.

Rani fidgets but doesn't wake up, and after a while she stretches her legs out so that her feet are draped over my thighs.

I'm hyper-aware of every little hair on my legs, and of the places where my skin is extra sensitive, like the tops of my knees. Any move I make could wake Rani up, so now I can't move at all. It's like when a cat falls asleep on your lap, and you just have to stay really, really still. Not that Rani's a cat.

After a few minutes, once it's clear that her legs are probably going to stay put, I start to relax and the whole day catches up with me. Suddenly, I can't keep my eyes open. And with the weight of Rani's legs on top of mine, I fall asleep.

When I wake up, we're still driving, and Rani's still asleep, though she's moved so that her feet are curled under her again.

Alexa and Dhruv are whispering in the front seat. It sounds tense, so I close my eyes to try to make it seem like

I'm still asleep, in case they look back here. I angle my head so I can hear them better.

"I'm sure things are fine," Dhruv says.

"Maybe, but she's being weird." That's Alexa.

Is she talking about me?

"Yeah, but she's always weird when you're not in the same place."

Well, probably not about me, then. Maybe someone they both know from college.

"I just wish we were back at school," Alexa says. "It's not that I wanna keep an eye on her, but . . ."

"You wanna keep an eye on her," Dhruv finishes. Alexa doesn't respond to this. "When David and I started dating," Dhruv starts to say, but then I stop paying attention.

Because Dhruv is dating someone named David? That must mean . . .

Well, it could be a girl's name, but all the Davids I know are guys. I think that means that Dhruv must be, you know . . .

I guess that also means that Dhruv and Alexa aren't dating.

This is a lot of new information to process. I look over at Rani, who's still asleep. If she were awake, I would totally be texting her about this.

So Dhruv has a boyfriend.

Huh.

CHAPTER THIRTEEN

"**WAKE** up, kids." Alexa slams her door shut. "We're here."

I must've fallen asleep again, because for a minute I forget where I am, the way you do when you first wake up.

But then I see Dhruv walking toward the car with two room keys, and everything comes back to me. We're at the motel in Connecticut. Still a weird place to be, but at least I remember.

Dhruv opens the back door and hands me one of the keys.

"If anyone asks, you two aren't sharing a room," he says to me and Rani. "There's supposed to be an adult with you at all times, according to motel policy."

"Dhruv and I are sharing a room," Alexa says. "Obviously. Anyway, just don't burn the place down or get abducted or whatever and we'll be fine."

I don't respond to Alexa. This is the best possible scenario. I won't have to deal with Alexa until the morning, *and* I get to share a room with Rani.

I just hope there are two beds. I don't think I'd be able to fall asleep if there was only one. I'd be too worried about rolling over or, like, hitting Rani in my sleep.

"How about we check out the rooms?" Dhruv asks Rani. "I think Alexa and Dalia have to call their parents."

Oh, right.

"Let's FaceTime them from here," Alexa says, motioning for me to move up to the front seat. "So we can just get it over with."

Dhruv and Rani walk off toward the motel, and Alexa pulls out her phone. Her finger hovers over her mom's contact, but before she presses the button to make the call, she says, "Don't mess this up for me. When they ask, we had the best day ever. They need to think we're practically family already. Got it?"

"Why do you even care?"

"I don't," Alexa says, but then she sighs. "Things with my mom haven't been so great since I got back from college. I need this to go well. I need her to know we had, like, a calm, fun day."

It surprises me a little, that Alexa would tell me this.

Before I can think about what I'm saying, I blurt out, "But your mom seems so chill," because I'm thinking about the bowling alley, and how weirdly nice Vanessa was to me about coming on the trip.

Alexa scoff-laughs. "You don't know what it's like to live

with her. All she's talked about for the past six months is your dad."

I don't really get why that's such a bad thing, other than the fact that it's gross and I don't want to hear it. At least Alexa got to know that her mom was dating someone.

But I don't say anything. It's too much to talk about.

"I'm calling now," Alexa says, then taps the button. "Remember," she hisses at me, "things are great, I'm taking amazing care of you."

Vanessa picks up a moment later. "Hey!" She sounds so excited. It's almost like she thinks this is actually going well. "Steve, the kids are calling!"

I can hear my dad in the background, and when Vanessa moves to adjust the camera, my heart sinks.

Because she's in my apartment. Maybe the only reason my dad agreed to let me go on this trip was so he could have some alone time with Vanessa.

Brain, no. We're not going there.

"Here they are," my dad says as he sits down and puts his face way too close to Vanessa's screen. And even though I can almost see up his nostrils, and Vanessa is sitting with him in *our apartment*, it's still kind of nice to see his face. Maybe it's just because I'm used to seeing it every day. "My two favorite future-stepsisters. How's the bonding going? Are you BFFs forever yet?"

Alexa and I don't say anything.

"Well, how was the first day?" Vanessa asks, rushing to start the conversation back up.

"It was great!" Alexa says. "Right, Dalia?"

When I don't say anything right away, Vanessa asks, "*Was* it great, Dalia?" She raises her eyebrows in a way that reminds me of Alexa.

I briefly forget how to make sounds with my mouth because I'm stressed that I'm getting involved in Vanessa and Alexa's fight.

But then Alexa elbows me in the stomach, and I say "Ow" before adding "Yup! So great!" through gritted teeth. And, I mean, it *was* great. But I still feel like I'm lying to my dad. Or at least not telling him the whole truth.

"Awesome!" my dad says, and he sounds sincere, which annoys me because, like, can't he tell that I'm not being completely honest?

"Well, thanks for checking in," Vanessa says. "We don't want to keep you from getting some good shut-eye!"

Of course they don't even want to talk to us for that long. They just wanted to see that we were alive, and now they can go back to hanging out in *my* apartment *without me.*

Alexa's smiling as she waves into the phone and says "Bye!" She doesn't even wait for her mom to respond before hanging up and twisting her face back to her trademark Alexa scowl.

Is this what my life's going to be like from now on?

Awkward conversations with people I barely know and definitely don't like? Alexa's already, like, a constant reminder that everything's going to be different when I get home from this trip, and the call with our parents only made it worse. My life's never going to be the same, and it sucks.

We both get out of the car, and Alexa walks toward her motel room. Before opening the door, she turns back to face me. "Don't die."

And then she's gone. I let out a long, slow breath and my whole body unclenches as I open the door to my motel room.

Most of the room is taken up by two twin beds, so, phew. They're separated by two identical bedside tables with two identical lamps. The walls are beige and prickly, and the carpet is almost exactly the same color as the walls.

"Hey!" Rani says when she sees me. She's walking around the room, examining things. She already put her stuff on the bed farther from the door, and she even brought her laptop. Maybe we'll watch roller coaster POV videos on it. I mean, no, that's silly. Why would we do that? We've ridden actual roller coasters.

But I think about that day, back in the secret room, when we were watching the Boulder Dash video on her laptop with our legs touching and . . . I don't know, it might be nice if that happened again.

Rani moves over to her bed and fluffs the pillows. She

picks up the weird old phone with a cord that's hanging on the wall between our beds and puts it down. Then she opens the drawer on the bedside table and pulls out a Bible.

"Some light bedtime reading," she says, hoisting the giant book over her head.

"I'm Jewish," I say. I know she was joking, but stuff with Christianity always makes me a little uncomfortable.

"And I'm Muslim," she says.

We laugh, because the Bible isn't a religious book for either of us. I mean, I guess it's good they have a Bible in here, because a lot of people who come to stay at the motel are probably Christian, and they might want to read a Bible before they go to bed. But shouldn't they also have books for other religions?

Rani lies back and scrolls through her phone for a minute. I sit on the edge of my bed, looking around the room. It's exciting to be so completely alone with Rani, without little kids on the swim team or my dad in the other room or Alexa and Dhruv watching over us.

"I just need to call my mom," Rani says. "I promised I would call every night."

"Sounds good."

I'm sure Rani's mom *wants* to talk to her. I'm sure she's excited to hear about Rani's day. Unlike my dad, who just wants to make sure I'm getting in sufficient bonding time with Alexa. And definitely unlike my mom, who doesn't even have my phone number.

Rani holds the phone tight to her ear and says, "Salam, mami jan," in a higher and sweeter voice than usual. After that she mostly listens to her mom talk and responds with one-word answers in English.

I knew that Rani speaks Farsi, but I've never talked to her about it. It's so cool. All I know are a few sentences in Yiddish and like two words of French.

There's probably a lot of stuff that Rani and I haven't talked about. Things I haven't even bothered asking. How am I supposed to catch up and learn everything about Rani in the same way that I know everything about Abby?

I mean, I've been friends with Abby for basically forever. Or I *was* friends with Abby for basically forever. I don't even remember how I learned things like how she's afraid of bees but not allergic to them, and that you have to climb into the back seat of her dad's car from the front because the doors are broken. I just knew.

I feel like I don't know anything important about Rani. Or even just the little details about her. I don't always know how to talk to her the way I talked to Abby. It's like my brain can't communicate properly with my mouth and I just spew word vomit.

And now Rani and I are sharing a room in a motel, which seems like something you should only do with someone you know really well. Somehow, being alone with Rani is exciting and awkward and nerve-racking all at the same time.

When Rani's done talking to her mom, she puts her phone on the bedside table and plops down on the mattress, smiling at me. "Today was awesome," she says.

My mood turns around instantly. Maybe it doesn't matter how well you know someone, just that you get along well and you have fun hanging out. Maybe that's enough sometimes.

I'm sitting cross-legged on my bed, facing Rani. She has her arms laced behind her head, and she's staring up at the ceiling.

"Except for Alexa," I say.

"But Dhruv's nice," she says. "I was talking to him before, when you and Alexa were calling your parents. And maybe Alexa's warming up to you?"

"Maybe."

Wait—she was talking to Dhruv before? I guess they're sort of becoming friends or something. Which is cool, but I feel a twinge of jealousy.

"Oh, I forgot to tell you." I lean forward. Now that she brought up Dhruv, I need to let her know what I overheard in the car. "Alexa and Dhruv were whispering, when they thought I was asleep, and guess what?"

"What?"

"Dhruv's . . . You know . . ."

"Know what? What is he?" She turns over and props herself up on an elbow, facing me.

"He's, um . . ." Suddenly I'm embarrassed. I don't know

why, but it feels weird to be saying this to Rani. "He's gay," I whisper.

"Oh, yeah," Rani says, smiling a little. "I knew that."

"What?" How did she know? "Did he tell you?"

Maybe they really *are* becoming friends.

"No," Rani says, looking down at the motel comforter. "I just knew, I guess."

She just knew.

Is that something you're supposed to just be able to tell? Does everyone know when someone isn't, like, a boy who likes girls or a girl who likes boys or whatever? My face gets hot, and I'm worried that Rani can see into my brain. I mean, if she already knew about Dhruv, what other kinds of things does she know?

Like, can she tell that I've been thinking a lot about her and about getting to know her and that I was sort of watching her sleep? Because I don't want her to know that stuff.

Not that thinking about those things means anything.

I think.

I need to change the subject to something that's totally safe. "Are you nervous about eighth grade?"

"Not really," she says. "I guess I'm nervous about starting a new school, though."

"Yeah, that seems like it would be really scary." Even if Madison Middle is the worst place in the world, at least it's *my* worst place in the world. I'm used to it.

"And I miss my friends from back home," she adds. "They all knew me super well, and we could talk about anything . . ." She trails off and looks away from me.

Does that mean she doesn't think *we* can talk about anything?

Then Rani says something so quietly that I can barely hear her: "What if no one likes me?"

"Well, I like you," I say. And then I want to take it back. Because I know how it sounds. "I mean, I'll hang out with you." I have to keep talking, to fill the space, so that she doesn't even remember that I said it. Because I didn't mean it that way. I didn't. "And like I'm sure everyone will like you. Because you're cool and nice and pretty—"

Why does my mouth say things before my brain can think? It's not even like my brain does much better, most of the time. But I would hope it would tell my mouth not to say that.

"Pretty?" she asks.

I can't look at her, but it sounds like there's a smile in her voice. Or maybe she's just trying not to laugh at me.

"Like, the popular girls will like you, is what I meant," I say. "They'll think you're cool. That's what I was trying to say."

I don't know why I'm saying this either. It's not like I *want* her to be friends with Cassie, but I guess it might happen. And if it does, I want to be prepared. Because I wasn't prepared for Abby to ditch me. Maybe I shouldn't even be getting to know Rani, maybe I should just—

"I'm not trying to be popular," she says, picking at the hem of her flouncy skirt. "I just wanna have, like, a few friends."

"I'm sure you'll have *tons* of friends," I say, because of course she will. She's so nice and cool and fun to hang out with. I'm just a stepping-stone to better friends.

"And, I'll have you." She sits up and looks at me. "Right?"

I beam at her. Talking to Abby never made me feel so jealous one minute and so completely happy the next.

And if Rani still wants to hang out with me after all the silly things I just said, then maybe there's hope.

So I say, "Right."

Rani yawns, and then I'm yawning too. I'm even more tired than I was in the car.

"I think I'm gonna brush my teeth and go to bed," she says, digging through her bag. When she finds her toothbrush and toothpaste she walks into the bathroom and shuts the door.

I lie faceup on the bed. I don't want to get up, maybe ever.

When Rani steps out of the bathroom, I pretend like I'm typing something on my phone, but really, I'm just thinking about our conversation.

After a minute she says, "I think you're my only friend

here." And I know she means like back on Long Island, not in this motel room. Though I guess that's true too. "I don't want you to think I'm not happy to be your friend, since I'm saying I also wanna have other ones." She flops over so she's facing me. "I just wanted to say that."

I don't tell her that, really, she's my only friend here too.

CHAPTER FOURTEEN

"RISE and shine, kiddies," an angry voice shouts through the door.

This is followed by a loud banging sound. I rub my face and stretch my toes, and I'm confused for a second even after I open my eyes. I look around in the semidarkness, once again trying to remember where I am.

"If you're not dressed and in the car in fifteen minutes, we're leaving without you."

Oh, right. Alexa. As my eyes adjust to the early morning light streaming in through the window, I remember that I'm in a motel room. And that Rani's sleeping in a bed five feet away from mine. The conversation we had last night comes back to me. I can't believe I called her pretty.

But I don't think about that for too long, because I remember something else: We're going to Lake Compounce today.

And you know what that means?

Boulder Dash.

It's only around ten a.m., but there are already tons of people streaming into the park. To reach the entrance gate, we all have to walk through a long concrete tunnel with a giant sign stretched across the wall that says "FUN THIS WAY!"

"I think I'm still nauseous from that funnel cake yesterday," Dhruv says. His voice echoes around us, bouncing off the concrete.

"Well, suck it up," Alexa tells him, but she's smiling. That doesn't stop her words from repeating back to us, echoing until all of Connecticut knows that they should be sucking something up.

When we make it to the end of the tunnel and step outside, the sunlight is almost blinding. Once my eyes adjust, I get my first look at Lake Compounce.

It's not like Great Adventure, where everything around us was hulking and made of steel. Lake Compounce feels different. The minute you walk in, it's like you're on the main street of some town from a hundred years ago. There are all these pastel-colored shops, with a clock tower sticking up from the center one.

The only thing that makes it clear that this isn't just some old-timey town is that, towering above the quaint houses, there's a huge wooden roller coaster. It's not Boulder Dash, though, because Boulder Dash is way bigger and built into the mountain that sticks up behind this other roller coaster. But it's still pretty cool.

"We gotta go on Boulder Dash," Rani says, hopping up and down a bit.

I've been worried that things might be weird with her since my mouth betrayed my brain last night, but so far everything seems normal.

"Yeah," I agree, walking away from Alexa. "We'll meet up with you two later."

"Whoa, whoa, whoa," Alexa says. "Slow down." She crosses her arms. "What's this Boulder Dash thing, and what if me and Dhruv wanna go on it too?"

"It's only the best roller coaster of all time," Rani says, looking over at me.

"You can just go on it later," I tell Alexa. "Rani and I are gonna go on it now." It comes out way whinier than I mean for it to, but I want to go on Boulder Dash with Rani.

Alone.

"No, I think we'll go on it now," Alexa says in a way that makes it clear she's already made up her mind. "Don't you, Dhruv?"

"Don't drag me into this," Dhruv says, but he follows as Alexa starts walking toward the mountain.

Toward Boulder Dash.

"How's the line this long already?" Rani asks. "The park *just* opened."

It only took a few minutes for us to walk over to Boulder

Dash, but now that we're here it's clear that everyone else had the same idea. There's a sign near us that says "Wait Time From This Point: Forty-five Minutes."

"Do you think we should wait?" I ask.

"Yeah, of course," Rani says. "I've been looking forward to this ever since we watched the video."

Well . . . who cares about forty-five little minutes, anyway?

Alexa sighs and rolls her eyes like it's my fault that there's a line for the most popular ride at the park. She takes out her phone and starts typing some really long message. I wonder if this has something to do with what Dhruv and Alexa were whispering about last night in the car.

I still have no idea what's going on with that, or who she was talking about. I don't even know why I care.

The line inches forward, and Alexa barely looks up from her phone.

"Let's play a game," Dhruv suggests after a few minutes of total silence.

"What kind of game?" Rani asks.

"How about one-word story?"

"What's that?" I ask.

"What do you think it is?" That's Alexa. "You go around and make a story by saying one word each." She's not even looking up from her phone. She's so good at being mean to me that she can do it while she's texting someone else.

"I'll start," Dhruv says quickly. He thinks for a second. "The . . ."

It's Rani's turn next. "Little . . ."

Now it's Alexa's turn. She even puts her phone away. "Badger . . ."

The little badger. Okay, that's actually pretty funny.

Hm, what's next? I can say any word I want, which is both freeing and terrifying.

"Can't . . ."

I guess I'm feeling like the badger needs a challenge.

Back to Dhruv: "Feel . . ."

"*Her,*" Rani says, making it clear that she *decided* that the badger would be a girl. And I feel bad for automatically thinking that the badger would be a boy.

Alexa: "Tail . . ."

"Oh, I forgot to add," Dhruv says. "When you think a sentence is over, you can say 'period,' but that has to be your word."

Well, "The little badger can't feel her tail" seems like as good a way to start a story as any, so I say "Period."

The line moves forward a bit, and Dhruv starts the next sentence. "She . . ."

Rani: "Loves . . ."

Alexa: "To . . ."

What does the badger love to do? What even are badgers? I think maybe they're like ferrets, but I can't be sure.

So, I make something up. "Dance . . ."

I put my hands above my head and do a little spin, like I'm the dancing badger. Rani giggles.

Dhruv continues with "But . . ."

"I'm gonna say 'she,' but this is totally unfair," Rani says, crossing her arms. "I keep landing on the boring words."

"We're all making up the story," Alexa says. "And we need all the words for it to work. *She* is just as important as anything else."

That might be the first helpful thing Alexa's said this whole trip. She wasn't saying it to me, of course. But it's something.

"Fine. She . . ."

Alexa: "Doesn't . . ."

Me: "Have . . ."

Dhruv: "Shoes . . ."

We all laugh at that. Poor shoeless badger.

Then Rani says "Period," and we're about to start a new sentence, but the line moves a bit and Alexa's back to checking her phone.

"I hope the badger gets to be a dancer," Dhruv says.

"Me too," I say. "I think she's probably very graceful."

"And she likes to tap-dance," Rani adds. "Because she thinks ballet is too slow."

I look over at Alexa. She's still at it with the typing, but it doesn't seem she's doing it to avoid talking to us. Her eyebrows squeeze together as she taps her thumbs on the screen.

"You okay?" Dhruv asks her quietly, rubbing her back. "Is it Sara?"

My brain perks up. There's that name again. The one that almost started a fight between Vanessa and Alexa at the bowling alley.

So, Sara must be the person she keeps texting. Maybe Alexa got into a fight with a friend too. Maybe Sara's, like, Alexa's Abby.

But I don't want to think about Alexa having a friend who ditched her, or Alexa being anything like me at all.

She puts her phone in her back pocket. "Uh, yeah. I'm fine," she says to Dhruv. But she doesn't sound it. "I'm ready for the ride, that's for sure."

After a bit more waiting, we're finally in the station, lining up for a spot on the next train. Rani and I stand behind a gate, while Dhruv and Alexa wait behind the one next to ours. That way they'll be in the seat in front of us and we'll all be in the same car.

"Do you think it'll be as good as the video?" I ask Rani, trying to distract myself from the pre-coaster jitters.

"I mean, it's gotta be, right?"

And before my brain can shut it down, I say, in a half-annoyed voice, "Does it, though?"

It's something I would say to Abby, but not Rani. Not a

new friend. Not someone who I could so easily scare away. Who I *have* almost scared away, probably.

But then Rani says, "Well, I guess we'll just have to see for ourselves."

She looks over at me and wiggles her eyebrows all mysteriously and grins.

I grin back.

Today, Rani's wearing striped overall shorts that don't look like any other article of clothing I've ever seen. She's like a cool train conductor. They're loose and bright and fun.

"I love your overall things," I say, because I want her to know. Because it's a normal thing to say. I think.

"Thanks!" She puts her hands in her pockets and lets her torso swing back and forth a bit. "You can try them on later if you want."

Her eyes go wide and she looks down at the ground, and I quickly look away too.

A moment later, the gates open.

The four of us rush into the car. Rani and I lower our lap bar, and the jitters come on even stronger, on top of the pang I felt when she told me I could try on her clothes.

"All clear," the park employee says after a minute. "Have a fantastic ride."

Then the roller coaster starts moving.

We're moving.

"Are you ready to riiiiiide?" the park employee asks as we go down the tiny hill that greets you right outside the station.

Everyone cheers, and I cheer right along with them. It's so weird to finally be on the actual coaster, after watching other people go on it so many times on YouTube. It's almost like I'm watching myself on a video.

The climb to the top is way bumpier than I imagined, and also way slower. Alexa and Dhruv look back at us while the coaster's inching up the track, and they both make silly faces. Which just proves my point that it's hard to be mean or miserable or on your phone when you're on a roller coaster. Like, it's basically impossible.

"WOOOOO!" Rani shouts, bouncing as much as she can with the tightened lap bar and looking over at me.

I want to scream along with her, but I'm way more nervous than I thought I'd be. My whole body's shaking.

Then Rani says, "Let's try to put our hands up. At least for the first drop."

"I don't know . . ."

If she had asked me before we got on the ride, I would've agreed in a heartbeat. But now that we're almost to the top, I want to hold on to the lap bar and never let go.

"Come on," Rani says. "We have to do it. Together."

And since I somehow always feel braver when I'm with Rani, I say, "All right. Let's do it."

We reach the top of the lift hill, and the ride almost seems to stop. There's a stretch of flat track that curves around so you can't see the drop. And we're going so slowly on this part that it feels like we could step out of the roller coaster and have a picnic or something.

And then—

"Here we go," Rani says, her leg bouncing next to mine.

We're at the drop now, which looks way higher than it did in the videos. Way, way higher.

In the split second before the coaster crests the hill, I chicken out. I can't lift my hands in the air. I can't do it. I absolutely can't.

But as we're about to fall, I feel a pull on my hand.

It's Rani, lifting mine up with hers.

She's holding my hand.

Then we drop.

AND I AM SCREAMING AT THE TOP OF MY LUNGS. I HAVE NEVER SCREAMED HARDER. NOT EVEN ON KINGDA KA.

BECAUSE I'M ON BOULDER DASH.

AND RANI'S HOLDING MY HAND.

After the first big drop, the ride jerks us to the left, and Rani lets go of my hand and grabs onto the lap bar. And, okay, she was clearly just grabbing my hand because I was chickening out on my promise. She was just making me put my arms in the air.

But it's almost like I can still feel her hand in mine, even when I'm gripping the bar.

The ride jerks us hard to the left again, then to the right, then to the left.

We're speeding through the trees, going up and down and up and down over tiny hills that throw us into the air. Alexa and Dhruv are clutching their lap bar for dear life, but I can see they're both laughing.

I should be thinking about how much I'm enjoying the ride, but I keep thinking about the way Rani's hand felt in mine, clammy and solid. I don't know why. Because really, it's not weird. Friends hold hands.

Well, I never held hands with Abby. But then again, we never went on a roller coaster together.

But also, I was never nervous around Abby the way I am around Rani.

And then these thoughts are knocked out of me, because we reach the bumpiest section and I'm screaming and Rani's screaming and Alexa and Dhruv are screaming and the wind and the woods are whipping past us, impossibly fast and loud.

For a moment, I don't have to talk or think or worry. The train clatters over the wooden track and my hair flies up from its ponytail.

After what feels like no time at all, the roller coaster train stops short and the ride comes to an end.

Dhruv and Alexa look back at us with windswept hair and huge smiles.

I only have the windswept part.

I'm too stunned to do anything except grip the lap bar, but on the inside I want to scream with joy. My whole body's warm, like I just downed a hot cup of decaf coffee at Bagel Boys.

"So," Dhruv says, "how was it?"

This time, I don't know what to say.

CHAPTER FIFTEEN

WHEN we get off the ride my whole body's covered in sweat.

"It's literally so humid," Alexa says.

I mean, I guess that's part of the reason why I'm, like, damp. Seriously, I'm drenched in sweat. It's awful. And my hands. Well, my hand, mostly. The one hand that Rani held. Or grabbed onto. Or whatever.

That one's particularly sweaty.

"We could go to the water park," Dhruv says. "It'll probably be less crowded now than later in the afternoon."

Last week, when I was researching all the amusement parks we'd be going to on this trip, I saw that Lake Compounce has a whole water park section.

It's important to do research, I think. To know exactly what you're getting yourself into. Not that I knew what it would feel like to go on an actual roller coaster, or to be at an amusement park. And not that I knew the hand thing was going to happen. But still.

From where we're standing, I can almost make out all these tall water slides and stuff. It looks like fun, and if I don't cool off I'm gonna melt into a puddle of sweat.

Rani says, "I'm down," and Alexa says, "Let's do it," and we're all in agreement that now is the right time to get into the water. Well, I don't actually say anything. But I nod. Or at least I think I do.

I'm a bit distracted.

"Let's get changed and meet out in front of the wave pool," Alexa says, mostly for Dhruv, since he's going to a different locker room.

I wish I could go somewhere and change by myself too. I know Dhruv's not changing by himself, since he'll be in a locker room with other guys. But I really don't want to have to change in front of Alexa and Rani. I've never felt comfortable changing in front of anyone. Abby always said it's because I'm an only child, and that if I had siblings I'd be fine changing basically anywhere, but I don't know if that's true. I think I'm just always a little uncomfortable.

We go into the locker room and I walk right into a bathroom stall, even though there's a sign that says "Please Change in the Dressing Area," which makes it sound like we're all salads and we need to be covered in ranch or balsamic vinaigrette.

Changing in the stall sucks. I press my back up against the grimy plastic wall so that I'm as far away as possible from the toilet, but it's still better than peeling off my sweaty clothes in front of other people while hiding under my towel.

When I'm done, I make my way toward the changing area. The locker room is full of little kids walking around in their little kid bikinis, and they don't look stressed about it at all. Yet here I am, thirteen years old, sporting the one-piece that I wear to swim practice. I don't even own a bikini. And I would never ask my dad to buy one for me. That would be the most embarrassing thing in the entire world.

When I get over to the changing area, I see Alexa. She's wearing a bikini top with board shorts, like the ones boys wear. Well, anyone can wear them, obviously. Because Alexa's wearing them.

They have sharks on them, and I actually think they're pretty cool. I guess she has a bunch of cool shorts. I didn't even know that was an option, to wear board shorts. They seem way more comfortable than my swim-practice bathing suit.

"Um, I really like your swim shorts," I tell her, saying it as quickly as I possibly can to get it over with. It was one thing complimenting Rani's overalls, but it's another to tell Alexa that I like what she's wearing.

She looks at me questioningly, then nods and says, "Thanks."

We're both quiet for a second.

"You ready?" I turn around and there's Rani. She's wearing an orange tankini, and for some reason I feel like I shouldn't be looking at her, so I stare at the wet tile floor instead.

I don't know why I'm so embarrassed. She wears her fancy sports bikini to practice most of the time, so she's more covered now than she usually is for swimming.

I feel exposed too, even though Rani's just looking at my face. It's like she's waiting for an answer.

Oh wait, she is. Because she asked a question. Where's a brain when you need one?

"Yup," Alexa says, responding to Rani for me.

I'm really not ready to be out in the park in just my bathing suit, but I'm grateful that I don't have to talk.

Alexa shoves our stuff in an empty locker and we go outside to meet up with Dhruv. He's wearing the same board shorts as Alexa.

"We bought a matching set so we'd be able to find each other in case we got lost," Dhruv says, and I don't know if he's joking or not.

We walk over to the Lazy River, which snakes through the whole water park area. There are about a million inner tubes stacked on top of each other, and everyone's rushing to grab one and jump in the water.

"Lazy River" is kind of a silly name. Are other rivers not lazy? Are they hard workers? I wonder what makes a river lazy. I guess just that it's a slow-moving body of water at an amusement park. Honestly, I think the Lazy River deserves to be lazy. Not everyone needs to be a hard worker all the time.

"Grab a tube and get in," the lifeguard shouts at us. She has a whistle in her mouth and is blowing it even though no one's doing anything wrong. There are some people who really shouldn't have the power to make such a shrill and loud noise whenever they want.

"She's worse than Leah," Rani whispers to me. She's standing very close.

"At least she's not making us swim laps," I say, still trying not to look right at Rani and her tankini.

She laughs a little, and she's close enough that I can feel her breath. My cheeks get hot.

Dhruv is the first of us to grab a tube. He hops onto it gracefully and starts floating down the river.

It's too hot to not be in the water, especially with my whole face blushing, so I go next. I wade into the super chlorinated river, keeping my arms above my head and trying not to think about how many kids (and probably adults) pee in it every day. I pull a tube in behind me, and attempt to hop up onto it backward like Dhruv did.

And it's totally not happening. My butt slides off the plastic tube, which makes a high-pitched squeaking noise as I fall back into the water.

Then I try to belly flop onto it, but that doesn't work either.

The lifeguard blows the ear-piercing whistle. "Get in a tube or get out," she shouts at me.

"Jeez," I say under my breath.

"Just get into it from underwater," Dhruv says. He's paddling against the flow of the river to reach me, and he grabs onto my tube, keeping it steady.

I don't want to just dive under. I can't. Even into the overly warm water of the Lazy River.

But then the horrible whistle blows again, and if I don't go under now, I'm never gonna do it.

I hold my breath and duck under the lukewarm water, and for that brief moment, I can't hear anything from above the surface. There's only the sound of water rushing past my head. And even if I'm just in three feet of water at the beginning of a Lazy River, for a few seconds, everything feels better. Even my brain gets quiet. There's nothing to do, or focus on, or think about. I'm just . . . underwater.

That's the best part of swimming, really. The feeling that you're somewhere completely different, where you don't have to worry about saying the wrong thing, because you can't say anything at all.

And now that I think about it, I actually have two places where I don't have to worry about every little thing I say: underwater, and on roller coasters. Maybe I can just hold my breath and/or be on a roller coaster every moment for the rest of my life. That way I won't say something wrong and mess everything up.

But as much as I think it might solve all my problems, I physically can't stay underwater forever. So, after a few seconds I pop up into the hole of the tube.

"I was worried a shark got you," Dhruv says, and I laugh a little.

He's still holding on to my tube, so we start to float down the river together, away from Alexa and Rani, who are still grabbing their tubes.

"They'll catch up in a bit," Dhruv says. "Or not. It's a Lazy River. Let's just let the current carry us."

He closes his eyes and rests his head on the tube. He looks so peaceful, and I start to wonder how he became friends with Alexa in the first place. She's so . . . bossy, I guess, and Dhruv seems like more of a go-with-the-flow type of guy.

I decide to ask him. "So, like, how did you and Alexa become friends?"

He opens his eyes and looks over at me. "She's pretty nice, you know." He props himself up on his elbows. "Underneath the parts that seem a little prickly."

That's not an answer to my question, but I don't push it, because I don't want him to get mad or stop talking to me. We drift down the river for a minute.

"We lived on the same floor," he says, finally. "Our dorm rooms were right next to each other."

He doesn't say anything else, so I kick my feet gently

in the water and think about how sometimes the fact that someone's just sort of around can be as good a reason to be friends with them as any. That's how Abby and I became friends. We were both waiting for the swings at recess, and that was that.

"Is Alexa your best friend at college?"

We're about to pass under a big waterfall that's smack-dab in the middle of the Lazy River. Some people are frantically trying to move their tubes away from the falling water, but Dhruv is just calmly floating toward it.

"Yeah, pretty much," he says, heading straight for the waterfall. "I also do theater stuff, so I have a bunch of friends from that. But Alexa's my best friend, for sure."

I try to imagine what it would be like to have different friend groups. Or even just more than one friend. Maybe it's easier for people like Dhruv and Rani, people who are nice and fun and don't overthink everything they say.

Dhruv gets soaked by the waterfall, and I follow right behind. It's very loud for a moment as the water beats against the hollow plastic tube.

"That felt nice," he says. "Refreshing." He shakes his hair so that it sprinkles me with water.

I splash him a bit too, but then I steer the conversation back to Alexa. "What's she like at school?"

"Alexa? She's . . ." Dhruv waves his hands in the air, as if the answer is floating just above the Lazy River. "Calmer,

I guess. Less stressed." He puts a hand into the water and lets it flow with the current. "This isn't such a great time for her."

"Because of me? And my dad and stuff?"

"No, no," Dhruv says quickly. "Well, that might be part of it. But it's something else, don't worry."

"Oh."

But of course, my brain is saying *WORRY!* Because that's what I think whenever someone tells me *not* to worry.

"Did you know that I have a stepsister?" Dhruv asks.

I can tell he's trying to change the subject, but I'm still intrigued. "You do?"

"Well, I don't remember a time when I didn't have a stepsister, so it's not really the same as you and Alexa, but still."

"Do you like her?"

"Of course," he says, then laughs when he sees my face. I bet he can tell that I'm thinking it's not really an "of course" situation for me and Alexa.

And we're not even stepsisters. Yet.

"It was just me and my mom, at first. She came here with me from Mumbai when I was a baby, and she met my stepdad a few months later." He gets sprayed by a water mister from above and wipes his face down with his hand. "I've known my stepsister for basically my entire life, so she's really just my sister. But it's a normal thing, having a stepsister. Lots of people have them."

"But you were just a baby, so you didn't even know it was happening," I say. "I'm thirteen. I don't know how I'm supposed to just go along with the fact that I didn't have a sibling for my entire life and now I'm about to have . . . Alexa."

"You just do," he says. "And I'm not saying this to be mean, but you don't really have a choice."

"You're like the millionth person to tell me that," I mumble, slapping the water a little with my fist.

The first person to tell me that was my dad. I don't even want to think about that, though. I always thought that even if everyone else on Earth stopped wanting to be my friend—like Abby—or stopped wanting to be my family —like my mom—that at least I'd have my dad. That he'd always be on my side, and we'd make decisions together, like what to do on a Sunday afternoon and where to get bagels. But now he's on Vanessa's side.

I should've realized I was wrong. I don't know how my brain actually thought something positive, like, ever.

"But not having a choice isn't always a bad thing," Dhruv says, and I look over at him. "Sometimes it brings new experiences or people that we wouldn't have met if we were able to choose for ourselves. Like my boyfriend, David." I perk up at this because he's telling me, not just whispering about it to Alexa. "We met in a class that I didn't even want to take. It was scheduled for super early on a Monday morning, but then David sat next to me on the first day, and the rest is history."

So, I guess it's not a secret that Dhruv has a boyfriend. And now that he's mentioned him, I really want to know more. But maybe he'd think it's weird for me to ask. After all, he's Alexa's friend, not mine.

But I need to know everything. Like how he *knew*. How he could be so sure about who he likes.

"So, like . . ." I start to say. Dhruv looks at me expectantly, and I can't back out now. "When did you know that, like, you know . . ."

"That I'm gay?" Dhruv finishes.

My face gets hot. "Yeah."

"I'm not really sure," he says. "I guess I've just always sort of known." He swings his legs so that his feet splash a little in the water. "And can I say something?"

My heart leaps into my throat. "Uh, sure."

"You should just say the word," he tells me. "You should just say 'gay' if you mean gay. Because that's what I am. You don't need to say 'you know' or whatever. It's not a bad word."

I can feel tears forming in my eyes. He's being so nice, but I'm still ashamed.

I splash water over my face so Dhruv can't see the tears. We're both quiet for a minute as the river carries us forward.

"It's easier," he says gently. "In college."

"What?" I ask.

"Being gay. It got easier. For me, at least."

Why is he telling me this?

And then I have a scary thought: Did he see when Rani held my hand? Because that was just because I chickened out on putting my hand up for the drop!

Or is he looking inside of me, and seeing something? Like how Rani just knew *he* was gay. If the Lazy River wasn't moving my tube along at a sensible speed, I'd be frozen to the spot.

Dhruv must see that something's wrong, because he asks, "Are you okay?"

I feel even more nauseous than I did after the funnel cake yesterday. But I don't want to tell him that.

I'm about to lie and say I feel fine, when Dhruv says, "You don't have to answer that. And you don't have to be okay."

A knot untwists deep in my stomach as I relax back into my tube.

We're coming to the end of the Lazy River. Up ahead, there's this giant frog sculpture that's spitting water out of its mouth. My tube drifts away from Dhruv's, but he grabs onto the two handles of mine and pulls it next to his so that we're connected.

"You grab on too," he says. "We'll make a double tube."

So I do, and we float together toward the frog.

The lifeguard blows her whistle. "HEY! NO DOUBLE TUBES!" But she can't really do anything, because the ride's almost over.

I'm struck by how weird this is, being in the middle of the Lazy River with a college student I barely know.

As I'm thinking this, the frog soaks both of us, and Dhruv and I look at each other, then burst out laughing. And even though the lifeguard yelled at us, he doesn't let go of my tube. And I don't let go of his.

CHAPTER SIXTEEN

DHRUV and I drop our innertubes back at the start of the Lazy River as the lifeguard shakes her head at us. We wave at her like nothing happened, all casual.

There's a slight breeze, which feels nice as it passes over my soaking wet hair and bathing suit. I close my eyes for a moment, and when I open them, Alexa and Rani are walking toward us.

And they're laughing. With each other. The twinge of jealousy I felt when I found out Rani and Dhruv were becoming friends is even stronger now. Except it's not jealousy, really. It's anger. I don't want Rani to get along with Alexa. She *can't* get along with Alexa.

I hate that I feel this way, but I do.

"Where'd you two go?" Alexa asks when she's within speaking range.

"We were just a little ahead of you on the Lazy River," Dhruv says, smiling over at me.

Alexa looks suspicious, but she doesn't say anything. Which makes sense, because I'm suspicious too.

Rani walks over to stand next to me, and I can't help but smile at her. "Hi!" she says, standing on her tippy-toes and rolling back onto her heels. "Um, so, how come you ditched me for Dhruv back there?" She asks it like it's a joke, but now she's not looking at me.

"Looks like you were having a fine time with Alexa." It comes out harsher than I mean it to, but did she forget that Alexa's the enemy? She's the supervillain to our secret agent.

"She's kind of cool, actually. We ended up talking about the weird family group chats we have with our cousins."

"Oh," I say, because I can't form any other words.

"And, like, she was saying how she just sort of sends stickers back and forth to her cousins in Colombia, because she doesn't really speak Spanish and they don't really speak English." Rani gets more and more excited as she tells me about their conversation. "And *I* was telling *her* about my cousins in Iran and how we have a group chat where we complain about how our parents force us to video chat, which is kind of funny because if we're complaining about it to *each other* we're obviously not *that* upset—" Rani finally looks over at me, and she stops talking. "What's wrong?"

I look down at the asphalt. I don't know why I say it, but I'm thinking it, and, you know, brain-mouth communication problems. "Maybe you can be her stepsister instead of me."

"What?"

I know I shouldn't have said that. I know Rani will be angry, and that's obviously the last thing I want. But I can't stop myself. I thought I had Rani to myself, which is silly because Rani can clearly get along with anyone. It's like I was thinking earlier: Some people can make friends so easily, even with people who are mean and would never even try to be friends with me. It's not fair. I just want Rani on my side.

I continue to stare at the ground like it's the main attraction at the amusement park. "I mean, if you're such good friends with her now, you should probably just be her stepsister. She clearly likes you more than me, anyway." I hate the words coming out of my mouth, but I don't know how to stop them.

"That's not fair," Rani says, which gets me to look up. Now *she* seems mad too. I want to take everything back. "*You* ditched *me*! You were talking to Dhruv!"

"That's different!"

"How?"

I try to think of how it's different—because it obviously is—but before I can, Rani stomps off toward the locker room.

I don't follow.

If Abby were here, she'd take my side. She wouldn't even *talk* to Alexa. Or she'd, like, yell at her for me. Well, the old Abby would've. The old Abby could be loud and mean and yell until she got what she wanted, but she'd never yell at me.

I miss the old Abby. I miss the way she'd get angry in my honor. The way she'd defend me. It's silly, though, because I know that I'm missing someone who doesn't really exist anymore. Like, obviously Abby exists, but not in the way I want her to.

I shake Abby thoughts out of my brain as Alexa and Dhruv walk over to me. We head toward the locker rooms in silence, where we once again split up with Dhruv. I give him a little wave, grab my bag from the locker, and run into the bathroom.

When I'm safely hidden in the stall, I check my phone.

I have six texts.

All from Abby.

My eyes go super wide. Maybe she knew I was thinking about her. And she must've been thinking about me too. It's like best friend telepathy.

I open my phone, hands shaking.

> Abby: heyyyy
> miss u

I almost start typing a response. I almost tell her that I miss her too.

But then I see the rest of the message:

> Abby: cassies having a party tomorrow

it's a boys + girls thing
can i tell my mom i'm sleeping at your house?
otherwise she won't let me go

My brain's about to short-circuit.

I can't respond.

Abby thinks she can just text whenever she wants, that she can just ask me to do her a favor. Even though we haven't spoken for months, even though she ditched me.

Well, she can't.

And sure, maybe I miss her. But the messages about the boy-girl party remind me of parts of Abby that I super don't miss, especially from this past year.

Like when she told me about Dylan.

It was the start of last school year, the beginning of seventh grade. Back when Abby and I walked home from school together, like we'd done every day since we were little.

She told me about how she and Dylan kissed behind the multipurpose room. She told me they *had* to kiss then, because he was about to get braces. "And if we kiss with tongue when he has braces on, my mouth will get all cut up," she said, as if it were the most obvious thing in the world.

Before Abby told me this, I hadn't even thought about what happens when you kiss someone with braces. I'd always thought the thing with a kiss was that you put your lips on someone else's lips. But then Abby made me think about tongues and braces and all the other parts involved in kissing. The whole thing seems like more trouble than it's worth. Probably.

I mean, I didn't even know if there was anyone I'd want to kiss. Not that there's anyone I want to kiss now. I'm not saying that.

Ugh.

I don't want to think about Abby and her boyfriend. Or how I felt like a complete baby when Abby would talk about him.

I don't want to think about anything at all. I want my brain to shut off, even if it's just for, like, five minutes.

I throw my clothes back on and run out of the locker room, not even waiting for Rani or Alexa. I leave the water park area and just keep running. I don't even know where I'm going, but I end up in front of a ride right by Boulder Dash. It's called Thunder and Lightning, and it's this huge yellow tower. I watch it in action; it's like if the pirate ship ride did extreme sports.

Mostly I decide to go on it because of the name. My brain's feeling way more Thunder and Lightning than Boulder Dash right now. Plus, the ride doesn't fit in with the rest of the park—it's too big, too metallic, too yellow— and I really feel that.

When I get to the front of the line, the ride attendant

doesn't even question the fact that I'm alone. I run over to the line of seats and hop on.

I strap in, and the ride starts with a mechanical whir as we're pulled back, like when you run a few steps backward on a swing to try to build momentum. We start off fairly low to the ground, but after a minute we're swinging so high and so hard that at the top of the arc I'm staring directly into the sun. It feels like we're gonna spin all the way around, like how some kids say they can make a swing flip over the bar even though that's definitely not true.

And we almost do flip, but then we swing down. We go all the way around so that now I'm suspended in midair in the other direction, staring down at the ground. I close my eyes and let the ride lull me. We go back and forth, back and forth, and the wind feels nice on my face and arms and legs.

While the ride's in motion, it's my whole world. I don't worry about anything else. I wish things could be like this forever.

Then the swinging stops.

I push my harness up and walk out of the ride area, and when I take a deep breath, I do feel slightly better.

I know I need to apologize to Rani. What I said was completely unfair. She doesn't deserve that.

In the distance, I spot her, Alexa, and Dhruv. They're all running over to Boulder Dash. At first, I'm worried that they've been riding rides and having fun without me, but then I see that they all look sort of panicked, so I walk toward them.

Alexa sees me first. She's too far away for me to hear exactly what she's saying, but she looks mad.

"Never, *ever* do that again," she says. "My mom would kill me if something happened to you." And I might just be imagining things but she sounds . . . worried?

No. I don't think Alexa's capable of worry. And, I mean, mostly she just sounds mad. Like, really, really mad.

Dhruv and Rani run over to us.

"Where were you?" Dhruv asks. "We were so freaked out." I believe that Dhruv was concerned about me, even if I highly doubt Alexa was.

"You okay?" Rani asks, and I'm surprised she's even talking to me.

She's looking down at the ground, and I wonder if she's still mad about how I yelled at her for being on the Lazy River with Alexa.

I'd still be mad at me if I were her. I'd probably never talk to me again.

"I'm fine," I say, even though it's not true. But I don't want to tell her about Abby's texts. She doesn't need to know that the only best friend I've ever had is just using me to try to go to a party.

Rani looks up. "We almost had to get them to say your

name over the loudspeaker. They were gonna mark you as a missing child and send out a search and rescue team."

I start giggling at that, because the thought of a search and rescue team looking for me when I was just riding Thunder and Lightning is kind of hilarious. Rani starts laughing too. Maybe things aren't completely ruined between us.

But then Alexa says, "Can you two be quiet for a second?" and Rani and I stop laughing. "This is serious. I'm in charge of you, you can't just run away."

She sounds more scared than anything else, and I don't know what to say. "*Someone* needs to be responsible here," she adds, but it doesn't sound like she's yelling at me, or at Dhruv or Rani. It's like she's just yelling.

After a tense moment, Dhruv says, "Why don't we go on Boulder Dash again?" He looks at Alexa, then at me. "There probably won't be as long of a line as there was earlier."

"Fine," Alexa and I say at the same time.

It turns out Dhruv's right, there's basically no line. And even though I'm still thinking about Abby's texts, and even though Alexa probably wants to punt me into the sun, I'm actually sort of excited again. Because we're still at an amusement park, and we're about to go on the best roller coaster of all time.

"Okay, what if for this ride Dhruv and Alexa sit up

front, and me and Rani go in the back, and then we switch next ride?" I say. "We can test out how it feels, like which is the bumpiest or the most fun or the scariest."

I've always wanted to do this, to test out a roller coaster like the people do in the videos I watch. It's like an experiment.

"All right," Alexa says, which surprises me. Then she adds, "I wanted to sit up front anyway," and things feel more normal.

Once we make it to the station gates, Dhruv and Alexa wait for the car at the very front, and Rani and I wait for the one in the very back.

There are only a few people ahead of us, and my heart starts pounding because we don't have much time before the ride. I'm not really scared for Boulder Dash, but my palms are sweaty and it's hard to breathe.

I need to get something off my chest or I'm gonna explode.

"I'm really sorry, Rani," I finally manage to say when we're next up to get on the ride. "I shouldn't have gotten mad at you for talking to Alexa on the Lazy River. That really sucked. Like, I mean, what I said sucked. Not you going on the Lazy River with her."

"It's okay," she says, holding my gaze and smiling a little. "I know you and Alexa don't get along that well, but she's really not so terrible." I don't know if I agree with that, but Rani doesn't sound that mad, which is good. It's great, actually. Then she adds, "It's just that I wanted to go on the Lazy River with *you*."

I turn away. I seriously don't think I've ever blushed as much as I have in the last two days. It's like my cheeks are permanently red.

Luckily, the roller coaster comes back into the station from the last ride, so it's our turn to get on. And that's good, because when we're on the coaster we don't have to look at each other or anything. We'll both just be staring straight ahead, and she won't be able to see if my face bursts into flames.

Once again, going on a roller coaster is saving me from having to talk. Or saying the wrong thing. I would kiss Boulder Dash's wooden tracks if I could.

Rani and I sit down, and Dhruv and Alexa stand up from the front and wave to us. We wave back, like they're about to go off on a boat trip around the world and we're sending them off from the docks.

"Everyone please sit down," the ride operator says, but they're really just talking to Dhruv and Alexa. "And wait for someone to come secure your lap bar."

They do, and then the ride is off.

It's still scary riding Boulder Dash the second time. Maybe even scarier, because I know from all the videos that the back of the coaster is the roughest ride.

"What if the coaster is so bumpy, we break through the lap bar and fly away?" I ask.

Rani laughs. "I mean, that would be bad." I snort, and she looks over at me. "So, I guess we don't have to put our hands up this time," Rani says. "It might be too rough."

"Oh, yeah, good," I say. "Cool."

But that means we won't be holding hands. And that's fine, of course. I just thought we might.

The videos weren't wrong: The back of the coaster *is* super bumpy. It feels like my spine is jumping out of my body as we tear through the woods. But even though it's a rough ride, it's incredible. Completely worth the brain juices sloshing around in my head.

"That was amazing," Alexa says. "The front is totally the best spot." She looks at us with her eyebrows raised. "How was the back?"

Rani and I must look like we both got a cartoon anvil dropped onto our heads, with our aching necks and dazed expressions. Alexa smirks.

"Ready to go again?" Rani asks. "We have to be in the front this time. You two can go in the back."

"Oh, we can?" Alexa scoffs.

"You have to," I say. "That's what we agreed on."

"I don't know if we agreed on anything," Alexa says innocently.

That's so unfair.

I don't say that, though. Instead I ask, "Are you not coming with us?"

"Eh, not really feeling it," Alexa says. "But, like, whatever.

You can still sit in the front. Dhruv and I will just go get food or something."

"We're old," Dhruv says as an explanation. He's like Alexa's niceness translator. "I don't think our ancient bones can handle riding in the back."

"Let's just go," Rani says to me, an excited glint in her eyes. "There's no one in line."

"Fine," I say, but my heart sinks a little. It was really fun when we all rode Boulder Dash together.

Not that I want to spend more time with Alexa. But maybe with Dhruv. And I guess I just like the four of us as a unit.

Rani and I run up the empty line area and into the station. It's starting to drizzle outside, and it's late in the day, so we're the only people waiting on line for the entire ride. It'll just be the two of us, and I'm so excited, I'm practically buzzing.

We hop into the front seats, and the park employee says, "Enjoy your private ride!"

Rani and I giggle at this, and then we're off, riding Boulder Dash for the third time today.

"We have to do something good for when they take the picture," I say as the train clicks up the first hill. "Since we're the only two people on the whole coaster."

"You're totally right," Rani says. She thinks for a few seconds. We're almost at the top now, moving higher and higher into the woods. "Okay, I know what I'm gonna do."

"What?"

She looks over at me and smiles. "If I tell you now it won't be as fun."

Maybe she's going to do a really silly pose, so I try to think of something good. I could point finger guns at the camera, or maybe pretend I'm asleep. I guess I'll decide when we get there.

And then the coaster drops. Being in the front of Boulder Dash is the best feeling ever. There's nothing but track in front of you and blurred trees all around you and it really feels like you're flying out of your seat.

When we get to the little hills before the big drop where they take your picture, I get a bit nervous, because I still don't really know what I'm gonna do. And I don't want to disappoint Rani.

In no time at all we're at the drop, and right before the camera flashes its blinding light, Rani grabs my hand.

That's what she does, I promise you.

She grabs my hand.

She holds it and lifts our arms up, together.

The light goes off.

They took our picture.

With our hands clasped.

And even after that, when we put our hands down, she holds on to mine almost until the ride stops.

So, it probably wasn't an accident.

I don't know what to say when we get into the station.

Actually, I can't say anything. My heart is beating so, so fast.

"That was such a good ride," Rani says. She hops out of the roller coaster like nothing even happened. Like we weren't just holding hands for a full thirty seconds.

When we get down to the area where they show you your ride pictures, Alexa and Dhruv are waiting.

"Nice picture," Dhruv says, smiling at me.

I blush a little, which is like whatever at this point because my face is just a blushing machine.

We walk toward the area where there's food and a bunch of other rides, but Alexa taps my shoulder, and I hang back with her. She waits until Dhruv and Rani are a bit ahead of us.

"I got you this," she says in her snippy voice. She hands me a keychain, and on it is the picture of me and Rani from the ride, our hands clasped.

In the picture Rani's smiling, and I'm in total shock.

"I thought you'd want to have it," Alexa says, looking at me. "But don't thank me or anything. I used your dad's money."

Alexa walks ahead toward Dhruv, and Rani looks back to where I'm standing. I'm pretty surprised that Alexa did something that could almost be considered nice. And kind of embarrassed. What does it mean that she thought I'd want to have it?

I stare at the keychain for a little too long, then jog to catch up to the group.

"What's that?" Rani asks, grabbing the keychain.

She laughs when she sees the picture. Not a mean laugh, though. But I still feel my heart drop into my stomach, like we're back on Boulder Dash.

"This is such a good pic," she says. Then she opens her phone and scrolls through her camera roll. "It's almost as good as this one," she says, showing me a picture. It's the selfie of us that she took that first day I went over to her house and we watched the Boulder Dash POV video.

"Yeah," I say. Because I can't say anything else.

It feels like my heart's gonna explode.

I never felt like this around Abby. I never felt nervous or scared or anything like that. I mean, I'm pretty sure Rani and I are friends, but . . .

Maybe there's something else to it.

CHAPTER SEVENTEEN

IT'S been a whole twelve hours since Rani held my hand on purpose on Boulder Dash, and my heart has just barely calmed down and my face has just barely stopped blushing.

Now, Alexa's sipping her coffee and sighing at the traffic, and Dhruv's napping. It's a peaceful kind of quiet in the car as the sun rises over the highway. We're driving from Lake Compounce to Pennsylvania for the next stop on our trip, Dorney Park.

Last night, after we left Lake Compounce, Rani and I slept in the same motel room again, but we didn't talk much. When she asked if I wanted to watch a roller coaster POV video before we went to bed, I said I was too tired.

It *was* true that I was too tired, but it was *also* true that I was scared our legs would touch again, like they did in the secret hideout, and I wouldn't know what to do. Holding hands on a roller coaster is one thing, but it's much scarier to think about that happening on solid ground.

I was ridiculously grateful for the five feet or so that were separating our beds.

I almost jump out of my seat when Rani nudges my shoulder with her index finger. She makes a look-down-at-your-phone hand motion, so I do.

Rani: are we gonna stop for breakfast?
i'm starving

Of course it's not about holding hands yesterday or anything like that. Why would it be? I didn't think that's what the text would be about, obviously.

Me: i'm hungry too
wanna ask if we're stopping?

Rani: can u ask

I look out the window on my side and sort of roll my eyes, because I don't want to ask Alexa, but I know I will since Rani asked me to.

"Are we stopping for breakfast?"

"Yeah, we're gonna meet our friend at a diner near Dorney in a couple hours," Alexa says.

Wait, what? "What friend?"

Dhruv wakes up and stretches his arms, almost hitting Rani in the back seat.

"Just one of my and Dhruv's friends from school, don't worry about it," she says, sounding annoyed, as if I should know this already. Dhruv yawns while giving her a Look, and Alexa is like, "Okay, listen, *maybe* I should've mentioned it. I'm just sort of stressed about this whole thing. Okay?" Then she says "okay" a few more times under her breath.

I didn't even know Alexa got stressed. I thought her only emotion was anger.

Dhruv turns around in his seat. "What if we all take a calming breath?" He sucks in a bunch of air through his nose and then breathes out with a loud sigh.

I'm not really in the mood to breathe, so I ignore Dhruv. "You didn't say there was gonna be someone else coming," I say to Alexa. We're just barely getting along as a group, and now she wants to add another person into this mess?

This pretty much proves my point that Alexa's just a horrible reminder of everything that's waiting for me at home, where I'm not gonna have a say in my own life anymore.

She looks in the rearview mirror and meets my eye. "What, are you gonna tell on me to your dad?" Dhruv rolls his eyes at this, but doesn't say anything.

"No," I say defensively, "I just wanna know about these things."

"My friend's coming with us to Dorney," Alexa says. "Just for the day." She's quiet for a minute. "Don't tell, kid. Seriously." And she almost sounds worried, which makes me think that for the first time I might actually have something over her.

"I'm not gonna tell."

Dhruv continues taking deep breaths until Alexa says, "Can you stop that?"

Maybe she really is stressed—I've never seen her snap at Dhruv.

Of course, at that moment my dad decides to check in.

Dad: Everything good?
Heading to Dorney now?

I could tell my dad that Alexa's bringing another friend, one that she didn't tell me about, and probably didn't tell our parents about, either.

But I'm not going to. I don't want to give Alexa any more of an excuse to hate me.

Me: yup

It's not much, but at least it answers both of his questions.

Another notification pops up on my screen. Rani's texting again.

Rani: what can we do to make the drive go by faster lol i'm gonna pass out i'm so hungry

I look up, and she's leaning against the side of the car and has her hand over her forehead and her tongue sticking out of her mouth like she's fainted. I put a hand over my mouth to stifle my laughter so Alexa doesn't hear. Rani opens one of her eyes and smiles when she sees me trying not to laugh. It feels like we're on the same side again, and it's amazing.

> Me: we could watch pov or makeup vids
> but i feel sick when i watch vids in the car
> we could listen to music or something?
> oh wait i don't have headphones lol
>
> Rani: wait i brought my airpods let's do it

I open Spotify, and the first thing that comes up is my amusement park playlist. It's pretty much exactly what it sounds like—songs that play in amusement parks, songs about amusement parks, that sort of thing. But the songs aren't exactly what you might call *cool*.

Rani pulls on her seat belt and leans over the middle seat so she can look at my screen. Her shoulder brushes against my arm, and I tense up. It's the closest we've been since Boulder Dash, and I don't know how to react. It scares me that she's this close, but I don't want her to move away either.

Once Rani gets a look at my screen and sees the playlist, she tilts her head up at me and gives a thumbs-up. She hands me one of her earbuds and settles back on her side of the car.

I'm half relieved and half sad that she's not looking over my shoulder as I start the playlist. The first song is this old one my dad likes called "Amusement Parks U.S.A.," about going with all your friends on a tour of amusement parks. It sounds super old-fashioned—people are singing "oooooooo" in the background—but it's a really fun song. Rani does this silly thing with her fingers where she makes them look like they're dancing in her lap so that Alexa can't see. And then I start doing it too and we have to look away from each other so we don't laugh out loud.

When the song ends the playlist switches to a German orchestra march with trumpets and strings, and it's definitely not as fun as "Amusement Parks U.S.A." I have a lot of songs like this on the playlist, because some German amusement parks have their own soundtracks, which is pretty cool. But after the fifth wordless song full of slow horns playing a slow tune, my playlist starts to feel super boring.

> Me: let's listen to something else
> what about ur music?

It takes Rani a minute to respond, but then she does.

> Rani: yeah let's do it
> we can switch to my phone
> i'll put on a new playlist

I thumbs-up her message and she scrolls through her phone. A minute later, we're listening to this amazing song that's all upbeat and dreamy, but the words are kind of sad. They might as well have come right out of my own brain. The singer is a girl with a low voice that sounds far away, and she sings about how she's thinking too much, about how she can't sleep, and it beams straight into my heart in a way the songs on the amusement park playlist never have. Rani has her eyes closed and her head is bopping along to the drums and the guitar. The song ends with the girl repeating that she thinks too much, and I only want to listen to music like this from now on.

After the song's over, Rani opens her eyes and looks over at me quickly, then down at her phone.

Rani: do you like it?

Me: i love it
let's listen to more

She grins at me, then puts on the next song.

A few hours later, we pull off the highway and into a diner parking lot. It's one of those old-fashioned ones, with a metallic exterior and a neon sign that says "Mama's Diner."

"Grab a table," Alexa says to us after she stops the car. "I'm gonna wait out here."

Dhruv looks at her in a sort of funny way, but he gets out

of the car, so Rani and I follow. He holds the swinging red doors of the diner open for us, and says "After you," in a silly British accent, which makes all of us laugh.

There's a sign that says "Please Seat Yourself—We're Busy!" even though we're the only group in the whole diner. We pick a window booth with bouncy red seats, and Dhruv and Rani sit on one side of the table and I sit on the other. A waitress comes by and drops menus in front of us. She calls us all "dear" and tells us the breakfast special is a sausage and cheddar frittata.

"I *really* want a milkshake," Dhruv says once the waitress leaves.

"It's like nine in the morning." Rani looks over at him and opens her menu.

"It's never too early or too late or too . . ." Dhruv tries to think of a word. "Afternoon? Anyway, it's always the right time for a milkshake."

"'Too afternoon'?" Rani asks, laughing.

They keep talking, but just outside the window Alexa's excitedly waving her hands over her head to an orange car pulling into the parking lot.

After a minute, the person Alexa was waving at steps out of the car. They're wearing a T-shirt with the sleeves cuffed and athletic shorts, sort of like me. I can't tell from here if they're a boy or a girl or maybe neither of those things. They have short hair, and they're running toward Alexa, and they're . . .

Kissing?

I quickly look away, but not before my face goes red.

"This all looks so good," I say in a really high-pitched voice, flipping through the pages of the menu faster than I could possibly be reading them.

My eyes must be like ten times wider than normal, because Dhruv gives me a weird look.

Okay, I might be wrong, but I think even in college when you greet someone by kissing them *like that* it means you're more than friends.

I glance back up, and now Alexa and her "friend" are hugging. They hug for what feels like a long, long time. And then they let go and walk into the diner.

I pretend like I wasn't just watching them.

"Hey," Alexa says, pulling a chair over from a nearby table so that her "friend" can sit in the booth next to me while she sits in the chair. "This is Sara."

Oh my god.

Sara.

The person Alexa was fighting with her mom about at the bowling alley. The one she's been texting nonstop, all week.

I guess I was wrong about Sara being Alexa's Abby. I don't think most people *kiss* their ex-best friend.

Sara nods at me and Rani. I look away, but I keep glancing at Sara in my peripheral vision. I'm not trying to be creepy or anything. It's just that if Sara's a girl, that means . . .

Okay, what's happening? I mean, seriously. Have I just been living the most sheltered life ever? Is this why Abby stopped being my friend? Not because I didn't grow boobs and refuse to wear The Shorts, but because I don't know anything about the world?

How did I not pick up on the fact that Dhruv is gay? Or that Alexa—well, Alexa's dating another girl, so she's clearly not straight. I feel silly for not being able to just *tell*. My skin is tight and the booth is too small and I have no idea how I've made it through thirteen years being so completely oblivious.

Dhruv makes some sort of meaningful eye contact with Alexa, who rolls her eyes, but then she looks down at the floor. She seems nervous.

"Um, so, Sara's my girlfriend," Alexa says. Then she looks up at me. "Just please don't tell your dad, okay? I mean, my mom knows about Sara and everything," she says. "But she doesn't know that I'm bringing her on the trip. So just be cool, okay?"

"How come she doesn't know Sara's coming?"

Alexa doesn't say anything, and after a beat Dhruv says, "Vanessa has some . . . thoughts about Sara. And about Alexa dating Sara."

Alexa scoffs. "'Thoughts' is putting it nicely. She treats me like a kid when it comes to dating, like I'm still too young. But then she expects me to be the responsible one the rest of the time . . . whatever. It's a whole thing."

And, okay, I know Alexa told me to be cool, but right now I'm being the opposite of cool. Or at least, I'm feeling the opposite of cool.

Because now I kind of *want* to keep this particular secret.

Alexa has a *girlfriend*.

CHAPTER EIGHTEEN

IT'S only the third day of the trip, but I feel like I've been away from home for a million years. Everything's changing.

I'm walking into Dorney with Rani, Dhruv, Alexa, and Sara—four people I didn't know existed at the beginning of the summer. And one of those four I didn't even know existed until this morning. *And* I have to keep her a secret from my dad.

I feel bad for thinking this, but it's all kind of exciting.

"I'm boiling," Dhruv says as he fans himself with his hand. "How is it this hot already?"

He's right, it's the hottest day of the trip so far.

"Make sure you're wearing sunscreen," Alexa says, handing me the tube when she's done putting some on her nose. "I don't want your dad yelling at me for bringing you home with a burn."

"I can tell for myself when I need to put on sunscreen," I say. But I grab the tube and start rubbing it on my arms, because I *can* tell when I need sunscreen. And now is one of those times.

To get inside Dorney, we walk through something that looks like an old-timey train station. I guess a lot of amusement parks want to look like they're old-fashioned and fun. I don't really get it, but maybe parents like it or something.

"What should we go on first?" Dhruv asks me. He turns to Sara. "Dalia's a roller coaster expert. I bet she has some rides in mind."

"Um, maybe," I say to Dhruv. Everyone's staring at me like I have the answer to all the roller coaster questions in the universe. It's too much pressure.

"She really is an expert," Alexa says. "Come on, kid." She looks at me expectantly. "What do we go on first?"

Alexa's probably just playing nice so that she doesn't look mean in front of her girlfriend. But it doesn't matter, because there *is* a cool ride that I've been wanting to go on.

"Well, there's this ride called Demon Drop, and it's like this super scary elevator sort of thing. And it's the only one like it left in the country." Once I start talking about rides, I really can't stop. Even if I don't want to be talking at all. It's like someone's pushed a button in my brain. "I think the rest of them maybe closed down because they were unsafe. This one might be unsafe too, because you just sort of drop from, like, super high in the air, and you're inside this metal cage. Anyway, I've been wanting to go on it for basically forever." I stop to take a breath so I can keep talking, but I realize I don't actually have anything else to say about Demon Drop. I'm just really excited to ride it.

"Sounds awesome," Sara says, smiling at me. "Let's do it."

I smile back, and I want to keep watching Sara, to try to figure her out. But I know it's rude to stare. There's just something about the way she carries herself. I don't think I've ever seen someone who looks so cool without trying, not even Cassie and the popular girls.

We all head over to Demon Drop, which is a longer walk than I expect. Something I didn't know about amusement parks before this week is how big they are. I guess because I had only ever watched videos of single rides.

But seriously, these parks are like their own little worlds. They're cities with roller coasters instead of trains and fried food stands instead of houses.

When we get to Demon Drop there isn't much of a line, but the cage where you sit during the ride can only hold four people at a time, so we split up, with Alexa and Sara going on first, and me, Dhruv, and Rani going on second. When it's our turn, we climb into the cage, and Dhruv sits between me and Rani.

They've been talking a lot, both at the diner and afterward, and now it seems like they're kind of friends. The unfairness of it makes my stomach hurt. It's not that I want

Rani to only talk to me. It's just that I hate how easy it is for Dhruv to talk to Rani, when for me it's a whole ordeal. I have to think about what to say, or not say. And I get so nervous. *That's* the part that doesn't seem fair.

"You two are gonna have to keep me safe," Dhruv says as we're locked into the cage. He looks genuinely nervous.

Rani swings her legs so they hit the chain-link bars with a high-pitched clink. "Oh, don't worry. We'll protect you."

She turns her head toward me and we almost burst out laughing when our eyes meet behind Dhruv's back. It's like we're secret agents again, sending each other on missions, reporting back. Everything feels good between us.

Before I have time to prepare, the cage rises up, above most of the other rides, above the entire park. At the top, the cage clicks into place and pushes us forward, so it feels like we're on the edge of a never-ending cliff, one switch away from falling into nothingness.

Which I guess we are.

My heart pounds, and for an incredible moment, my brain is only focused on when the switch will release.

And then we drop, and my screams mix with Rani's and Dhruv's as we free-fall. It's completely exhilarating.

But there's something else too, an almost familiar feeling.

Maybe because I've felt like I've been free-falling off the top of some old, clanky ride for the past three days.

"So, how are you feeling about all this?"

We're off Demon Drop now, and we're all walking to a ride called Wild Mouse.

I tense. "What?"

I look up and Sara's walking next to me, so I turn my focus to the ground.

"About being Alexa's stepsister," Sara says, laughing a little. "How are you feeling?"

I breathe out. I thought Sara somehow knew about my weird feelings for Rani.

"Um . . . I guess I'm feeling okay."

Ha. Super funny joke, Dalia. If Sara could see inside my brain, she'd be laughing too.

"Okay is better than bad." Sara smiles and runs a hand through her short hair to push her bangs back.

The path we're taking to Wild Mouse leads us under a bright orange-and-purple roller coaster, and there are people screaming directly above our heads.

"I like your shorts," Sara says after the riders zoom past. "We're sort of matching." She grabs a bit of the mesh navy blue fabric of her own shorts and holds it out toward me to prove her point.

I look down at my shorts, which do look like Sara's. Just without the set of white stripes that are running down the side of hers. Usually my long shorts from the boys' department mark me as different from the girls who wear The Shorts. A bad kind of different. But I don't know, Sara seems really cool. And *she's* wearing them.

"Thanks," I say. "There aren't that many other girls who wear shorts like these." I don't actually feel like talking right now, but Sara found the topic that takes up most of the space in my brain, other than roller coasters. "Like in my grade, the popular girls, and also the girls who aren't really popular but are cooler than me . . ." I stop for a moment because I realize I've just told Sara that I'm not cool. But maybe she already guessed that. "Like, they all wear these short jean shorts."

"I know the kind," Sara says. "But these are way more comfortable, and way more swishy." She stops walking and swings her hips back and forth, so that the mesh of the two legs of the shorts rub against each other. "Swish, swish, swish," Sara says as her shorts swish along with her.

She's being dorky, but it makes me laugh. "Do a lot of other girls wear shorts like these in college? Like the ones we're wearing?"

"Some do," Sara says. "Like people who play sports." She's quiet for a moment, and then says, "And other queer women."

My heart starts beating really fast, and I don't know what to say. I've heard that word before, but I don't think I've ever heard someone use to it describe themselves. Dhruv called himself gay, and now Sara's saying something about other queer women, so she must call herself queer.

They both have labels for themselves. Maybe that's something everyone has in college. Like, if I was in college and introducing myself, I would say: "Hi, I'm Dalia. I like roller coasters and I'm Jewish and I'm . . ."

I don't know what that last part would be. But Sara knows about herself. And Dhruv knows about himself. And for all I know maybe Rani knows about herself too.

Since *she* brought it up, and since Dhruv and Alexa and Rani aren't in earshot, there's no harm in asking Sara something that I've been thinking about a lot lately. "Um, so," I start. There's no turning back now. "How do you know if you have, like . . . a crush on another girl?" I say the last part really quickly. But then I realize how the question sounds. "I mean, how *did* you know? I'm not asking for me, or whatever. I don't have a crush on another girl."

Sara looks at me and pushes her bangs back again and says, "I guess it's kind of hard, with other girls. Because you don't really know if what you're feeling is friendship, or if there's something more."

"So how did you know there was, like, something more with Alexa?"

"Well, I did something pretty wild."

"What?" And even though we're walking, I'm on the edge of my seat. Not a real seat, obviously. That's just how I feel.

"I told her I liked her. That I had feelings for her," she says. "And she had feelings back." Sara looks at me again. "It's not always that simple, but for us it was."

"But how did you know that Alexa also likes girls? Like, *like* likes them?"

"I didn't know for a while, but I just had a feeling."

There it is. I wish people and their feelings would go away. Everyone on Earth has these feelings. Everyone except me.

I know every type of roller coaster, but I don't know anything about people.

"Also, I knew she '*like* likes' girls because we were friends before we started dating and we talked about that kind of stuff," Sara says. "Sometimes you just need to talk. Even if it's hard." She nods a little, like she's agreeing with herself. "I guess that's sort of the whole thing."

"I think I'm gonna sit this one out," Dhruv says right before we're about to get on line for Wild Mouse. "I might get one of those Extreme Milkshakes with a Twinkie on top."

"Those what?" Sara asks.

"It's a Dorney Park specialty," Dhruv says. "There's a bunch of other stuff on it too. It costs like twenty bucks, but I've been looking forward to it since Alexa and I first planned this trip."

"He really has," Alexa tells Sara.

Before Dhruv walks away, he looks between me and Rani and then meets my eye. I look away, my face getting hot. It's probably nothing, but when I look back up, he gives me a thumbs-up and walks away. What's going on?

The line for Wild Mouse is pretty long, so Sara and Alexa settle in to wait a few steps ahead of me and Rani. I keep sneaking glances at them. They're leaning against the guard rail, and Sara has her arm around Alexa's waist. For the first time in three days Alexa doesn't look pissed. And since Sara's been here, she hasn't been sending any frantic texts at all.

Seeing my dad's arm around Vanessa's waist and seeing them kiss and stuff made me want to throw up. Probably because he's my dad. But I don't feel that way seeing Sara and Alexa be all touchy-feely. I mean, it's kind of embarrassing, but I can't look away when Sara and Alexa hold hands or things like that. I like seeing how Alexa smiles at Sara and the way they fit into each other just right. It's like they don't even notice we're waiting on line for a ride. They probably stand like this, pressed against each other, everywhere they go.

We're all being pretty quiet. It's too hot to talk or play games to pass the time. That doesn't stop me from getting nervous about what Sara said, about having to talk through your feelings. How can I do that when I don't even know what my feelings are?

When we get to the front of the line, a ride attendant opens the gate and we pile in the car, which looks like, well, a wild mouse. Being on the ride isn't that scary or exciting, really. The whole point is that you go up pretty high on this track, and once you get up to the top the whole thing is flat, but you make a bunch of these really sharp turns. And right before the turn, you feel like you're about to be flung off the edge of the world.

It's like the roller coaster can't catch up to where it needs to be.

"What should we go on next?" Sara asks once we're off Wild Mouse and back with Dhruv. She looks over at me. "Any ideas?"

I'm so distracted by all the thoughts pinging around in my brain that I almost want to say I don't care. I had hoped the sharp turns of Wild Mouse would knock some of the thoughts out of my head, but that definitely didn't happen.

But because I'm me, and I really can't pass up the opportunity to pick a roller coaster, I say, "We could go on Hydra?"

We can see Hydra from where we're standing—it's green and steel with lots of inversions. It's at the very center of the park, so you can see it from pretty much anywhere. There are flags lining the midway directing people to the ride, since it's basically the main attraction. Everyone agrees that it'll be way better than Wild Mouse.

As we walk over to the line, Sara and Alexa start talking

about how they need to recruit more people to some club they're both in—a film club or something—in the fall, but then they go on and on about boring stuff like putting up flyers, so I shift my attention to Dhruv and Rani, who are walking a little bit ahead of me. Rani's holding her phone out for Dhruv to look at, and he bends down to see the screen.

"Oh my god," Dhruv says, looking at the picture Rani's showing him on her phone. I crane my head so that I can see what he's looking at. It's Rani in her zombie mermaid makeup. "You *have* to meet my friend Piper. She does makeup for the theater program at my school and she would die if she saw this." He looks at the picture again and uses his thumb and index finger to zoom in. "You should totally do theater makeup, you'd be so good at it."

"Really? You think?" Rani asks, looking pleased. "I mean, I've done a little, but I don't know . . ."

"No, you have to," Dhruv says. "I mean, I'm just on stage crew, but you're clearly super talented."

Even though I've been too nervous to really speak to Rani today, and even though everyone is talking without me, I feel, like, proud to know her. I feel proud that a college student is telling her that the makeup she did last Halloween looks good enough to be professional.

There's a pang in my chest, an aching feeling, like how my arms and legs feel after a particularly hard swim practice.

I wish I could tell Rani that I feel proud of her, but if I open my mouth my brain might give me away. Can regular friends be proud of their friends? Like, so proud that your heart feels all warm and fuzzy? Or is that different? Is that only a thing when you have . . . you know . . . a crush on someone?

As we move toward the front of the line, we can clearly see Hydra up close and personal. It's so wide that it covers like half the park, with its giant green loops framing the sky.

"Whoa, wait," Rani says, pointing to the ride. "We're gonna go upside down before the lift?"

We all look up to see what she's talking about. The ride leaves the station and then immediately enters this really slow roll, so that everyone's inverted right away.

"Yeah, isn't it so cool?" I say before I can stop myself.

It's just that Rani noticed the most unique thing about Hydra without me pointing it out, which is pretty amazing. So obviously I have to explain more about the pre-lift roll, since she's the one who brought it up. "Okay, so, that's called a JoJo roll, and Hydra is actually the only roller coaster on Earth that has one. It's really cool because it's a heartline roll that happens even before the lift hill, so people are screaming and stuff before the first drop. That, like, *never* happens."

"What's a heartline roll?" Rani asks.

For some reason my face gets hot from her just asking

me a question. Something feels different, talking to her right now. But maybe it's just my brain panicking.

It really is the worst organ in my body, my brain. And that's *including* my appendix.

I don't fully meet Rani's eyes as I say, "It's this kind of roll where you go, like, three-sixty, all the way around. It's not a loop or anything. I think sometimes it's also called a barrel roll."

"Wait, so we're about to go on a ride that has something that no other roller coaster in the entire world has?" Rani asks. I nod, and she smiles at me and says, "That's awesome," and my heart feels like it does its own JoJo roll.

As we get farther up in the line, we all see that the ride can only hold four people in a row, so we'll have to split up again like we did on Demon Drop and Wild Mouse.

"Why don't you four try to sit up front and I'll go right behind you?" Alexa suggests. "I don't really wanna be in the front row, anyway."

I lift my eyebrows at Alexa, and she just shrugs and smiles a little. Nice Alexa is weird, and it's hard to hate her, with her agreeable seating arrangements and such.

When it's time to get on the ride, I climb in so that I'm on the outside edge. I'm sitting next to Sara, who gives me a thumbs-up. Beside her, Dhruv and Rani are talking and swinging their legs and the sun is starting to set. I don't feel like I did before, on Wild Mouse. I'm way more relaxed.

I twist around to look back between the seats to the row behind us. Alexa gives me another small smile, and I give her one back.

I turn forward when the ride attendant comes to lower our harnesses, and once we're secured, we take off, all of us screaming before the first drop.

CHAPTER NINETEEN

EVEN though I never stopped worrying about being weird around Rani, the last few hours at Dorney were super fun. I added about a dozen more roller coasters to my credits list, and everyone got along surprisingly well.

Now we're pulling into another motel, which looks pretty much exactly the same as the last one. Even the font on the sign is the same.

There is one difference, though: Sara's here.

"This is how the room situation's going to work," Alexa says as she steps out of the car and stretches her arms. "Sara and I will be in one room. *Alone.*" Sara shakes her head and smiles at Alexa, and *I* smile at Sara shaking her head.

I sort of figured that Sara would be going home after Dorney, not staying overnight with us. Is it normal that Alexa and Sara are sharing a motel room? Are college students who are dating allowed to sleep in a bed together?

I guess that's a silly question, because when you're in college you're basically an adult. I'm obviously not going to tell my dad about Sara being here, but now that I know that Alexa's sharing a room with her, it feels like a bigger secret.

Actually, everything's starting to feel like a big secret. Before this summer, the only part of my life I didn't tell my dad about was watching roller coaster POV videos. But then, you know, all *this* happened, meeting Dhruv and finding out about Alexa's girlfriend.

I don't even *want* to tell my dad.

So maybe it's time to start keeping secrets from him. It's not like *he* had any problem keeping dating Vanessa a secret from *me*. And who knows, maybe these secrets will mean it won't hurt as much when I get back from the trip and he's spending all his time with Vanessa. Because I'll have my own stuff going on.

"I've already talked about this with Dhruv," Alexa says, "and the three of you are gonna share the other room." She motions to me, Rani, and Dhruv.

"Do you two mind sharing a bed?" Dhruv asks me and Rani. "There are only two beds in the room, and I figured neither of you would want to share with me."

I absolutely do mind. I mind it the most anyone could ever mind anything. Because I don't think I can handle sleeping in the same bed as Rani.

"That's fine," Rani says.

Well, never mind, then. I guess it's fine. Rani clearly

doesn't have any weird feelings about me the way I might for her.

"We have to call our parents before we go to bed," Alexa says to me.

I forgot about that. It's pretty much the last thing I want to do. But we promised them we'd call every night.

Dhruv and Rani start to head over to the room I'll be sharing with them. I wonder if they'll talk about me while I'm FaceTiming my dad.

Or maybe they *won't* talk about me at all, which would somehow be worse.

But if they *do* talk about me . . .

Like, okay, does Dhruv know how I feel about Rani? I'm worried he does, especially after that Look he gave me before Wild Mouse. The thought makes me want to vomit, but at the same time it's kind of exciting.

And I don't *think* he would say something, but who knows. Maybe it wouldn't be the worst thing in the world if he *did* say something, because then I wouldn't need to tell her myself. My heart's pumping so fast that I can feel it beat in the tips of my fingers.

Before Dhruv and Rani go into the room, though, Rani whispers something to Dhruv, who nods. "Lex, darling," he says in an overly sweet voice.

Alexa rolls her eyes and laughs. "Yes?"

"Could we possibly borrow some of your makeup?"

I look over at Rani, trying to ask with my eyes what's going on, but she's focused on Dhruv.

"Uh, sure, go wild," Alexa says, clearly a bit distracted. "But don't use my eyeliner. I don't wanna get pink eye." She sticks her head in the car for a second and emerges with her makeup bag.

"Thanks." Dhruv grabs the bag, and then he and Rani run into our motel room.

"You coming?" Alexa asks.

"Oh, um, yeah," I say, and follow her and Sara into their room.

Alexa plops down onto the bed and motions for me to sit next to her. "Remember, Sara's *not* here," she says to me when we're both positioned with our backs to the headboard. She doesn't even say it like she's angry. It's more like she's scared, which sort of scares me, so I just nod.

Alexa presses her mom's contact and the phone rings. Sara's sitting in a chair in the corner of the room, out of view of the camera.

"Look at our girls!" my dad says when he picks up. Vanessa's behind him, pouring them both a glass of wine.

Ugh.

I wish we had never agreed to call our parents at all. Because now it's just a reminder that when the trip is over, this is gonna be my life. I'll have to watch Vanessa pouring glasses of wine all the time and I'll have to escape to my room, except that won't really be an escape because it's technically my dad's office.

"Are you having fun, Dals?" my dad asks. But before I can answer he adds, "Vanessa and I got bagels this morning and I almost ordered one for you before I remembered you weren't here!"

My eyes go wide, and I turn away from Alexa's phone, making a *hm* noise in the back of my throat.

I don't understand why he thinks I want to hear about that. A little over two weeks ago, *we* were getting bagels, and *we* were biking around and searching for horseshoe crabs, and things were good. It was just me and my dad. That was it. That was our whole family. But now that I know that Vanessa's been in his life for six whole months, everything we did together in that time feels tainted. He could've told me about her but he didn't. And the worst part is, he doesn't even realize that anything's changed now that I know.

My dad hands the phone to Vanessa and I can hear him opening the fridge in the background.

"Wait, Ale, did I tell you about the Weinsteins?" Vanessa asks as she takes a sip of wine.

"Nope, you didn't." Alexa's voice is tight, like she's holding back what she really wants to say, but then she glances up at Sara and seems to calm down a bit.

"Oh, you won't *believe* —" And then Vanessa launches

into this whole long story about a friend of hers who had an affair with another teacher at the high school where Vanessa also teaches.

It's weird to hear a mom talk to her kid like that, like Alexa's a friend she ran into at the grocery store. But maybe it just seems weird to me because I have no clue what a normal mother-daughter relationship looks like.

"Cool for the Weinsteins," Alexa says.

"No, not cool for the Weinsteins. *Especially* not for Pauline. Were you listening to what I was saying?"

"What?" Alexa asks. "Yeah."

There's a pause, and my dad comes back into frame. "Anyway," Vanessa says. "Isn't it *so* nice to be spending some time with Dalia? She's *such* a great kid."

I want to ask Vanessa how she'd know that, since I've only met her a whopping two times, but I keep my mouth shut.

Vanessa sighs and says, "You're growing up too fast, Ale. I really think it'll be good for you to be friends with Dalia."

Alexa leans forward and puts her head in her hands, then takes a breath and says, "Mom, I'm an adult. I'm not growing up too fast. And Dalia and I aren't friends."

That stings a little, even though it's definitely true.

Alexa keeps going, not trying to hide her anger as much now. "You wanted us to bond so badly, but I think you know that what's *actually* going on right now is that I'm babysitting your fiancé's kid for you."

Not true, I want to say, but I don't. Because even though Alexa is definitely *not* my babysitter, I weirdly feel like I'm on her side in all this.

Alexa keeps talking, getting even more heated as she goes: "You can't gossip to me about Pauline's affair and then tell me I'm growing up too fast. Pick one: Are you my mom today, or my needy friend?"

Sara shakes her head and pushes her hair back, and when Alexa looks up at her, her face softens.

"I can't talk to you when you're acting like this," Vanessa says, clucking her tongue.

"That makes two of us."

I haven't seen Alexa and Vanessa have a real fight before. It's kind of scary. But at least Alexa's anger isn't directed at me.

"All righty then," my dad says, too cheery, too loud, "maybe you girls need to get some rest. Big day of driving tomorrow, right?"

Alexa loses a bit of the fight she had in her a moment ago, and she exhales, "Yeah."

"All right, well, good night girls," my dad says.

"Good night," I say. It's more a reflex than a true statement.

"Night," Alexa says with her teeth clenched.

And the call is over.

Alexa bends forward and puts her head on her knees. She stays that way for several seconds, but when she sits up, she looks over at me. "Are you okay?"

I'm surprised she even asked. I nod, and I don't say that I want to ask her the same question.

"I know I shouldn't have said all that." Alexa turns to Sara. "I told myself I wasn't gonna go off on her."

I stand up from the bed as Sara walks over to Alexa. She takes my spot and pulls Alexa close, rubbing her back. "It's okay," she says reassuringly. "Your mom said things she shouldn't have said either."

"Yeah, I guess," Alexa says.

I hover awkwardly while Alexa and Sara talk quietly for another minute. I need to leave.

I sneak toward the door, trying not to disturb them, trying to make it so that they forget I'm even here.

"Dalia," Sara says, stopping me mid-sneak. "Why don't you stay for a minute?"

I don't respond, but I turn around and look at Alexa, who meets my eye and nods.

I move away from the door slowly, like if I make any sudden movements, they might kick me out. And the thing is, I really don't want them to. There's a part of me—a big part of me—that wants to stay in here. I like that they're including me, and I feel kind of safe in the room with them. Plus, I'm definitely not ready to face sharing a bed with Rani just yet.

I sit down on the chair Sara had been sitting in while Alexa and I called our parents. It's hard and dusty, with a dark-orange cushion. I pull my knees to my chest and wrap my arms around them, trying to get comfortable.

And then it's quiet. So, so quiet. There are crickets chirping outside and maybe frogs too and other things you'd never hear at night on Long Island.

I hold my breath, because I don't know what else to do. I figure if I don't make a peep, they'll hardly even notice I'm here, and no one will ask me to leave.

Sara and Alexa look comfortable, like it's not an awkward kind of quiet for them. Alexa's leaning against Sara, who's rubbing her fingertips gently along Alexa's inner forearm. I don't know why, but it makes my heart hurt to watch them like that, so comfortable with each other. But it's not a bad hurt.

I look away and trace my fingers lightly against the skin on my own arm. It feels really nice. But then my face gets hot and I stop touching my arm, because I'm worried they'll notice and I shouldn't have even been watching them in the first place.

After a minute of this, I have to look back up, and when I do Sara looks at *me* and smiles. I smile back, but inside I'm freaking out. Maybe she saw me touching my arm and she thinks I'm a complete weirdo.

"So, Dalia was asking how we started dating," Sara says to Alexa after another minute of silence.

My heart starts beating really fast. "No I wasn't."

But then Sara gives me this questioning look and Alexa raises her eyebrows, so I'm like, "Okay, yeah, I was, but not for, like, any reason."

"Well, I don't think I told you the full story," Sara says.

"That's fine." I let go of my knees and sit forward on the uncomfortable cushion. "I don't need to hear it. Like, it's fine."

"Well, the thing is," Sara says, "I really like telling the story." Alexa looks up at her and smiles.

I shrug and say, "Um, all right," because I'm obviously actually really curious about what Sara did to make Alexa want to be her girlfriend.

Sara clears her throat, and Alexa adjusts her position against Sara's chest and closes her eyes, looking way more relaxed than I've literally ever seen her. Then Sara starts telling the story.

"All right, imagine, my first day on campus: a naive first-year—never say 'freshman' when you get to high school or college, Dalia, because it's a gendered word and it's not inclusive of women and nonbinary people."

I nod my head really hard, even though I'm not sure why. I feel ashamed, I guess. I hadn't ever thought of that. It's not like I have to worry right now because I don't think eighth grade is a gendered word, but maybe it is and I have to worry about that too. But I'm glad Sara told me because if she hadn't, I'd just go around saying "freshman" and that wouldn't be inclusive.

Sara keeps talking as if she hadn't just said something that was completely new to me. Hopefully that means she doesn't realize how little I know about literally anything.

"So, I found my group for first-year orientation, and the first person I saw was Alexa, and she was yelling at this guy for who knows what reason—"

Alexa sits up and bumps Sara's shoulder, scoffing. "That's not what happened," she says, but she doesn't sound angry at all.

Sara laughs and rolls her eyes. "That's exactly what happened!" She looks over at me. "Don't let Alexa's lies cloud your judgment of the story."

Alexa shoves Sara again and they both laugh, and I feel like I'm intruding on something even though Sara's telling the story to me.

"Sara can't be trusted," Alexa says. "I'll tell the rest of the story."

Sara shakes her head and Alexa starts saying something about the first time she saw Sara. And maybe it's just because of how hot it is, but the motel room starts to feel super cozy. Alexa leans her head all the way back on Sara's chest, and I wrap my arms around my knees again. The air in the room is thick with the day's humidity, and even though the chair isn't that comfy I lean back, and my eyes sort of slip closed.

The next thing I know, there's a hand on my shoulder and I jump up from the chair, but it's just Alexa.

"Maybe you should head into your room," she says. "I think it's time for bed."

"I'm not a baby," I say, "you don't need to tell me when it's time for bed."

She raises an eyebrow. "I just mean because you fell asleep."

Oh.

I didn't even realize I had been asleep. I guess she wasn't trying to be mean.

"Um, sorry for bothering you," I say to Sara as Alexa opens the door for me.

Sara shakes her head. "Dalia, you're no bother at all." She smiles at me. "I hope you dream about a roller coaster with a million JoJo rolls."

My face gets hot and I laugh a little and mumble a quick thank-you as I walk outside.

The air is even stickier out here, and it almost sounds like the crickets are putting on a concert. Like, that's how loud it is.

But Alexa doesn't close the door on me right away. Instead, she walks outside and leans against the wall. "Thanks for listening to Sara tell that story," she says, smirking a little. "I think she really likes talking about it." When I don't say anything she adds, quietly, "I mean, I do too."

I'm not sure how to respond. Alexa's been sort of—and

I know this sounds so weird—*nice* today? She might stop being nice the second Sara leaves, but still.

I nod, and Alexa takes a breath and crosses her arms. Then she uncrosses them and taps her fingers against her thighs. "And if you ever want to talk about stuff like that, I'm, like, here. Obviously."

"Uh, okay?" And then, because things are oddly good, I ask the question that's been on my mind since Alexa first mentioned it. "How come Vanessa didn't want Sara to come on the trip?"

Alexa sighs and looks down at her feet. "Of course that's what you ask."

"You don't have to tell me," I say quickly.

"No, no."

I don't know if she's agreeing that she doesn't have to tell me, or if she's saying she *wants* to tell me. Alexa's sort of confusing like that. But then she says, "My mom thinks Sara's the reason I've been angry at her all summer."

"*Is* she the reason?" I'm pretty sure I know the answer, but I ask anyway.

"No," Alexa says. "No, of course not." She stacks her hands on top of her head and exhales. "Sara's the only person who makes me calm." When I don't say anything, she keeps talking. "My mom's always acted like I'm her friend, not her daughter. She lays *everything* on me. And then she got mad when she realized I grew up, and that she wasn't my number one priority anymore." She sighs. "So, remember how I told you on the first day we met that college is just . . . fine?"

I nod. "Yeah."

"Well, I just said that because I was annoyed at you." Somehow this doesn't surprise me. Alexa takes a breath. "The truth is, college is pretty incredible. It's the place where I feel most like myself. I didn't realize until I got there how much I was taking care of my mom even when she wasn't really taking care of me. She would just use me as a sounding board for gossip. She'd tell me all these things that I didn't understand, or didn't need to know, and I'd have to listen and give advice and tell her what she wanted to hear. Like, she uses me. It's exhausting. But Dhruv and Sara really take care of me. We take care of each other. And when I came home for the summer, I couldn't stand it anymore, the way my mom spoke to me. But she didn't see anything wrong with it. She just thought I had changed too much at college, because I wasn't taking all of her crap anymore. And she thought me dating Sara was part of that." She laughs a little, even though nothing's funny. "I probably shouldn't be telling you any of this."

My shoulders relax a bit from their position up near my ears. I hadn't ever really considered that Alexa might not be angry *at me*. That she might just be angry.

Alexa leans back against the motel room door and stares

out at the parking lot. I'm mad for her. I hate that I ever called Vanessa chill. Maybe all parents are annoying, or mean, or hurtful, in their own special way.

"All right," Alexa says after a moment. "Go to sleep, I don't want you complaining that you're tired tomorrow."

"Fine," I say, rolling my eyes. But then I look back up at Alexa, and she's smiling at me, so I smile at her.

Maybe, deep down, Alexa's the nicest person in the world.

But that doesn't stop her from slamming the door.

CHAPTER TWENTY

I walk the two doors down to my motel room and stop. The lights are on, and Rani's and Dhruv's muffled voices leak through the door and out into the motel parking lot.

It feels wrong to barge in while they're talking, so I knock on the door. Rani opens it a crack and there's a giant grin on her face. "*Perfect* timing."

I can't see inside the room because the door is still mostly closed.

"Perfect timing for what?"

"We'll show you in a second, but can you close your eyes?"

"Okay?" I follow her instructions, and a second later, Rani's hands are on my shoulders, steering me inside. I hope she isn't looking at my face right now, because I'm definitely blushing.

Rani has me sit down in a chair and while I'm adjusting in the seat, a door across the room opens and closes. A moment later, she says, "All right, open your eyes."

When I do, all I see is Rani standing in the middle of the room, holding a makeup brush covered in blue pigment.

"So," she says, swinging her arms, "Dhruv and I have been working on something, and you're our test audience."

For a second, I'm a little annoyed that they didn't include me in . . . whatever this is. But the feeling goes away quickly because I'm also super curious.

"Are you ready?" she asks.

"Uh, sure?"

She turns toward the bathroom. "All right," she calls, "we're good to go when you are."

The bathroom door opens, and Dhruv walks out.

Only the person in front of me doesn't look anything like Dhruv.

The top half of his face, from his mouth up, looks like a painting: blue and green and teal blended seamlessly from one color to the next. Toward the edges of his face there are drawn-on black lines made to look like feathers. It's like his eyes are wings and they're taking off from the side of his head.

Dhruv holds a hand under his cheek and poses.

"So, what do you think?" he asks. And there's something that sounds like nerves under his usually confident voice.

I'm almost too in awe to speak. "It's incredible," I manage, even though "incredible" doesn't even begin to describe it. Dhruv looks like a high-fashion bird. I turn to Rani.

"You did all that with Alexa's makeup?" She nods. "Did you watch a tutorial?"

"Um, not really." Rani shrugs like it's not the most amazing makeup I've ever seen.

"She's a literal artist," Dhruv says, jumping in. "It's unreal."

Even though she's looking down, Rani's beaming. "I mean, Dhruv told me the kind of look he wanted, and this is what I came up with."

"If I was as talented as you, I wouldn't be so modest," Dhruv says. Then he turns to me. "In case you're wondering why I look like this . . ."

I nod; I'm *definitely* wondering.

"There are all-gender drag shows every weekend at school, where tons of different people wear these amazing costumes and do really creative makeup, but I've always been too nervous to perform," Dhruv says. "Partially because I know nothing about makeup."

"That's not true," Rani says. "You knew exactly what you wanted me to do."

"Yeah, but *you* made me look like *this*." He gestures to his face and poses again, and we all admire Rani's work.

It's so cool that Rani helped a *college student* with something. I feel that warm burst of pride again, like the one I had earlier today when Rani was showing Dhruv her makeup looks in the first place. Except this time I don't just have to look on from a distance.

"I was thinking for my drag name I'd either call myself Dame Judi Finch or Jay Walker," Dhruv says as he looks at his makeup in the dirty motel mirror.

"How come you wanted to look like a bird?" I ask.

"Well, first of all because I love them," Dhruv says, "but also because they're so dramatic. And the birds with the most colorful plumage are usually male, which is pretty fabulous and very gay."

"Can I take a picture of how it turned out?" Rani asks Dhruv.

He agrees and poses for her, and after a minute he says, "Let's get one of all of us."

Dhruv and Rani pull me in for a selfie, and I feel very plain compared to Dhruv's done-up face and Rani's giant smile, but I'm glad they included me.

"Do you think you'll perform at the show once you go back to school in the fall?" I ask Dhruv.

"Maybe," he says. "But I don't know . . . not even my boyfriend knows that I want to do drag."

"Wait, what?" Rani asks. "Why?"

"It's not like I think he'd be mad," Dhruv says quickly. "But he's in the acting program at school, and I'm on stage crew. I actually joined *because* of him. I feel like it'd be weird to tell him I want to perform when I've been working backstage the whole time I've known him. I don't want to take that from him." He rubs the back of his neck. "Anyway, it's fine. I just wanted to see what the makeup would look like."

I honestly can't imagine Dhruv just working backstage. He's so funny, and I feel like he needs to be in the spotlight.

"You should send him one of the pictures," Rani says. "He might think it's cool."

"I want to . . ."

I can tell that Dhruv wants to add a "but." I wish I was as bold as Rani and could just say, "Totally! Tell him! It'll be great!" but I have no idea if it will be.

"Alexa doesn't know either," Dhruv says. "It was just something I was thinking about. And now I guess you two know."

I like that Rani and I are in on one of Dhruv's secrets, even if it is kind of wild that he told us. I mean, we're just two middle schoolers he barely knows.

But maybe that's *why* he's telling us. Sometimes it's way easier to talk to someone when you don't really know them.

"I think you'd be amazing," Rani says, and Dhruv smiles.

I love that there are all these different combinations of people, with Dhruv and Rani and Alexa and Sara, and that talking to them and hanging out with them feels so completely different from one person to the next. We can have secrets with one combination of people or texts with another, and it's weirdly . . . nice? Like, usually it would stress me out if I found out I wasn't included in something, but I like that we're all connected, like five little bubbles on a mind map.

Dhruv checks his phone. "Oh my god, it's so late."

"It's only midnight!" Rani says.

"Well, unlike you two, I'm an old man, and I need my beauty sleep." Dhruv yawns and flops onto his bed, faceup, then closes his eyes. "Anyway, Rani, this is incredible. *You're* incredible." He stretches his arms and then folds them over his stomach. "Sweet dreams, you two."

After a few seconds, his breathing slows.

Rani stifles a giggle. "Is he already asleep?" she whispers. "With his makeup on?!"

We're frozen for a second as we listen.

"I think he might be," I whisper back.

We both have to hold in our laughter.

When the moment passes, it's just me and Rani in this quiet motel room. Well, us and an unconscious Dhruv.

I go to the bathroom to brush my teeth, and when I get out, Rani's lying on the bed we have to share, facing away from me. She's curled on her side, her hair like a waterfall streaming down her back.

I can't bring myself to walk closer to the bed. I don't know how I'm going to fall asleep tonight.

What would Rani do if she were me? She'd probably jump right in. She'd plop onto bed next to me and not worry about accidentally brushing her leg against mine while we're sleeping, because she definitely isn't thinking about me the way I've been thinking about her.

I take a deep breath and move closer to the bed. It's like

getting into the pool at the beginning of practice: I just gotta do it.

I sit as lightly as possible on the edge of the bed farthest from Rani.

I don't hear her move; maybe she fell asleep as quickly as Dhruv. But then she turns over to face me, and I almost scream because I'm already way too jumpy.

When my heart calms down a tiny bit from the surprise of Rani being awake, it picks right back up again because, well, Rani's awake.

I honestly wish that she *was* asleep; then I wouldn't have to worry about anything.

Like, I wouldn't have to think about how being friends with Rani feels different from being friends with Abby, and what that means or whether I should talk to her about it.

I don't think I'll ever say anything.

Scratch that: I'm *definitely* not gonna say anything about how I feel, because the only two possibilities are that she doesn't feel the same way and I'll have zero friends, which is depressing to think about. Or she *does* feel the same way, and that option makes me so nervous, I literally want to throw up.

"Dhruv's already snoring," Rani says. "I don't understand how he fell asleep so fast."

I nod because I can't form words right now, and stretch one leg out on the bed. I don't go under the covers or anything, and only half of my butt is actually on the mattress.

Rani must see the pained look on my face, because she whispers, "We can talk under here," as she pulls back the fluffy off-white motel comforter and motions for me to get under it with her.

I really don't want to be in a confined space with Rani right now, but I don't think I have a choice. Because otherwise Dhruv might wake up and hear us.

I crawl under, and Rani pulls the comforter over our heads. We're both lying on our stomachs, and it's stuffy and dark. She turns on her phone's flashlight, but doesn't say anything.

I decide to play it safe. "So, how'd you like Dorney?"

"It was cool," Rani says. "I think I liked it more than Lake Compounce. Like, I obviously loved Boulder Dash, but the rides at Dorney are way better."

Great, so she had more fun today—when we barely spoke—than she did yesterday. But, like, she's right—Dorney has some great rides.

Neither of us says anything for a minute, and then Rani's screen lights up to tell her that she got a snap. I try to read who it's from, but I don't recognize the name.

Rani looks at her phone and puts it back down.

"You can snap them back," I say, "it's whatever." Obviously it's not whatever, though, because she has better people to be talking to than me.

"No, it's fine," she says, resting her head on her arms, "it's just one of my friends from home."

Even though I know it'll make me jealous hearing Rani talk about all the friends she has and her life before she ever met me, I still want to know everything I can about her. I want to collect every piece of Rani trivia. So I ask, "Is it hard to keep in touch with your friends from your old school?"

She flips over so she's facing me and props herself up. "Kind of, but I FaceTime them a bunch and we message on Snap all the time."

"Do you miss them?"

Rani nods. "I miss that I never had to explain anything to them. Like, because they've known me since kindergarten."

It's my turn to nod. That's how I felt about Abby.

"Do you miss Minneapolis too? Or just your friends?"

Rani flips over again so she's lying on her back, and I keep the comforter held up like a tent above us. "I miss going to the farmers' market every weekend with my parents," she says. "And I miss how we lived super close to downtown."

"We have farmers' markets on Long Island," I say quickly. "And you can get into Manhattan in like forty-five minutes on the train."

I don't know why I'm defending Long Island. I don't even like it that much. But I want Rani to like it and not be sad she moved here or miss her old friends. And I want her to be friends with me when we get back to school.

"I mean, there's other stuff I miss about my friends too," Rani says. "Like how we all told each other the second we had a new crush." She looks at me then, and my face gets so hot that I have to look away and pretend it's just because it's really stuffy under the blanket.

My heart must be working harder than it's ever worked in its entire life.

Rani turns over onto her stomach and I can almost breathe again. "Plus, my mom had a ton of Persian friends in Minneapolis. I mean, mostly everyone I knew in Minnesota was white, but we still knew a bunch of people from Iran. Like, we would go over to each other's houses all the time. That was pretty nice too, I guess. Not the part where almost everyone was white, though."

"Are there a lot of people from Iran on Long Island?" I ask, feeling kind of embarrassed that I don't know the answer even though I've lived there my whole life. "Like, more than Minneapolis?"

"I mean, I think more than Minnesota, but still not a ton," Rani says. "But my mom'll find them all." She laughs a little at that.

I laugh a little too, but it's not a real laugh. Because if her mom makes new friends, those friends might have kids, and Rani will be friends with them over me, because they'll understand what it's like to live on Long Island and have parents who are from Iran, and I barely even understand one of those things. I have no idea what it's like to live somewhere where there aren't a million other people who look like me. *So* many other people on Long Island are white and Jewish.

I'm pretty sure I'm the only person on Earth who doesn't understand how to make friends. I only have one friend right now, and I'm not even sure if we're *actually* friends, or if these feelings mean we're something else.

"Hey, Dalia?" Rani says quietly, pulling me out of my thoughts.

My heart explodes in my chest. "Yeah?"

"Are you mad at me?"

"What? No. Why would you think that?"

She looks down at the sheets. "I mean, you were pretty much ignoring me all day today."

My already-exploded heart drops down into my stomach. I didn't think she'd notice. "I wasn't trying to ignore you," I tell her. "Like, it's not because I'm mad at you or anything, I promise. Really, I *promise*."

"That's good to hear." She smiles at me, then looks down again. "I guess I was just kind of worried, though."

"Worried about what?"

"Worried that, like—are you sure there wasn't *any* other reason you weren't talking to me? Like, if you weren't mad?"

I think my heart just, like, lives outside of my chest now.

Does she suspect something? Is she trying to get me to tell her about . . . like, how I feel?

I almost laugh, because that thought is *so* wild.

"Um, no," I whisper, even though I'm pretty sure Dhruv's not waking up any time soon.

"Then you have to actually talk to me tomorrow." She shines the flashlight under her chin so that her face is illuminated with yellow light. "You can't ignore me."

And even though it seems like there are still things that neither of us are telling the other, being under the comforter makes it feel like our own private world, like it did when we were in our secret hideout.

Except this time there's a snoring college student in the room with us. But whatever, he's fast asleep.

Rani responds to the snap from her friend from Minneapolis and I lay my head on my arms and look at her. But, like, not in a creepy way. She's just the only thing to look at under the comforter, other than the scratchy motel sheets.

For some reason at that moment my heart starts to actually hurt. The way it did earlier today when we were on line for Hydra, except even stronger. Kind of like when I was watching Alexa and Sara in their motel room. And it's weird because right now I'm probably happier than I was all day. I think it just hurts because . . .

Well, I'm not sure, really.

"Let's watch a video," Rani says.

"Okay," I say, feeling somehow much more than okay

now. "Can it be a makeup tutorial, though?" I *really* don't feel like watching a POV video right now. It would remind me too much of watching Boulder Dash with Rani in our secret closet, and I don't think my heart can take that.

Rani smiles this huge smile, which makes my insides melt.

She puts on a video that she's already shown me, one where a boy around our age makes himself look like a vampire Barbie. I don't tell her that we've already seen it, though, because once the video starts, she sort of nestles into me. I mean, she might just be getting more comfortable, but one whole side of her body touches one whole side of my body, from our legs to where we're propped up on our elbows. I don't want to do anything that makes her move away from me.

After a minute, she pauses the video, and I'm worried she's going to ask me again why I was being weird today.

But then she says, "I still really think we should do a roller coaster makeup tutorial."

"How?" I ask, laughing a little, mostly from relief that it wasn't about anything else.

"The loop could go around your nose," Rani says, smiling.

I look down. I don't really like drawing attention to my nose, because it's big enough to do that itself. My dad calls it our schnoz.

But then Rani reaches up under the blanket and taps my nose. "It would be hilarious," she says. "The costume of the year."

I smile and put my hand where hers had been, on the bridge of my nose. "Definitely."

She starts the video again. "Can you see?"

"Yeah," I say. But it doesn't really matter whether or not I can see the video. Because even though my eyes are sort of pointed toward the screen, all I can think about is how my heart is pounding and how her leg is touching mine.

My whole body tenses up, and I start shaking and sweating all at the same time. I'm worried that Rani can feel me shaking or hear my teeth chattering. She has to feel that my body is like a coiled spring. That I might explode at any second.

I can't help but think about what Abby said about kissing Dylan. Not the stuff about his braces or anything like that. But the rest of it. Back when she told me about what it was like to kiss someone, I was so scared of the idea of putting my mouth on someone else's mouth. It's still the scariest idea in the world, because 1) it's sort of gross, and 2) I don't know if I'd do it right.

But when Abby was telling me about the kiss, I couldn't think of anyone I would even *want* to do that with, so it didn't matter. But now I'm worried that maybe it does matter. Because maybe there's someone I would want to kiss.

And someone who I probably, most likely, almost definitely have a crush on.

Rani.

And I don't know what to do.

CHAPTER TWENTY-ONE

"YOU sure you can't come to Ohio?" Alexa asks Sara, hugging her very tightly. It's the next morning, and we're in the parking lot of the motel, about to leave for a day of driving. "We can just put you in the trunk."

"Or the middle seat," I say. "That's open too."

"I was joking, kid," Alexa says, rolling her eyes.

"So was I," I tell her. But I wasn't, really. It was nice having Sara here, especially since it meant that Alexa mellowed out a bit. Now that Sara's leaving, I'm sure it'll be back to grumpy Alexa.

Sara—who's still squeezing Alexa as hard as she can—gives her a look, and Alexa stops her eyes from rolling all the way back into her skull.

"I wish I could come," Sara says, running a hand through her bangs. "But I have to go to this show my brother's in. He's like a tap-dancing sailor or something? I think it's a pretty big part."

"Fiiiiiiiiiine," Alexa sighs. "Text me when you get home." She kisses Sara quickly, and I look away.

"Dalia," Sara says. I look up. Why is she saying my name? "I have something that I wanna give you. Walk with me to my car?"

I look over at Alexa, who just shrugs. Dhruv and Rani are pretending like they're busy talking, but I can tell they're really looking over at me and Sara and Alexa to see what's going on. They're trying to be sneaky about it, but it's not working.

Dhruv fell asleep in his makeup last night, and it took a ton of motel soap and scrubbing before it all came off. He said he didn't want to have to explain to Alexa or Sara why part of his face was blue. Luckily, Alexa didn't ask any questions when Rani returned her makeup. She was too distracted by Sara leaving.

Sara's still looking over at me, and my heart's pounding. I don't know what she could possibly want to give me.

When we get to her car, she climbs into the driver's seat and motions for me to sit up front on the passenger side. I get in and shut the door.

"I don't actually have anything for you," she says. "Sorry."

"Oh, that's fine—"

"I just wanted to talk to you alone before I left," she says, interrupting me. "You know, to wish you good luck with the girl you definitely don't have a crush on."

She winks at me, and my face goes red. Can Sara tell that I realized I have a crush on Rani last night?

No, that's silly.

But because I don't think I'm ever going to see Sara again in my life, I do something kind of wild: I tell the truth.

"Actually, I, um, sort of do, um, with Rani, like, you know . . ."

I don't finish the sentence, but I think Sara understands what I'm saying, because she says, "I remember the first crush I had on a girl. I was around your age. I don't know if I even realized it was a crush back then, though. So honestly, you're like ten steps ahead of me."

I don't feel ten steps ahead of her. I feel awful. I feel sick. I feel like I don't want to talk about this, but at the same time it's the only thing I ever want to talk about.

"Is it bad that I kind of want to, like"—I take a breath— "tell her?"

I realize it's true when I say it. Once again, my mouth is ahead of my brain.

Sara laughs a little, but not in a way where I think she's making fun of me. "It's definitely not bad. If I were you, I'd also want to tell her. It's easier than just thinking forever about what could happen."

I look down at the black rubber floor of Sara's car. It's like she's seeing into my brain.

Then she adds, "I'm gonna put my number in your phone, just so you have it in case you ever want to talk about this or anything else. You can text me whenever."

After we exchange numbers, I start to leave the car, but Sara's like, "Wait, one more thing." I freeze with my hand on the door handle. When there's "one more thing" it's usually serious. And I've had enough serious conversations to last me one hundred lifetimes. But it's Sara, so I listen.

"I know you might not agree, but I think you and Alexa should talk." She takes a breath. "Maybe not about Rani, but about other things. She has a lot going on too, and you might be able to see eye to eye on more stuff than you think."

I nod, and Sara doesn't add anything, so I say goodbye and leave the car.

But now I'm sort of worried, because the more I think about it, the more it seems like Sara might be right. Alexa's the only person who's in pretty much the exact same situation as me: She's also dealing with a parent getting remarried; she's dealing with having a new stepsister. She has a *girlfriend*.

Oh, god. Sara's *definitely* right.

"What were you two talking about?" Alexa asks when I get back to the car. "What did she give you?"

"Nothing," I say. Because it's technically true, even if it's not really.

I spend the first two hours of our drive thinking about what it would be like to have a real conversation about, like, serious topics with Alexa.

More unbelievable things have happened.

I mean, I can't think of any.

But still.

A few hours later, we pull into a rest stop in a town called Burnt Cabins, which is a pretty amazing name for a town.

Rani and I go to the bathroom, and I finish before her and walk out into the main rest stop area, where Alexa is pounding her fist against a vending machine.

"Hey, Dalia." Alexa calls me over to the machine she's currently whacking. I stop when I get a few feet away from her. "Wanna ride with me in the front for a bit?" That last part comes out like a grunt, because whatever she bought isn't budging.

I eye her suspiciously. "Why?"

Sure, we were getting along fairly well yesterday. But that was probably just because of Sara. Plus, she basically told me on the first day of the trip that I was never gonna be allowed to sit up front.

"If I say 'quality time' you won't believe me, right?"

I shake my head.

"Yeah, figures." She leans her back against the vending machine and crosses her arms. "All right, here's the deal. My mom texted me to say they're gonna FaceTime us while we're on the road instead of at the motel. They're gonna call your phone since I can't pick up while I'm driving, and it'll be easier to talk to them if we're both up front." She shakes her head. "Just do this for me, okay? Yesterday's FaceTime . . . could've gone better."

"Whatever," I say, walking back toward the car, where I'm planning on sitting in the back seat like I have been for the past three days. I had thought that *maybe* things would be a tiny bit different with Alexa after yesterday. But of course they're not.

But then I hear footsteps coming toward me, and after a second there's a hand tapping my shoulder. I turn around, and Alexa's holding out two cans. "Seltzer or ginger ale?"

"Um, seltzer."

She nods and hands it to me.

"So, also . . . Sara thought that maybe it would be a good idea if we—"

"Talk?"

"Yeah." She smiles a little and shakes her head.

"That's what she said to me too."

The highway ahead of us is flat, and the yellow lines on the road get blurrier and blurrier the longer I stare at them. Rani and Dhruv are both napping in the back. They fell asleep like five minutes after we left the rest stop.

I wanted to fall asleep too, but I couldn't because Alexa and I had to FaceTime my dad and Vanessa. I held the phone, and I didn't even try to smile at my dad this time. I mostly pointed the camera at Alexa, who didn't pick a fight with Vanessa, but I think that's probably just because she was concentrating on driving. The whole call lasted about two minutes.

Two endless minutes.

"They're both asleep," Alexa says, looking in the rearview mirror.

"Yup."

"You were good," she says. "On the call."

"It's kind of terrible seeing them like that. Like, I hate that they're all couple-y. Talking to them on FaceTime just kind of sucks." I turn toward Alexa. "Don't you think?"

"Honestly, it's whatever." She takes a hand off the wheel to grab her ginger ale. "My dad and I have a weekly check-in and we never have anything to say to each other. So I have practice at this kind of thing."

It's the first time I've heard Alexa mention her dad. "Does he live on Long Island?"

"No, he lives in LA with his new wife and their babies."

"You already have stepsiblings?"

"Half siblings, but yeah."

Even though it's only been a year or so officially, it feels like my parents have been split up for a long time, so I have the whole child-of-divorce thing down. But Alexa's already been through the whole having-a-parent-remarry thing.

"Was it hard?" I ask. "When your dad got married?"

"Not really," she says. "I never saw him that much after my parents got divorced, since he moved away."

"Same with my mom," I tell her. "But I don't think she's remarried."

"You don't think?"

"We don't really talk," I say. "She moved to New Jersey like a year ago and I haven't seen her since."

"That sucks."

"It's whatever."

"It's not whatever." Alexa sounds mad, but not at me. "She's still your *mom*. Like, what did you do when you got your period?"

"I don't know," I say. "I don't have it yet."

I never actually thought of that.

"Well, tell me when you get it, okay?" She looks over at me for a second, then back at the road. "I'll buy you tampons and tell you how to put them in."

Ew, ew, ew. But also, that's weirdly . . . sweet? "How come you're being so nice to me?"

She frowns. "I don't wanna be mean. I've actually been wanting to say that I'm, like . . ." She takes a deep breath, then mumbles the word *sorry*.

"What?" I ask. I know what she said, but I want her to say it again. I want proof that it's not all in my brain, that she really has been kind of terrible to me, and she knows it.

"Sorry," she says, almost yelling. Then, more quietly, "I'm sorry."

She checks the rearview mirror, but Rani and Dhruv are still asleep.

"I'm gonna try to be more chill about everything," she says. "And I really am sorry that you saw me fighting with my mom yesterday." She takes a breath. "*And* I'm sorry that I've been taking it out on you. My mom and I were already having a tough summer, and then she was completely fine with you coming but wouldn't even think about letting me bring Sara. Not that that was your fault or anything."

"At least your mom talks to you," I say. "My dad didn't even tell me he was dating your mom until, like, a few days before I met you."

"Wait, what?" Alexa asks, taking her eyes off the road to look at me. "He didn't tell you about my mom at all before then?"

I shake my head. "Nope."

"What? Why?!"

"I don't know, I guess it just never came up."

But that gets me thinking, which, obviously, is never good. Why *didn't* he tell me? The only answers I can come up with are that he thinks I'm a baby who can't handle it, or else he thought I didn't need to know.

"Aren't you mad?" Alexa asks me.

Huh.

I think about that. Like, *really* think about it.

"I don't know," I say, pulling my legs up onto the passenger seat. "Like, maybe he had a good reason for not telling me." But even as I say it, it sounds like an excuse.

"Oh, yeah?" Alexa asks. "What was it?"

I try to come up with one. I can't.

"Okay, fine, maybe I *am* angry. But I can't really be mad at my dad. Like, I can't show him I'm mad at him, you know?"

"Why not? If I were you I'd be so mad. And I'd let him know."

Somehow that doesn't surprise me.

After a minute Alexa says, more gently, "You're allowed to be angry."

"I know," I say, crossing my arms and turning toward the window.

Obviously Alexa thinks it's okay to be angry. She's angry all the time. People probably expect that from her. Like, it doesn't change how people see her.

"Do you?" She looks over at me quickly, then back at the road. After a minute she adds, "It feels nice to get angry, sometimes. To yell and scream."

"I can't."

"How come? Don't you want to yell?"

I shrug.

"You should yell. Trust me, it feels *so* good."

"Now?"

Alexa pushes a button on her door, and my window goes down a few inches.

She raises her voice so I can hear her over the wind. "Stick your head out a little bit. It won't wake them up, I promise. No one will hear but you."

It's my turn to raise my eyebrows at Alexa, but she just lowers the window the rest of the way.

I scooch over so I'm on the edge of the seat, and turn my head so it's partially outside the window.

The wind pushes super hard against my face, and I twist my neck back and forth and back and forth. I stick out my tongue. I test how the air feels when it flows over my nose, and my chin, and my forehead. I reach my hand out and let it float, and it slices through the air like it's water. I think of Rani's long fingers sliding over the surface of the pool, never dipping under.

And then I think of my dad, mistaking Rani for Abby when they couldn't be more different. And how he didn't tell me about Vanessa for six months. And how Vanessa thinks Sara's the reason Alexa's mad, because apparently when your parent falls in love they only care about themselves and they don't know anything about you anymore.

I turn my head forward, to face the highway ahead of us. I open my mouth, and I can feel it getting cracked and dried out from the air, but it doesn't matter. I scream a little and I can't even really hear myself, so I scream louder. I can still barely hear over the wind slamming into my face, but the sounds mix together, my scream and the watery air whooshing by, and my chest feels light and my throat hurts and it's like being on a roller coaster, except I'm not screaming because I'm going downhill, I'm screaming because I can and because Alexa told me to and because, fine, yes, I'm mad.

When I'm done, I raise the window. The car is so, so quiet now that the wind is gone. But it's not uncomfortable. It's actually kind of nice. I look over at Alexa.

"Feels good, right?"

I nod. "Feels great."

CHAPTER TWENTY-TWO

"WE'RE gonna stop in Pittsburgh," Alexa says. "I need a break from driving."

Makes sense, because it feels like we've been in the car for about a hundred hours. But I think it's only been, like, four.

"Why doesn't Dhruv drive?" Rani asks, leaning forward from the back seat.

"I can't," he says. "Never got my license."

"So yeah," Alexa says. "We gotta stop somewhere."

"Well, if we're going to Pittsburgh, you know what I wanna do." Now Dhruv's leaning forward from the back seat too. He puts his hands on Alexa's shoulders, but she shimmies them off.

"No," she says firmly. "It'll be too expensive. Dalia's dad didn't give me that much extra money."

"What is it?" Rani asks. "Maybe I can pay."

This time I'm the one who says a firm no. I don't want Rani paying for me. She already paid for the Slingshot, and I shouldn't even have let her done that.

"It's not even me paying," Rani says. "It's my mom. I'm telling you, it's totally fine."

She leans back into her seat after saying that, and I look out my window.

It doesn't feel totally fine. It feels like every time Rani offers to pay for something, she gets one step closer to being the kind of rich Hillcrest girl who'd want nothing to do with me when school starts back up in the fall. When I get nervous around Rani my heart beats too fast, but when she offers to pay for things it feels too heavy in my chest.

But I don't want to fight with Rani, especially when things are actually almost good with everyone (if I don't think too much about the crush).

"Okay," I say. "But where are we even going?"

"What?" Dhruv asks, raising his eyebrows at me as he holds open the door to the National Aviary in Pittsburgh. Inside is bright and airy, with giant ceilings and marble tiles and tiny birds flittering about.

Dhruv told us last night that he likes birds, but apparently that was a total understatement.

"You think you're the only one with a weird obsession?"

"My thing with roller coasters isn't weird," I tell him.

"Yeah, *okay*," Dhruv says, and I stick my tongue out at him. "Hey, hey, I'm not saying it's a bad thing. Being weirdly obsessed is the best feeling in the entire world." Dhruv inhales deeply. "I could sniff that bird smell for hours."

"Ew," I say, laughing.

From the moment we step inside the aviary, we're enveloped by the stench of musty feathers and bird poop. But Dhruv clearly loves it.

"You're so weird," Alexa says.

"I know." Dhruv turns to us. "So, here's the game plan." He goes on to explain how we should start our trip in Condor Court. "Andean condors are the biggest raptors in the world. Their wingspan is just about ten feet. And there are three condors in the exhibit: Lurch, who's fifty years old; Lianni, who's thirty-seven; and Precious, who's sixty-two. And Lurch and Lianni are paired, so they're sort of married."

"What about Precious?" I ask. "Who's she paired with?"

"Precious is by herself," he says. "But I don't think she really minds."

When we get to Condor Court, I'm surprised by how big and ugly the birds are. There's a sign near the exhibit that tells us that they're the largest flying birds in the world. The sign also says that they defend themselves by vomiting, but I'm choosing to ignore that part.

I can't even imagine how they can keep themselves in the air. They have these weird bald heads with a tiny bit of hair poking out, and jet-black feathers with a white ruffle around their neck that makes them look like they're all dressed up with nowhere to go.

Okay, fine. I guess they're sort of cute.

Dhruv starts talking to them in this high-pitched voice. "Well hello wittle birdies," he coos, "aren't you just the cutest wittle things?"

"Dhruv, they're bigger than you," Alexa says, but she's laughing. "And didn't you say they're like sixty years old? They're middle-aged. Stop doing that baby talk."

"I mean, Precious is older than middle-aged," Dhruv says. "Andean condors only live about sixty or seventy years in captivity."

"That's so sad," I say.

"Well, they don't even live *that* long in the wild."

The poor birds. It must suck to be a condor in captivity, because you can't fly wherever you want.

And that's when someone behind me screams.

I turn around and see a loose peacock encircling Rani. I tell this to Dhruv, who doesn't seem concerned.

"Oh, that's not a peacock," he says, walking over to Rani and the large bird squawking at her. "It's a peahen. You can tell because she's not brightly colored. Peacocks are male, and peahens are female."

"Uh," Rani says, frozen in place, "I don't really care what it's called. Can you just get her away from me?"

"But she *chose* you," Dhruv says. "You're so lucky. Maybe she thinks you're a male because of your shirt."

Rani looks down at her bright blue shirt.

"ARE YOU SAYING SHE'S TRYING TO MATE WITH ME?" she screams, and then the bird does too.

"Shh," Dhruv says, speaking to the bird. "It's all right, lil' buddy." He walks slowly toward the long brown peahen and ushers her away from Rani.

The bird waddles away, and I can't help it. I start laughing. Not just a little giggle, but, like, complete hysterics.

"What?" Rani asks. "Are you laughing at me?"

I can't even answer because I'm laughing too hard. It's just so ridiculous, Dhruv and his thing with birds, a peahen trying to mate with Rani.

Then Dhruv starts laughing too, and Rani. Even Alexa joins in. And none of us can stop. I'm laughing so hard that tears run down my face and I have to bend over.

After a few minutes, we all calm down. My chest hurts, but a good kind of hurt. Like how I feel after screaming on a roller coaster. Or after a bird just tried to mate with the girl I have a crush on.

"Maybe it's time for the next exhibit," Dhruv says, wiping tears from his eyes.

So, we leave Condor Court and go see the penguins at Penguin Point, the brightly colored birds flying around the Tropical Rainforest, and some loud finches in the Grasslands. Dhruv tells us a bunch of fun facts everywhere we go.

I love walking around the aviary with him; it's so nice

to have someone who's super excited about something tell you about it. I hope that's how Dhruv and Alexa and Rani feel when I talk about roller coasters.

We only stay for a couple of hours, because we need to get back on the road, but Dhruv looks like he never wants to leave. I'm pretty sure he'd be fine if we left him here to live with the birds and become part of their flock.

"Rani, you want a turn up front?" Alexa asks when we get back to the car.

"Um," Rani says, looking over at me, "that's okay. I'll sit in the back with Dalia."

She smiles at me, and my whole body basically melts.

"Suit yourself," Alexa says, and she raises her eyebrows at me while Rani gets into the car.

Oh, god. Alexa knows.

I look away, but secretly I'm happy that maybe Alexa's picking up on something that's going on between me and Rani. Because that means it's probably not just in my brain.

Probably.

Rani's sitting on the edge of her bed in the motel, looking at something on her phone.

"My mom just texted me this thing Madison Middle sent over to our house," she says. "It's something about a pod?"

"Wait, no way." I get up from my bed and walk toward her side of the room. "They sent yours out already?"

I'm just standing near her bed now, which is even more awkward than sitting. I try to send a message to my legs to sit on the bed next to her and to not be so friggin' weird. But my body isn't listening to my brain at the moment, so I perch on the opposite edge of Rani's bed. Which is totally normal. It's obviously fine to *sit* near a *friend.*

"I guess?" Rani pushes herself all the way up onto the bed so that she's cross-legged on the comforter. And a little closer to me.

My heart speeds up, and I move my butt ever-so-slightly farther off the edge of the bed as I pull my phone out of my shorts pocket so Rani doesn't notice me shifting.

And I see that my dad texted.

Dad: Voila! Your back to school letter!

He attached a picture of the same mailer Rani's mom just sent her. He also added a second message.

Dad: Wish you were here, Dals.

I want to roll my eyes, Alexa-style.

I used to love spending the last days of summer with my dad—getting ice cream, talking about my new teachers, savoring the long days and the warm, salty air.

Maybe I miss him too. Or maybe I just miss, like, the good parts. But that's still a kind of missing, I guess.

But *then* I think about what it would be like if I were home right now—getting ice cream with my dad *and*

Vanessa, talking about my new teachers with my dad *and* Vanessa. The air would probably smell like fish, not salt. The ice cream would taste sour.

I want to scream again.

So instead of texting my dad that I wish I was there too, like he probably expects, I just thumbs-up his message. It's the best I can do.

Because the truth is, even though I'm still feeling nervous about Rani, and even though it was hard to deal with Alexa on the first couple days of the trip, I would rather be here. Maybe not in this motel room, specifically, but, like, on this trip. With Rani and Dhruv and Alexa and sometimes Sara.

Rani slides over from where she was sitting and kneels next to me on the bed. She nudges my shoulder and shows me the picture on her phone, zooming in on a particular line. "Okay, but what *is* a pod?"

I can't move away from her now, so I look down at her phone, like I'm super focused on reading the letter. But really I'm just thinking about how warm it feels where Rani's shoulder touched mine.

"Okay, so pods are sort of like classes, or groups. There's the red pod, yellow pod, green pod, and blue pod. It's just because Madison's too big to have everyone in one class." I read what it says on the picture her mom sent. "And it looks like you're in red!"

"Is that good?"

"That's amazing," I say, and then I look away because I didn't mean to sound that excited. But it is amazing, because, well, that's *my* pod. "I'm in red too."

"Awesome," Rani says as she lies back on the bed, legs dangling off the side.

It's safer like this, right now, when her head's nowhere near mine. I take a deep breath.

"So are you in, like, any clubs at school?" Rani asks after a minute of leg-swinging silence.

"Um, not really."

Ugh.

It sounds so uncool, to have to tell Rani that. No clubs. Nothing going on. So much free time that used to be filled with Abby. We were sort of like a two-person club. But I guess that's not even really a club, if there are only two people.

"You should start a roller coaster club," she says. "I'd join."

I look over at her, and it seems like she was looking at me too, because she meets my eye for like a millisecond, and then she looks back up at the ceiling.

When I'm sure my voice won't sound shaky or weird or anything, I say, "You should start a makeup club." Then I quickly add, "I'd join."

"Maybe we could start a combined roller coaster and

makeup club," Rani says. "That way we could show everyone our roller coaster makeup tutorial when we finally do it."

Her eyes flash over to me again. We both look away.

"Um, were you in any clubs at your old school?" I ask after that.

"Not really," she says. "I had Farsi school every Friday, which kind of sucked because I couldn't hang out with my friends after school, but that was, like, sort of a club. And some of my friends were in drama club, so I helped out a little bit with makeup for that. Nothing like what Dhruv had me do, but still." She sits up. "My school did *Legally Blonde Jr.* and one of my friends, Logan, he played a sorority girl because he asked the director if he could be one and she was like, sure, and so I got to put all this pink makeup on him. We did this amazing photo shoot." She opens her phone and scrolls for a minute, then turns it around to show me.

It's a picture Rani took of her and Logan in a dressing-room mirror, and they're both doing peace signs and Rani's holding a makeup brush and Logan has a bald cap on or something and his eye makeup looks amazing. I mean, obviously it does, because Rani did it. And then I notice something else. "Wait, is this the same guy from the vampire Barbie tutorial?"

She's shown me a few of his videos, and they're all amazing and scary and literally so funny.

"Yeah, he got super into makeup after that. I'm kind of

mad that he's getting all these views for something I taught him." She looks up at me. "I mean, not *actually* mad, obviously."

"Right."

I don't say anything else for a moment because I'm thinking back to the videos Rani's showed me of him. How come she never mentioned they were friends?

But then I think about the things he talks about in the videos, like boys at school he has crushes on and stuff (he uses fake names, like Carrot and Bob). But, yeah.

So, he's a boy who likes boys. And Rani is friends with him.

So, she can't be too closed-minded, right?

Like, maybe if I told Rani that I have a crush on her, it would be okay.

But if I tell her and she doesn't feel the same way, that's it. There goes my chance at ever having a best friend again, or any friends, really.

But if I tell her and she *does* feel the same way . . .

Maybe I'll tell her tomorrow. Maybe I'll just do it.

I think.

Maybe.

Probably not.

Who knows?

But I could.

The thought makes my stomach do a 360-degree flip.

CHAPTER TWENTY-THREE

IT'S the morning of the fifth day of our trip, which is hard to believe. That means I'm going to be home in two days.

I don't think I'm ready to go back.

Luckily, I don't have to worry about that right now. We're walking into Cedar Point, the biggest amusement park in Ohio. I can already tell it's going to be different from the other parks. It's not trying to be old-timey like Dorney and Lake Compounce. Instead, the first thing you see is this huge turquoise roller coaster, with a giant loop framed by a perfectly blue, cloudless sky. The park is in the middle of Lake Erie, so it almost feels like we're on a desert island and we somehow imagined a whole amusement park onto it.

There's a sign that reads "Cedar Point: The Roller Coaster Capital of the World," and I can see why. There are rides in every color of the rainbow, and they're towering above us in all directions.

I can't believe this is real.

"I know this is gonna sound like a wild suggestion," Dhruv says, "but what if we get a morning funnel cake? I feel like I didn't really get to enjoy mine the other day because I was too nauseous from riding roller coasters."

"So, your solution is morning funnel cake?" Alexa asks, raising her eyebrows and laughing a little.

"Um, I wouldn't say no to a funnel cake," Rani chimes in.

"But then you're not gonna be able to ride roller coasters for, like, half the morning!" I don't mean to sound whiny, but what's the point of going to an amusement park if you can't ride roller coasters?

"Okay," Alexa says, "how about this: Dalia and I will go on a few coasters, and Dhruv and Rani can have their morning funnel cake?"

I look over at Alexa. I don't want to spend time away from Rani, but then again, the less time I'm with her, the less time I have to worry about whether or not I should tell her about the crush.

"Let's do it," Dhruv says, and he holds out his elbow for Rani to take. "M'lady?"

Rani giggles and hooks her arm through his. I try to tamp down the jealousy that burns yet again in my stomach. It's literally so silly; I guess what I'm most jealous of is the fact that, for some people, it's so easy to link elbows or hold hands or whatever, but for me it's the biggest deal in the entire world.

So, Dhruv and Rani head off in search of a funnel cake, and Alexa and I stand in the entrance area for a second, watching families stream in past us.

"This one?" Alexa asks, pointing to the turquoise entrance coaster looming above us.

I nod, and we walk over to the line. It's called Gatekeeper, and I know it's going to be amazing because I've watched the POV. I want to tell Alexa everything about it, but I don't want to ruin the peace we have going now.

But then she's like, "All right, what do I need to know about this coaster?"

And obviously I'm so glad she asked.

We both look over at the ride as the line inches forward. "Okay, so see how the lift hill is really wide? Like, how it's got the track in the center and a platform on either side?" Alexa nods. "Well, that's because it's a wing coaster, so, like, the track is in the center and the seats are the wings, and I guess they put the floor there on the lift hill so people don't get super scared yet that they're just dangling over the ground with nothing under them."

"But don't you think they'd want to scare people?" Alexa asks, looking at the coaster. "Isn't that the fun part?"

"I mean, I'd want to be scared," I tell her.

"Me too."

The line keeps moving, and we don't really talk that much, but it's not awkward or anything. Alexa pulls out her phone and starts typing something.

"Are you talking to Sara?"

"Yeah," she says, not looking up. Then, after a minute: "She's asking how you're doing."

I nod and turn to face Lake Erie, in case Alexa looks up, so she can't see the huge grin on my face. "What did you say?"

"I didn't." She looks up from her phone. "What *should* I say?"

"Um, I guess that things are good? And that I'm maybe gonna do something about the . . . thing."

I know the moment it's out of my mouth I shouldn't have said it.

And this is confirmed when Alexa puts her phone in her back pocket and raises her eyebrows. "What thing?"

"Nothing," I say quickly. But then I remember what Sara said, about how Alexa might be the right person to talk to about a lot of things.

Maybe even this thing.

I take a shaky breath and say, "I sort of have a crush on someone."

"Oh, yeah?"

We're almost at the front of the line, and my heart is pounding. Maybe if I tell Alexa and get it off my chest, I won't feel like I need to tell Rani. And *then* maybe I won't be so nervous around her today.

"Um, okay, I'm gonna tell you who it is, but you have to promise not to say anything. Like, not even to Dhruv if you're alone with him in the motel or whatever, okay? You really, really can't say anything. You can't even *think* it, okay?"

"I won't say anything," Alexa says.

"So, the person I have a crush on is, um . . . Rani."

I watch Alexa's face closely, but she doesn't seem too surprised. "That's really cute," she says, smiling.

How could she possibly call the most important thing in my entire life "cute"?

She must see my face, because she says, "Not cute?" I shake my head. "Then it's exciting! Are you gonna tell her?"

"I don't know."

"Hm." She puts a hand under her chin and taps her fingers on her jaw. "That's really tough, because you two seem like such good friends. And it's hard to tell when you're good friends with someone whether or not they might have a crush on you too."

"Yeah, exactly," I say.

And now we're up next. We're about to get on Gatekeeper.

"How about this," Alexa says. "I'll keep an eye on Rani and see if I think she maybe has a crush on you too. That way we can talk strategy. When we're done with this ride, we can find Dhruv and Rani, and split up again. Then you two can ride roller coasters by yourselves for a bit."

"Yeah?"

"Oh, yeah," Alexa says. "It'll be great."

I guess Sara was right. Maybe Alexa *is* the right person to talk to about all of this.

We get on Gatekeeper, and it's even better than it looks. We twist and soar over Lake Erie, legs dangling. Me and Alexa.

A team.

CHAPTER TWENTY-FOUR

"**WHY** don't we split up for a bit?" Alexa asks when we're back with Dhruv and Rani after they get their morning funnel cake. "We can meet again for lunch."

She winks at me.

"Sounds good," I say, all casual and such.

"Yeah," Rani agrees.

"Just make sure you answer me if I text you," Alexa says. "And—"

"Don't die?"

"How'd you guess?"

I smile at her. "Maybe I'm learning."

She nods and smiles back. "All right, well, see you at lunch."

"Peace," Dhruv says, walking backward. He almost bumps into a family with little kids precariously holding ice cream cones, which makes the rest of us laugh.

"So, what do you wanna go on first?" I ask Rani as we walk down the midway, looking around at all of our roller coaster options.

I beg my heart to not pound so loudly in my chest. Because I'm definitely *not* going to tell Rani about my crush right now. I have to wait to see what Alexa says, so there's no point in worrying.

But I still feel nervous.

"You pick," she says. "Maybe something with a kind of long line, though? I can feel the funnel cake gurgling around in my stomach."

I laugh. "I definitely could've told you that morning funnel cake was a bad idea."

"Well, it was delicious."

"But was it worth the stomach gurgling?"

"Duh."

I'm about to respond when I get distracted by this super intriguing sign for a roller coaster called Steel Vengeance. The sign's a sculpture of a runaway mine cart on the side of a cliff. It's all very Wild West. I don't think I've ever seen a POV video of this ride before.

Rani and I both look up from the sign at the same time. Like, all the way up. And what we see is almost unbelievable: a huge wooden roller coaster, except there are parts of the ride where you go upside down (on a wooden roller coaster!!). And for the first drop you basically fall straight down to the ground.

So yeah, it's awesome. And we need to go on it.

We run to the line, which is long and Wild West–themed, just like the sign.

"This is gonna be unreal," Rani says.

"Well howdy there, partner," a voice from behind me says.

Rani laughs, and I turn around to see someone dressed like a cowboy. They must work for the park, because they're wearing a name tag that says "Steel Vengeance—Dan." So, I guess their name is Dan. Unless their full name is Steel Vengeance Dan.

"Howdy," Rani says, playing along. She even does a little southern accent. I know cowboys aren't from the south, but the way she says it is pretty incredible, actually.

"Mind if I tell you folks a few facts about this here ride?" Steel Vengeance Dan takes their cowboy hat off and uses it to point at the roller coaster.

"Surely," Rani says, still in character. Seriously, it's amazing.

Steel Vengeance Dan goes on to tell us about how the roller coaster looming over us is a hypercoaster (taller than two hundred feet) and a hybrid coaster (steel and wood), which is pretty epic.

Their description of the coaster also reminds me of Son of Beast at Kings Island, which I've read all about because it was the first wooden hypercoaster and it got shut down because it was too dangerous.

I tell Rani all about it after Steel Vengeance Dan moves onto the next group of unsuspecting people. "Son of Beast was supposed to be, like, a sequel to this other ride called The Beast, which is sort of hilarious because I don't think roller coasters usually have sequels, like that's definitely just a movie thing. But they shut down the ride because there were so many accidents and also it gave people really bad whiplash. Like, even on the POV you can hear people screaming and it sounds like they're in pain."

Rani looks nervously up at Steel Vengeance. "Is this one safe?" she asks. "Like, are all wooden hypercoasters dangerous?"

"No, I bet this one's super safe. Roller coasters only get shut down if there's something really wrong with them, and there's definitely nothing really wrong with this one." When I see her face I add, "It'll be okay. I promise."

It's just like I imagined back when we first watched a roller coaster POV video together. I'm the expert, guiding Rani and helping her feel safe.

I get that warm feeling in my chest, the one that hurts a little but also feels really nice.

Rani nods, like she's ready to go. And then it's time for us to get on the roller coaster.

The ride is just as awesome as Steel Vengeance Dan made it sound. But it's not the kind of coaster where you can put your hands up, because it's way too tall and scary.

I mean, maybe *some* people can put their hands up, but by the time we get to the top, I'm convinced we're about to fall through to the center of the earth, and that is not a time for hand holding.

No matter how much I might want it to be.

I scream even louder than I did out of the car window, and my stomach flips as the sky becomes a blue blur.

When we get off the ride, we're both laughing and trying to catch our breath. Rani leans against me to rest, and I can feel the post–roller coaster warmth radiating from her skin.

I never, ever want this trip to end.

After Steel Vengeance, Rani and I run from coaster to coaster. One of the best is Valravn, which is a dive coaster.

"Dive coasters are really cool because they have pretty much vertical drops and the trains have these long rows of like ten people, so that everyone can have a front-row seat!" I shout this to Rani so she can hear me over the metal chain as we're going up the lift hill on the ride—"And dive coasters pause at the top of the hill with the train tilting down to face the drop so that you have no choice but to see what you're about to fall into." But I don't think she hears me, mostly because she's too busy screaming at the top of her lungs in anticipation of the drop we're actually about to go down.

The whole time I'm alone with Rani, I feel like I can do anything. She runs faster than me, but I'm happy to lag behind her, watching her head bob in the crowd. I like it when she looks over her shoulder to make sure I'm still there. I can't help but think about how lucky I am that she came on this trip. How lucky I am that for this one week she's all mine. Well, not *mine*, but.

Yeah.

"Let's get ice cream," Rani says after our fifth or sixth roller coaster.

We're both sweaty and tired and ice cream sounds like the best idea ever.

"Yes please," I say. But then I realize something. "Oh wait, Alexa has my money."

"Dalia, seriously?"

"What?"

"I mean, I'll just pay for you. I told you, I can pay for whatever."

I look at her, and when I don't respond for a minute, she turns around to look at me too.

"But, um, I don't really *want* you to pay for me," I say quietly. Maybe it's how hot it is, or how sweaty and tired I am, but I feel a little annoyed. I force myself to push that feeling down. Everything's been going so well. I don't want her to know I'm mad. But I almost can't help it when flashes of her Hillcrest mansion play like a horror movie in my brain.

I try to take a deep breath, but my lungs don't feel right. Now that I know how nice it feels to yell when you're angry, it's, like, the only thing I wanna do. But I can't just go around yelling at people. Especially not Rani.

I just wish we were back on a roller coaster so I could scream. Or so we didn't have to talk. When we're riding on a roller coaster, I don't think about Hillcrest, or what eighth grade will be like, or how much money Rani's family has. I should've asked Steel Vengeance Dan if I could've just kept riding the roller coaster all day. Maybe if they knew what it was like in my brain, they'd make an exception for me, and I wouldn't have to wait on line or anything. I could just keep going and going and going and going.

"It's just ice cream," she says after a minute. "I don't see what the big deal is."

She starts to walk over to the ice cream stand nearby, but I don't follow. It would be so much easier to not say anything. To just be a little bit mad about this forever.

But seriously, does she *really* not see what the big deal is?

I'm going to lose her to the Hillcrest popular crowd.

I know it, I do. Because she doesn't even realize what it feels like for me when she tries to pay for stuff, like the Slingshot and the aviary and now ice cream. It's like I'm a little kid. Like I can't do anything for myself. Like she's my babysitter. The heavy feeling in my heart is back, but now it's mixed with anger.

So I do something that surprises even me. I look over at her, and I shout, "The big deal is that I wanna pay for things myself!" She turns around, confused. "I don't want some rich Hillcrest girl buying things for me!" Hurt flashes across her face. I want to take it back. I *need* to take it back. "I didn't mean—"

"That's what you think of me?" she interrupts. "That I'm just some rich Hillcrest girl?"

Now that I yelled, my chest feels looser, but I feel ten times worse. I never should've shouted at her. Why on earth did I think that was a good idea? I'm going to push her away. I don't want to push her away. I don't want her to leave. I don't, I don't, I don't.

"No," I say. "Maybe. I don't know."

We're both quiet for a minute. Tears start to prickle in my eyes, but I blink a bunch of times until they go away.

I shouldn't have said anything.

"I'm not really in the mood for ice cream anymore," Rani says finally, crossing her arms.

"Okay," I say. I don't know what's happening. "I guess, um, we have to meet Alexa and Dhruv in a minute anyway."

We walk in silence over to the main midway. It's worse than if we were yelling.

We agreed earlier that we'd meet Dhruv and Alexa at this place called Buckaroo's Burritos, and I spot them standing there, smack dab in the middle of everything.

I don't think Alexa sees us; she's saying something to Dhruv and laughing, and for maybe the first time this entire trip I'd *much* rather be with Alexa, or at least in a group with Alexa, than alone with Rani.

But that's when I hear it.

"Dalia and Rani sitting in a tree, *K-I-S-S-I-N-G*—"

"Alexa, don't," Dhruv says, laughing a little. He clearly doesn't see us either.

"But it's adorable!" she says, then starts singing again. The words carry to us from across the midway: "First comes love, then comes marriage . . ."

My heart stops. Like, I actually think my heart is not functioning right now.

"STOP!" I scream. My voice crackles and burns as I yell. I don't know what to do. What am I supposed to do?

Alexa stops singing right away when she sees me, and her eyes go wide. "Dalia, I didn't—"

But she doesn't finish that statement. She doesn't tell me what she "didn't."

Alexa is the one who told me that I'm allowed to get mad.

Well, now I'm madder than I've ever been in my entire life.

At her.

Why would she do this to me? Why would she sing that to Dhruv when I explicitly told her not to say anything?

I thought she'd understand, that maybe after our chat in the car yesterday . . . I don't know.

I look down at the ground. I feel like I might catch on fire from the heat rising in my face.

Dhruv looks between me and Alexa. "Maybe we should all go sit somewhere? We can talk, or . . ."

Alexa stares daggers at him. That's clearly not a good idea.

So then he's like, "Uh, Rani, why don't you and I go grab some food?" Dhruv walks over to Rani and leads her toward Buckaroo's Burritos.

I look up just as Dhruv pushes Rani through the swinging wooden doors. She turns over her shoulder and meets my eye, but the expression on her face is completely different from when we were running from coaster to coaster. I can't tell if she's angry, or confused, or what.

The only thing I can tell for sure is that I'm feeling some sort of red-hot rage.

I want to kick something. I want to pick up a steel roller coaster and throw it all the way across the country. No, all the way across the world, so that it lands back here and crushes Alexa and Rani and Dhruv and me.

This is the worst thing that could possibly happen.

I glare at Alexa, channeling every bit of rage into my eyes.

"Jeez, Dalia," she says, "It was only Dhruv."

"ONLY DHRUV?" I scream. "Rani CLEARLY heard, and you PROMISED not to tell him!"

I think my volume control is broken. Right now, I only have one setting: ear-piercing scream. And I won't switch off.

Alexa walks over to me and puts a hand on my shoulder. I throw it off and turn away from her, crossing my arms and making a scene in front of all these happy families who are just trying to have a good day at the Roller Coaster Capital of the World.

"I can't believe you would sing that," I say. "It's not even true. Why would you say that thing about me and Rani? I only told you I had a crush on her, not that I wanted to kiss her or anything. I literally don't understand why you would say that."

"I shouldn't have sung that song, Dalia. You're so right."

And then I don't hold back. "Well, I should've never kept the secret about Sara. Maybe I'll just text my dad right now and tell him that she came on the trip." I pull out my phone and hold it up.

"*Don't* do that," she says, and there's anger and maybe something like desperation in her voice.

I keep the phone held out. "I could!"

Alexa scoffs. She's cold again, her arms are crossed. "You know what? Fine. Go ahead," she says. "I bet my mom wouldn't even care if *you* told her." She looks at her nails and flicks dirt out from under them with her thumb. "But just wait. She'll turn on you. Once you're stuck with her, you'll see."

"At least you have a mom," I scream. "You don't know *anything*."

"Are you kidding me? You're telling me that *I* don't know anything? I know what it's like to have a parent who leaves.

And I know what it's like to have a mom who doesn't want to be a mom."

"If you know so much, how come you sang that song? After you *promised* not to say anything?" Alexa tries to butt in, but I'm back to screaming. "I didn't even wanna come with you on this trip. I just wanted to ride roller coasters. That's literally it."

Alexa and I are standing right in front of each other now. I'm tall enough that we're basically eye to eye.

"Well, I didn't want you to come period!" Alexa puts a hand to her forehead. "You know what? I'm done pretending to be nice to you. I tried. I really did."

"Pretending to be nice? Are you serious? You weren't nice to me this whole trip!"

Well, except yesterday. And this morning. But clearly she was faking it.

I should've seen this coming. Because it's what always happens when I start warming up to someone. Once my brain starts to care even a little bit, they leave.

"I don't have to stand here and take this from you, kid." And she says "kid" with so much hatred. "I'm going back to school in a few weeks. I don't have to deal with this."

"Exactly, you're going back to school," I say, my voice breaking. "I'm gonna have to deal with my dad and your mom and them getting married. You get to run away. This is my *life*."

Everything's going to be completely different when we get back from this trip. If my dad and Vanessa are getting married, that means they'll probably live together. And then I guess I'll live with them? I don't even know. I don't know anything.

Alexa laughs. "You don't get to say that I'm running away. You don't get to say anything about me." She shakes her head. "You know what? Have fun going home and being part of a happy little family. You'll get just as fed up with them as I am, and when you do, you're gonna have to deal. Alone. Because I'm never visiting. After this summer, that's it. You can have them."

"Fine," I say, even though it's definitely not. "I don't care," I say, even though I definitely do.

She doesn't need to tell me that I'll be all alone. I know I will.

I can't even bring myself to yell anything back at Alexa now, though. I'm completely numb.

"Just don't talk to me," Alexa says. "I don't care what you do. I don't care who you wanna kiss or who you don't wanna kiss." And then she says again, more quietly this time, "Just don't talk to me."

"Whatever," I say.

Everything is whatever. The whole world is whatever.

Alexa and I turn away from each other.

Of course, Dhruv and Rani choose this exact moment to

walk out of Buckaroo's holding burritos the size of a small child.

They walk toward us slowly, like we're bulls who might charge at any moment.

"So, how's it going out here?" Dhruv asks gently. He unwraps the foil and takes a bite, smiling hesitantly at me and Alexa. "Did you two get a chance to talk?"

We don't respond.

CHAPTER TWENTY-FIVE

I storm into the motel room and slam the door. I don't even check to see if Rani's behind me. I want to crawl into bed and never leave.

The rest of the day at Cedar Point was awful. My dad texted a bunch of times just to check in, but I didn't respond. I don't care if he's freaking out; I turned my phone off when we got to the car and haven't turned it back on.

I flip the comforter back and flop into bed, lying on my stomach. I put a pillow over my head and pull the comforter back over me.

Then I start to cry. It's not even a good cry, where you feel empty and clean afterward. It's a terrible cry, and I try to stop the tears from streaming down my face, but no matter how much I wipe them off onto the nice white motel sheets, they just keep coming.

Maybe my body knew that this would happen and it's been waiting to release the floodgates. Just add my physical human body to the list of people who know what's happening before I do.

I hear the door open, but I don't take the comforter off my head. It must be Rani. Maybe she won't even notice I'm here.

She tiptoes through the room, and then sits gently on her bed. I hear a tiny creak of springs. Then nothing.

And then: "Dalia?"

She says it so quietly that I think I imagined it. Maybe I cried so hard that I fell asleep, and now Rani's saying my name in my dream.

But no.

"Dalia? Are you okay?" I don't respond. "Are you awake?"

I hold my breath.

"Dalia?" She says it a bit louder.

I'm frozen.

"Um, so . . . what happened today?"

Yup, definitely not answering that.

"Well, I guess I just wanted to say sorry for trying to pay for stuff."

I especially don't respond to *that*.

"Can we talk?"

Yeah, right.

"Are you awake?"

"No."

"Oh, okay," she says, and I think I hear a smile in her voice.

I don't understand how she's smiling. My face is going to be in a permanent frown after today.

I throw the pillow and the comforter off and kick them to the bottom of the bed. Now that she knows I'm here, there's no point in hiding. Instead I just lie here, flat on my back, staring at the off-white ceiling.

"Do you wanna maybe watch something?" Rani asks, sounding really hesitant. "Like, a POV video?"

I grunt in response. I don't know if I want to watch a roller coaster POV video ever again. Or maybe that's all I ever want to do. Maybe I need to just stick to POV videos and give up on the real thing.

Last week, my life was fine. The only thing that's changed is now I've been on real roller coasters. I went on Kingda Ka, and everything was different, and now everything is terrible. So, yeah, no more roller coasters.

Rani gets off her bed and walks over to mine. She maneuvers around the whole thing, and lies on her stomach on the other side.

"Okay, well, I'm gonna watch the Boulder Dash POV," she says. "You don't have to look at it or anything, but I'm gonna watch." She takes a breath. "You know, I wasn't trying to avoid you after you got into that fight with Alexa. I actually, like, wanted to talk."

I don't say anything.

Then she says, "But I guess you don't."

My heart drops. What would we even talk about? What would I even say? *Oh, yeah, when Alexa was singing that song about us* K-I-S-S-I-N-G, *she got it exactly right and I'd like to kiss you now. Cool?*

Obviously not.

After a few seconds of silence, I hear the sounds that mark the start of the video. A fuzzy ride attendant's voice says, "Okay, folks, we're all clear for the ride."

I turn my head a bit to the side. I don't even want to do it, but I can't help it. It's like my body has an automatic response to Boulder Dash.

When I turn my head, Rani's looking right at me. And she doesn't look away.

Was she . . . staring at me?

No, that's something I would do. She wouldn't stare at me . . .

But she's still looking.

She's looking *at me,* and not at the video. She was lying on her stomach, but now she turns over onto her back and holds the phone straight up in the air, so that we can both see it.

And as she flips over, she scoots closer to me.

As much as I'm trying not to care about anyone in the entire world, as much as I want to be completely numb, my body is betraying me. Because my heart starts beating so fast.

I know her scooting closer to me wasn't an accident. She's so close that she could stretch her toes out and they would touch mine.

Oh my god.

She's stretching her toes so that they touch mine.

Our feet are touching. On purpose.

I pretend like I'm looking up at the screen, but really, I'm straining my eyes to try to look down at where our feet are pressed together.

Then she curls her foot over mine, so it's like our ankles are hugging.

And now I literally can't breathe. I can't. I can't. I can't.

So, I do something silly. I pretend to cough, this big loud bark, which makes Rani drop her phone and move her foot away.

"Are you okay?" she asks.

I know she's talking about the cough, but suddenly I'm crying again. Because I'm really not okay. I try to wipe the tears away, but they just keep dripping out of my eyes.

Rani turns onto her side, her cheek resting against the pillow. And I'm just lying here, tears streaming out of my eyes at such a high speed that my vision's watery and all I can see are shapes and colors.

"Dalia," Rani says. And she says it so nicely that it makes me cry even harder. Why is she being nice to me? I mean, we got into that fight about her paying for ice cream. I was kind of terrible to her. And then . . . She had to have heard what Alexa was singing. Why didn't she just run out of the amusement park right then and there? If I were her, I would've sprinted back to Long Island on my fish legs and never talked to me again.

I don't want Rani to see me crying like this, so I flip over to my stomach and bury my face into the pillow.

"Listen, you're right," Rani says. "I mean, my family is sort of rich." *Sort of?* Tell that to the secret closets. But I don't say anything, so she keeps talking. "And I don't understand how you felt today at the amusement park. But I want to." I look up from the pillow, then quickly turn away. "But you need to understand how *I* feel too. Like, I really wanted to pay for you. I'm able to pay, and . . . I don't know. It feels nice to buy you things."

And she sounds like she really means it. I'm still ashamed, but there's something else too. A warm, safe feeling.

I don't turn over to face her, but I say, "I'm sorry too. I'm sorry I yelled at you. I'm sorry for all of it. It wasn't fair." And then, because I can't help it, I add, "And I'm sorry we didn't get ice cream." Rani laughs a little at that, and my heart feels like it's being pulled in a million different directions.

After a moment, she whispers, "Um, so I talked to Dhruv about some stuff earlier."

I turn on my side and face her. I don't think my head's ever been this close to someone else's before. My heart has stopped and started and stopped and started one hundred times today. I should be in a medical study or something.

But it starts up long enough for me to ask, "What did you talk to him about?"

She shakes her head and says "Dalia," all soft and low. This time it sounds like the start of a longer sentence. And if it's the start of a longer sentence about what Alexa was singing, then I don't want to hear it.

So I say, "It's not true."

"What?" She looks confused.

"What Alexa was saying. It's not true."

"Oh," she says. But she doesn't seem happy.

She seems, I don't know, something else.

Disappointed?

"I don't even know why she was singing that song." I can't stop talking. I just need to keep saying things. "And after today I'm never, ever going to talk to her again, so, like, it doesn't matter."

"Oh," Rani says again.

"It's so ridiculous that she would even think that—"

"I don't really think it's ridiculous," Rani says.

That makes me stop talking. Now that I'm not filling it with words, the silence is almost too loud. It's practically buzzing.

"I actually, um . . ." Rani trails off, but she looks up at me. She moves her foot back so that it's touching my foot. And I know it sounds weird, but it's the nicest feeling.

But also, the scariest. She must be able to feel that my

whole leg is shaking. My whole *body*'s shaking. Somehow this moment is scarier than any roller coaster, because I have no idea what's going to happen next.

Why isn't Rani saying anything? Her face is so close to mine. And I'm just looking at it, because I can't look anywhere else.

"Um," Rani starts back up again, and I have to move my foot away because it's shaking so hard that I can feel Rani's foot vibrating along with it. "It's not really ridiculous because actually I think that, um. Because I actually might, like . . . *like* . . ."

And then, Rani touches my shoulder. Like, she reaches up with her hand and touches my shoulder. It feels like she's shocked me. I'm electric. I'm on fire.

I'm gonna pass out.

And then—I don't know where it comes from, since my brain has left the building—I say, "Me too."

Oh my god.

Did I just tell Rani that I . . .

And did she just tell me that . . .

It couldn't have happened just like that, right?

I must've fainted.

It's not possible. That can't have been what she was saying.

But maybe it was.

Because now she's smiling. She's smiling, and looking

down. And I don't know what to do. I don't know what I'm supposed to do.

Our faces are so close that I can feel her breath on my skin.

So, I do something that I don't think my brain would approve of. But I do it so quickly that I don't even give my brain a chance to object.

I put my thoughts on pause.

I lean in.

And I press my mouth against Rani's mouth.

Her lips are warm and soft and I've never felt anything like this before in my entire life. I open my eyes, and she opens her eyes, and we're both looking at each other and kind of smiling as much as we can while our lips are pressed together.

I close my eyes again after a second but now I'm thinking, like, what if I'm doing this wrong? What if she didn't want me to do this? What if this was the worst idea in the history of ideas?

I sit up. Rani must see the look on my face, because she sits up too.

And then she turns away from me.

And walks back to her bed.

And gets under the comforter.

Oh, god. I scared her away.

I made everything worse like I literally always do. Now

she's across the room, and I don't know what happens next. Maybe I should go over there and apologize or ask if she wants to watch a makeup tutorial or—

But as I'm thinking this, she turns off the lights.

CHAPTER TWENTY-SIX

WHY did I do that? Why did I do that? Why did I do that?

I've been thinking about that moment in the motel room since it happened last night. We're in the car now, and it's completely silent. Not the buzzy kind of silence like the one between me and Rani yesterday, but the kind that makes it too easy to hear yourself think.

So, yeah, *now* my brain decides to show up. And it's just as confused as I am. I seriously don't know what I was thinking. I'm not Abby, you know? I'm not bold enough to just kiss someone as popular as Dylan and not freak out.

Not that Rani's like Dylan. I mean, she's way, way cooler. And nicer. And everything-er.

I know Abby would've told me to go for it, to kiss Rani. She would've said I had nothing to worry about. Abby's advice for everything was to just do it, but only because almost everything worked out for her in the end.

I don't know if I miss Abby, exactly, but I miss having a

best friend. That was, like, the biggest part of my identity, back when Abby actually cared about me. Having a best friend and knowing that I was also hers.

Being around Abby made me feel like I was glowing. I liked knowing that if someone asked her "Who's your best friend?" she'd say "Dalia" with no hesitation. That felt really good.

What I definitely *do* miss is how things would just sort of work out for me too when I was friends with her. How she could come up with some silly scheme and we'd be able to convince her parents and my dad to let us have a sleepover on a Tuesday, or something wild like that.

And now I don't have a Tuesday sleepover friend. I don't have a friend at all. I have literally zero friends. I'm going to go back to school with no one, because I had to go and— ugh, ugh, ugh—*kiss* the only friend I had.

I'm leaning against the door in the back seat, and I can see from the reflection in the window that Dhruv's asleep. Rani's just been scrolling through her phone with her AirPods in, and Alexa wouldn't even look at me this morning when we walked from the motel to the car. Not that I was looking at her, either.

In case you're keeping track, that adds up to a whole lot of silence.

We've been in the car for three hours now, and I've spent most of that time trying not to look over at Rani. I want her to talk to me, to say something. But I don't think she's going to. Or maybe I actually don't want her to. I don't know.

I'm mad at Rani, I'm mad at myself, I'm mad that I thought this road trip might even be the start of something, when instead it just feels like an ending.

But most of all, I'm mad at my dad. I mean, the more I think about it, the more I'm like . . . he did this to me. He's getting married to a woman I *barely know*, and he let me go on a road trip with her daughter. He *wanted* me to go. To "bond."

I almost scoff, thinking about it, about how ridiculous it is that he thought Alexa and I could ever bond over anything.

The worst thing about this car ride, though, other than the overwhelming awkwardness, is that this isn't even the last day of the trip. We're supposed to go to Coney Island tomorrow. We were saving it for last, since it's near where we live.

But honestly, I sort of don't want to go to Coney Island. I want to go home.

Not that home will be much better. Because, you know, the whole dad and Vanessa thing. But still. I just want to be completely alone. Not in a silent car with three people who probably hate me.

I look at my phone for something to do, and, of course, there are three new texts from my dad.

> Dad: I miss you!!!!!!
> Can't wait for you and Alexa to come home!!
> We'll all go out for bagels!!!!

The thought of eating a bagel right now makes me nauseous. He clearly has no idea how mad I am. If Rani were actually talking to me, I'd complain to her.

I wish there was *someone* I could talk to about all of this, but my mind is coming up blank.

Wait.

Maybe there is.

I go to send a new message, and I type in Sara's name.

If there's anyone I can talk to about everything, it'll be Sara. I don't really know what to say, so I just write:

> Me: something happened
> do u have time to talk?

For the next half hour, I check my phone every two seconds. And every time there's nothing. But finally, she texts back.

> Sara: i'm at work so i can't rn
> but let's please talk later!!
> are you ok????????

Great.

Sara's not free, Rani and Alexa aren't talking to me, and Dhruv's asleep, but he probably wouldn't want to talk to me either. There are literally zero people I can talk to.

I scroll through my phone to make myself look busy. I think about maybe reading back through my old texts with Rani, from before the road trip. Back when we were secret agents together and everything was good. But then I see Abby's name.

And even though the last thing Abby sent me was about the boy-girl party, maybe *she's* someone I could talk to.

But no. We're not friends.

She tried to *use* me to hang out with Cassie.

I shouldn't text her.

But I mean, there's no one else. Literally no one. And maybe, even though we're not friends, she'll still answer. Maybe it'll be like a reflex. Like, she'll just start typing out a response before she forgets that we stopped being best friends—or friends at all—months ago.

No. I'm not going to do it.

But maybe . . .

Before I can make some sort of silly Abby-related decision, Alexa turns the car off the highway and we pull into a rest stop.

"Fifteen minutes." she says. It's the first thing she's said all day.

I don't really have to go to the bathroom or anything, but I'm not going to sit by myself in the back seat, that's for sure. I want to get as far away from the car and everyone in it as possible.

There's a tiny little patch of grass on the far end of the parking lot, so I trek over there. I look back to make sure no one's following me, but of course no one is.

I take a deep breath and unlock my phone.

Am I gonna do this?

Abby's the only contact on my favorites list, because she made me add her when we first got our phones in sixth grade. So if I wanted to message her or FaceTime her or whatever, she'd just be a tap away.

I shouldn't do this.

But on the other hand, if I don't talk to *someone* about all this, my head might explode.

I take another breath. And another. But I only have fifteen minutes, so I stop at two breaths. I mean, I keep breathing. I just stop with the deep, panicked ones.

And then I press her name.

My phone rings, and I immediately want to end the FaceTime. What am I even going to say to her? We haven't had a real conversation in months.

The phone rings, and rings, and—

"Dalia?"

I don't know why, but something inside of me breaks. Seeing Abby's face on my phone makes me cry.

"What's going on?" The connection isn't great, so she freezes for a second. But there's worry on her frozen face.

And that's enough, just that look. Just seeing her face. I

can't help it; I tell her everything. I tell her about my dad and Vanessa, about meeting Rani at swim practice, about Rani's house in Hillcrest, about Alexa, Dhruv, Sara, the roller coasters.

The kiss.

I don't know what Abby's going to say, but I need her to know. And it feels so good to be talking, to not be holding in all of these secrets, that I'm not even worried about it.

"That's a lot," Abby says. But she doesn't say it like she's mad at me. She says it like she really means it.

I sort of laugh and sort of hiccup, then snort all my snot back up my nose and wipe my eyes. I know it's gross, but it's the kind of thing you can do in front of someone who knows you as well as Abby knows me. Or, knew me.

"Why didn't you tell me any of this before?" she asks.

"Because we weren't talking!" She looks down, away from her phone. And when she doesn't respond I say, "Like, because you were hanging out with Cassie all the time."

She looks up now, and I watch her shake her head on the screen. "Just because I was starting to be friends with Cassie and hanging out with her and stuff didn't mean I didn't still wanna be your friend too." She tucks a piece of hair behind her ear. "Like, we couldn't have been each other's only friend forever."

That stings. But I know she's right. Even *I* made a new friend. Well, until I ruined it.

Then she says, "But actually, Cassie and I are sort of in a fight right now."

I know it's none of my business, but I'm curious. "What happened?"

Abby sighs. "She basically told Sanjana and Grace that I cheated on Dylan."

"Did you?"

"Of course not! But I think Cassie has a crush on Dylan and won't admit it, so she just made it up."

"That sucks," I say.

"Whatever, Dylan and I are over."

"What?! Why?!" I've missed so much. But then again, she's missed so much in my life too: meeting Rani, my dad having a girlfriend, going on this trip.

Even though I caught her up on my life, the space between us starts to feel bigger and bigger.

"He wanted me to go to all of his lacrosse games, but I told him I have other things going on." Abby tosses her hair behind her shoulders. "I think he thought that he was my entire life. And, like, obviously I couldn't just drop everything to watch him play."

"So he broke up with you?"

"What? No," Abby says. "I broke up with him." Abby's always been the cooler and bolder one between us, and this is no exception. "Now, what are we gonna do about you and this girl?"

"Who? Rani?"

"Uh, yeah. I mean, you two *kissed,* so she definitely likes you." She says this in her planning voice. I love when Abby puts on her planning voice.

"Maybe, but she won't talk to me," I say. "I think she thinks it was a mistake."

"You don't know that! You have to talk to her!"

"I can't do that."

"Why not?"

"I'm not you," I say. "I can't just talk to someone I have a crush on like a normal person."

"You're not me," Abby says. "But I think that's why we got along so well." My heart drops when she says "*got* along so well" instead of "*get* along so well." But she's right. Even though we're talking now, it doesn't feel the same. It's not bad. Just not the same.

Abby keeps going. "You're *Dalia.*" She says my name like it really means something. "You just need to talk to her. Seriously."

I look at Abby on the screen for a second before I respond, her pixelated face twisted with concern.

"I missed you," I say, because it's true even if I don't want it to be.

"I missed you too," she says. "And actually, Dals, I wanted to say something."

I try to swallow but my throat is dry. I nod to let her know I'm listening.

"I just wanted to say that I'm really sorry," she says. "About Dylan, and about not sitting with you at lunch and hanging out a lot with Cassie and all that stuff. I know we haven't been best friends for a while, but, like, you still mean so much to me."

I smile with my mouth closed. I'm glad to hear her say it, and I know what she means. I think about when we were little kids and all the sleepovers we had, about playing with her dog, going to the park. Those memories are still good ones, even if we might not make as many new ones with each other.

I must be broken, because even Abby's nice words make me cry. But I manage to say "Thanks, Ab." I sniffle the snot up again and look back across the parking lot, where Alexa and Dhruv and Rani are walking out of the rest stop. "I think I have to go back to the car."

"Makes sense," Abby says. Then she puts a hand on her cheek and smiles with her mouth closed. "Love you, my Great-Dane-slash-dachshund."

I give her a watery smile and can't help but say, "You too, you Old English sheepdog."

The FaceTime ends, and I stare at my phone for a few seconds, as if Abby might still be there. Then I stand up and walk back toward the car. Somehow, things don't seem as bad as they did when we pulled into the rest stop.

I called Abby because I was desperate, but I think it was the right thing to do, even if I don't know whether we're best friends anymore. We've been growing apart. But who knows, maybe when we go back to school, we'll wave to each other in the hall. I hope so.

But sometimes, I think, it's good to have someone you know will always pick up the phone.

CHAPTER TWENTY-SEVEN

IT'S evening now, and we're crawling through New York City traffic. But things are pretty okay. After the rest stop, I felt calm enough to take a nap, and I slept for most of the ride.

Alexa stops the car in front of a beautiful old brick building. I'm not quite sure where we are, but we must be in a quiet part of the city. No one told me the plan—that would require actually talking to me—but I think we're sleeping here tonight.

We all step out of the car, and Dhruv pulls me aside.

"Hey," he says in a quiet voice, "I just wanted to talk to you for a minute."

"Um, okay?"

"I'm really sorry about what happened with Alexa," he says. "I know a lot of this trip's been hard for you."

And because Dhruv is being nice to me, and because I haven't spoken to anyone except Abby all day, I start to cry. I thought I gave all my tears to Abby on our FaceTime, but it turns out I have more.

"Dalia, no." Dhruv gives me a hug, but I leave my arms dangling. "Listen," he says, letting go of me. "I talked to Alexa while we were at the rest stop, and I told her that you two really need to talk."

Um, why would he do that?

The thing is, I actually *don't* need to talk to Alexa. I just need to survive the next day and then I'll be home on Long Island. Things will go back to normal, and I'll ignore her whenever I have to see her, and everything will be fine.

"Well," I say, crossing my arms, "she should talk to me, because I'm not gonna talk to her."

"Yeah, that's basically what she said." Dhruv raises his eyebrows. "Are you sure you two aren't sisters?"

He smiles a little, but I don't. If the mark of sisters is that they're mean to each other and ruin everything, then I don't want one.

I decide to change the subject. "Where are we?"

"Oh, right," he says. "We're at my boyfriend David's house. I figured this would be a good place to spend the night since it's in Brooklyn and it's only like a thirty-minute subway ride to Coney Island."

"We're *all* staying at your boyfriend's house?"

"It's pretty big," he says, but he must see the look on my face, so he adds, "You'll have your own room, so it's better than a motel."

He's got a point. I don't think I could share a room with

anyone tonight, even if our beds were ten thousand feet apart.

"Cool."

"Okay, but can you please try to talk to Alexa?" Dhruv asks. "I just feel like, I don't know, your situations are so similar. Maybe *you* can even help *her*."

"Um, maybe."

I think Dhruv takes my "um, maybe" as a yes, even though it's definitely not, because he wraps me in another hug.

I really, *really* don't want to talk to Alexa. I don't see how it could possibly help.

But I might have to.

David's house is even nicer on the inside than it is on the outside. I thought it was like his family's home, because he's probably around Dhruv's age, but now I'm not sure. The décor doesn't seem like something adults would pick out. The walls are painted super bright colors and the whole place is decorated with pictures of Dhruv and David and all of their friends, and there are rainbow flags and murals with drawings of boys kissing boys and things like that.

He must be, like, super rich, but it's not like Rani's mansion. I think David's probably lived here for a while, because everything seems cozy and comfortable and, well, lived-in.

It's pretty awesome.

So then this guy—he must be David—comes out of his bedroom to greet us. He's tall and wearing these amazing super-short red-and-white athletic shorts, and the first thing he does is run over to Dhruv, lift him off the ground and pull him into a huge hug.

"You two must be Dalia and Rani," David says, grinning and not letting go of Dhruv's waist. "Dhruv's told me so much about you."

I feel two things: the first is embarrassed, because David said my name and Rani's together, like we're some sort of duo, which we're clearly not. But I also feel pretty happy, because that means Dhruv's talked about me to David. And even though he's a college student and I'm just his friend's future stepsister, I think we might sort of be friends too.

David and Alexa chat for a minute, but I'm distracted by Rani—surprise, surprise. I've been avoiding looking too much at her, but I see her moving from the corner of my eye. When I turn my head, she's looking up at Dhruv and pointing at her phone. Dhruv scrunches his eyebrows, and when he looks down at his phone his eyes go wide.

Rani mouths *Tell him,* and Dhruv grimaces.

Oh. She must be talking about the makeup look she did for him. The secret the three of us shared. I know Dhruv wanted to tell David, but once he does, it won't be something that only Rani and I know. And then that'll be one less thing connecting us. Even though Rani's not talking to me, we're still bonded, from this secret, from this trip. I don't want that to go away.

When Alexa and David are done catching up, Dhruv rests his head on David's shoulder and says, "Do you want to see a picture from the trip?" My heart's thumping for Dhruv right now. If he's nervous, he's hiding it really well.

"Of course," David says.

I want to look over at Rani, to be connected by this again, to have our secret-agent-mission eye contact, but I'm too scared.

Dhruv does actually seem a little nervous as he hands David his phone. "Rani's a makeup expert," he says quickly, before David can respond. "And I actually asked her to help me workshop some drag looks. Not that I'm ever going to perform, and I mean, it's just a first go at it, but—"

David puts his hand over his mouth, then looks up from the phone. "This is amazing," he says to Dhruv. "You look amazing. And obviously you should perform. People *must* see this face." David squeezes Dhruv's cheeks, and Dhruv laughs and grabs David's hand. They beam at each other. David turns to Rani and says, "You made my boyfriend look so gorgeous."

"Uh, did you think you could get away with not showing me?" Alexa asks, smiling, and Dhruv holds his phone out for her.

She's totally impressed too, and now all three of them are oohing and aahing over Rani's makeup skills. I want to feel proud of her again, like how I did when she first showed Dhruv her zombie mermaid makeup. And I *am* proud of her. But I don't think I'm allowed to feel that way anymore, because I ruined everything with Rani.

After a minute, Dhruv laughs and says, "I'm so relieved."

That makes one of us.

"Did you think I wouldn't like it?" David asks.

"No, but I was still nervous."

I'm glad Dhruv feels better, and that he's not nervous about it anymore. I really am. But if Dhruv was nervous to tell his *boyfriend*—someone who obviously likes him or else they wouldn't be dating—I'll never be able to talk to Rani about what happened between us. I would be so nervous that my whole body would erupt in flames.

It's quieter in the room now, and Dhruv is resting his head against David's shoulder.

"Um, I'm really tired," Rani says, breaking the silence. "Can you show me where I'm sleeping?"

"Of course," David says, leading Rani to a room down the hall.

I hate to say it, but I'm relieved. I can't talk to Rani about the kiss tonight. Or even be in the same room as her. It's too much pressure.

"I'm, uh, gonna go to bed too," Dhruv says as David

walks back over to us. Then he does this really big fake yawn. "Yup, super tired. It's definitely bedtime for the old Dhruvster. I guess it'll just be you two okay good night bye." He pushes David back into his bedroom and closes the door with a little wave of his fingers.

Super subtle.

So now it's just me and Alexa. She's standing across the room from me, not looking my way.

I move to sit on the couch, because I'm not sure what else to do. It's a big blue sectional that looks like it's been sat on by a lot of butts. It's worn, but seems maybe almost loved? I know that's a weird thing to say about a couch, but it's sort of what everything in David's house feels like. He clearly put a lot of thought into making the whole place homey.

I tuck my legs under myself and look over at Alexa, who's now fully facing away from me. She might be looking at one of the pictures on the dresser, or she might just be avoiding me.

And then: "Dalia, I'm so, so sorry."

"What?"

She walks over to the couch and sits on the opposite end, tucking her legs under herself too.

"I feel like garbage," she says, putting her face in her hands. "I shouldn't have said anything about you and Rani, even if I thought it was a joke. If someone did that to me when I was your age, I'd never talk to them again. I only said it because I thought it was kind of cute that you have a crush on Rani. But seriously, I *really* didn't think anyone but Dhruv would hear it."

There's that word again. It's cool that she ruined my life because she thinks my crush is "cute."

Cute might be the worst word in existence. My crush isn't "cute," you know? It's not, like, a bulldog puppy. Well, maybe it would be if the bulldog puppy was the size of an elephant and it was sitting on my chest and I couldn't move or breathe or think about anything else. And I wish it wasn't like that, but it is.

So, I don't say anything.

"Listen, Sara told me you texted her earlier."

My heart drops. I mean, we didn't even talk about anything, because Sara had other stuff going on. But if she had been able to talk, I would've told her about kissing Rani. And then what? Would she have just blabbed everything to Alexa?

"Don't be mad at her, okay? She only told me because *I* told *her* about the fight we got into. She said you were maybe going through something, and that we should talk. You and me." Alexa takes her legs out from under her and sits cross-legged, leaning forward. "I feel so terrible. I never should've sung that song. I'm really, really sorry, Dalia." She looks up at me. "I know some things are off limits to joke about, and I should've realized that was one of them. And the worst part is that I remember what it was like when

I first had a crush on a girl. It felt like the most important and terrifying thing that had ever happened to me. Even more than when I had crushes on boys."

"Then you shouldn't have made fun of me! If you know what it's like, then you shouldn't have sung that song."

"I know, I know." She puts her head in her hands. "That was super immature of me. But I was hurt, I guess. Not by you. Just . . . yeah. I should've remembered what it felt like to be thirteen."

I don't think Alexa's problem is that she forgot what it's like to be thirteen. I think she forgot how to be a decent human being.

She sighs. "I really am so sorry. I forgot how big of a deal having a crush on someone can be. Especially if it's on a really good friend—"

"Please be quiet," I hiss, because Rani's just in the other room.

Alexa lowers her voice. "Have you talked to her at all today?"

I shake my head. "No, because yesterday, uh . . . I just don't think she's ever really gonna want to talk to me again. Which is fine, obviously. It's fine."

"Hm," Alexa says, like she really has to think about how Rani's never going to talk to me again. Cool.

We're both quiet for a minute, then she asks, "Can I tell you a story?"

I don't know if I want to hear it, but I don't feel like talking. So I nod.

"So, here's the thing. When I first got to college, I didn't have that many friends. Actually, I had no friends. Like, not a single one. And then I met Dhruv, and he was so funny and nice. You know those people who you just wanna be around all the time?" I do know, because that's how I feel about Rani. Well, not right now. But up until yesterday. "Dhruv's one of those people for me. And he would do all these little things for me, like make me mac and cheese the night before I had a test, or buy shampoo when I ran out."

She takes a breath. "I guess what I'm trying to say is that, to me, Dhruv is family. He's not 'like' family. He just is. Last year at college, that was the first time I felt like I was part of a real group, like, where people cared about each other and listened to each other. Dhruv cared for me in a way my mom never did, and it finally felt like I had a real home."

I don't say anything, so Alexa keeps going: "And that was part of the reason I was so mad at you this whole week— which was completely unfair, but yeah—because you were sort of a reminder of what it was like at home this summer, when things were so rough with my mom."

It's not fair that she's saying I'm a reminder of stuff at home for her. Because that's not my fault.

But I guess in a way *she* was kind of a reminder of the fact that my life will be completely different when I get home after this trip. So I understand, even if I don't want to.

Alexa looks right at me and says, "Something I realized when I was away at college is that when you're different, like if you're queer, you need to be able to choose the people you love. To choose your own family." Alexa sighs and rubs her temples. "Do you get what I'm saying?"

I shake my head, because I really don't.

She takes a breath and tries again. "Like, how our parents are getting married? They're choosing each other, and now we're gonna be a family."

I scoff a little, and Alexa looks up at me and smiles with her mouth closed.

"No, yeah, I get it," she says. "That's gonna be rough. But even if we fight with our parents, *we* can still be a team, you know? Maybe we can be our own little family too."

"But it's not a choice on our part. We're being forced into it. My dad didn't even *tell me* about it for six whole months. That's not a choice. That's, like, the opposite of a choice."

"Yeah, that was honestly really terrible of him, and I feel like maybe I should give him a stern talking-to." I smile thinking about Alexa yelling at my dad. Then I wipe the smile away, because that's an awful thing to smile about. "But what if it *was* a choice?" Alexa continues. "I mean, like, for us." She scrunches her face up as she says, "Dalia, I'm choosing you to be my sister."

"What? You can't just do that."

"Why not?"

"Because family isn't supposed to be mean." I know it sounds like something a little kid would say, but it's true. "Family's supposed to support you and not make fun of you when you have a crush on someone."

"You're not wrong," Alexa says. She looks off into the distance, like she's deep in thought. "What if we do a test run?"

"A what?" I ask.

She lowers her voice. "Talk to me about Rani. I wanna hear about her. And I'll give you advice and maybe you'll see that actually I wouldn't be a bad sister." She shifts on the couch. "*So,* what do you like about Rani? Why haven't you two talked all day? What happened?"

I look at Alexa. There have been so many times on this trip that she's been mean to me, or treated me so, so terribly. But I've also seen another side of her. She's different with Dhruv, and with Sara. She can be nice. And it feels really good when that niceness is directed at me. So, I decide to give her a chance.

I tell her everything that happened with Rani, the way we were watching videos and then talking and then kissing and how she ran back over to her own bed.

"So she hates me, right?"

"I don't think that means she hates you at all," Alexa

says. "I think that just means she got freaked out. Having your first kiss is a huge deal."

"I don't know if it was her first kiss," I mumble. But now I'm thinking about how maybe Rani's first kiss was with me, and I feel all nice and warm or whatever.

"It was *your* first kiss, right?"

"Yeah." Is Alexa going to judge me for that? For not having my first kiss until now?

"Then it was probably hers too," she says. "I didn't have my first kiss until I was a senior in high school."

Really?

She must see the look on my face, because she smiles and says, "It's true. You're clearly way cooler than me."

"No I'm not," I say, but I'm smiling. And then I ask, "But what do I do? About Rani?"

"I hate to break it to you, but I think you're gonna have to talk to her," she says. "It might be scary, but the only way she'll know how you're feeling and you'll know how she's feeling is if you talk. Because you still have a crush on her, right?"

My face gets hot. "Yeah?" It comes out as a question, but it's true. I definitely still have a crush on Rani.

I have a crush on Rani that's so big, I feel like *crush* isn't even the right word. My heart hurts just thinking about the way we joke together, about her Halloween makeup looks, about how she really likes hearing me talk about roller coasters, about how she felt comfortable enough with me to talk about her family and friends from home.

"Then tell her!" Alexa says.

"That's the same thing my old friend Abby said when I talked to her earlier." It feels weird to call Abby my "old friend," but maybe that's what she is.

"Sounds like a smart person," Alexa says.

"Yeah, she is." And if Alexa wants to try to be my sister, then I want to tell her the whole story. "I was actually in a really big fight with Abby this whole year. She was my best friend, and I guess kind of my only friend, but then she ditched me." I take a deep breath. "So, I don't know . . . "

"But you two made up?"

"Kind of? But I don't know if we're even best friends anymore."

"Do you want to be?"

"Not really," I say, before I can think too much about it. And once I say it, I know it's true. I don't think I want to be best friends with Abby anymore. It's weird to admit it, but I think we're just going our separate ways.

"The same thing happened to me with my middle school best friend," Alexa says. "Well, we stopped being friends when high school started. But we talk sometimes now."

"Really?"

"Yeah," Alexa says. "Not a lot, but it's nice. We were both obsessed with wombats when we were in middle school for some reason, so we'll send each other wombat pics if we ever stumble across them." I laugh a little at that. "Just because you don't want to be best friends with her anymore doesn't mean you can't still care about her, you know? And it doesn't mean you'll never talk again. I honestly don't know anyone who's still, like, best friends with the same people they were best friends with in middle school."

I don't say anything, but I really do feel way better about the whole Abby situation.

"But to go back to what we were talking about *before*," Alexa says. "You're going to have to talk to Rani. And if you need my help, let me know. I promise I'm not going anywhere." I don't look up, so she keeps talking. I like that she's taking the lead on this conversation. "Dalia, I don't want you to end up like me. Or like how I was this summer, I guess. I don't want you to be angry, or to stop caring. Because you clearly care so much, about so many incredible things. Like roller coasters, and your friends, and probably a ton of other stuff that I don't know about." I do look up at her then, and she smiles at me. "Don't let that stop. I'm worried that after this week you're gonna feel like you shouldn't care, or like you can't. But you *need* to. And the people you care about won't always leave. *I* won't leave. And I'm gonna try to be better. I promise."

And that's when I really start crying. I wish my tear ducts wouldn't do this to me, but I guess it does feels nice to let everything out.

It *is* sort of wild that after everything we've been through this week, and after how mad I got at her and how mad she got at me, Alexa still wants to try being my sister. I got mad, and she didn't go away.

We sit in silence for a minute. It's not the cold silence of the car earlier today, or the buzzy silence like with Rani last night. This one's different. It's warmer, cozier.

"So, what do you think?" Alexa asks.

"About what?"

"Did I pass the test run?"

I think about it. If family really is something you choose, then I guess Alexa isn't such a bad choice. Like, I can get mad at her sometimes, and I can think she's super annoying sometimes—and I definitely will—but yeah. She's trying. She realized she messed up, and she apologized.

Weirdly, I want to care about Alexa. And what's even weirder is that I think she wants to care about me too.

"Yeah," I say. "I think you did."

CHAPTER TWENTY-EIGHT

"**THIS** is a Coney Island–bound Q train," the automated announcer voice says. "The next stop is Beverley Road."

"All right," Alexa says when the announcement's done. "It's gonna be about a half hour before we get to Coney."

We're on the subway now. Alexa and Rani and I are standing up, holding on to a pole, and Dhruv and David are sitting nearby, fast asleep. Rani and I didn't talk this morning. We haven't spoken at all since the kiss.

The train starts and stops, and after a minute Alexa meets my eye. I don't like the look on her face. It's like she's planning something.

And then she quickly drops down into the seat next to Dhruv and David, completing the three-seat row.

"Whoops, looks like there're no more seats over here," Alexa says, even though the subway car is basically empty. "I guess you two are gonna have to sit over there all by yourselves." She points to the opposite end of the car.

I give her a Look, but when Rani turns to gaze out the

window, Alexa gives me a thumbs-up and mouths *You got this*.

Okay, it might just be the jostling us back and forth, but I'm pretty sure my whole body is shaking, like it was before Rani and I kissed. My insides feel like they're made of jelly. But it's time. I'm going to talk to her.

"Should we, um, go over there?"

Rani nods, and we walk toward the other end of the car, swinging from pole to pole to keep from flying away as the subway speeds toward Coney Island.

I sit down at a spot where there are only two seats, rather than a whole bench. Rani sits next to me.

"So, I just wanted to say that, um, that . . ."

"What?" Rani has her arms crossed in a very Alexa-like way, and refuses to look at me. Maybe this is a terrible idea. Maybe I should just cut my losses and try to find a new friend in the fall.

But Rani isn't just another friend.

So even though it feels like my heart might rip out of my chest because it's beating so hard, I say, "Rani, I like you. Like . . . *like* like you."

And then, Rani does the worst thing I could possibly imagine: She giggles. I want to dissolve into the subway floor and live the rest of my life as a puddle. Because of course she doesn't like me. Of course she thinks this is ridiculous, and she's probably going to tell all of this to Cassie when they're best friends in the fall and—

"Dalia, I like you too," Rani says through giggles.

This is too much for my heart to handle. "What? Then why are you laughing at me?"

"I'm—not—laughing—at—you." She struggles to get each word out through a fit of laughter. Then she takes a deep breath, and the giggles stop. "I thought you hated me!"

"WHAT?" I basically shout this at her, because that thought is so completely ridiculous. "Why would you think that?"

"I mean, because after we, like, you know . . ." She looks away, but I know she's talking about the kiss. "I ran away. I know I shouldn't have done that. I didn't mean to, I just thought I did something wrong and you were never gonna want to speak to me again."

"I thought *I* did something wrong and *you* were never gonna want to speak to *me* again!"

She looks up at me, shaking her head. "I tried to tell you that I had a crush on you so many times."

"What?!" I shout again.

She laughs. "Yeah! Like, I was gonna tell you when I was showing you the makeup I did for my friend for *Legally Blonde Jr*. I was gonna be like, 'Oh, you know how he talks about having crushes on boys in his makeup tutorials, well I actually have crushes on girls, and I have a crush on you.'" She turns away from me and looks across the train at an ad for a toothbrush. "I mean, that would have been silly, and probably not a great way to say it. But, yeah. I wanted to tell you."

"I didn't realize!"

"I didn't realize either! I mean, I thought *maybe* you might *possibly* like me, but I was pretty sure I was just telling myself that because I have such a big crush on you."

I put the heel of my hand on my forehead and shake my head, scrunch my eyes up, and laugh a little. My brain is about to explode.

I guess everyone who was telling me I should just talk to Rani was right. Because apparently, we were both trying to give each other hints but we were too wrapped up in our own individual brains. So, like, I had no idea what her brain was thinking, and the whole time it was sort of thinking the same thing as mine.

We both just look at each other for a second, but then I turn my attention to the sparkly black subway floor.

"Well, if neither of us are mad at each other," Rani says.

"And we both *like* like each other," I add.

I'm smiling so big, I think my mouth is going to fly off my face. Rani's smiling back at me. And my heart is pounding again but for the first time since we kissed it doesn't feel like the world is ending.

Rani yawns, but then she laughs again. "I promise I'm not bored! Just super tired."

She looks like she could just fall asleep right here, on the subway. She leans back in her seat, so we're both facing forward. And then . . . she puts her head on my shoulder.

Oh my god.

Rani's head is on my shoulder.

I'm even more frozen than when she accidentally stretched her legs out on me in the car, because this isn't an accident. She wants her head to be there. And *I* want her head to be there too.

Rani yawns again, and I can feel her jaw move on my shoulder. It's solid and warm. "Thanks for coming over to my house that first time after swim practice," she says sleepily.

"Thanks for coming on this trip with me," I say, and I think my face might cramp up from how big I'm smiling.

"Hey, kids," Alexa says, tapping my shoulder. I must've fallen asleep after Rani did. Alexa gives me another thumbs-up, and then points out the window. "Look outside."

Rani takes her head off my shoulder and stretches her arms, then we both turn around and kneel on the yellow and orange subway seats.

I think I'm going to faint, because the view is the most incredible thing I've ever seen. We're aboveground, and it's like we're flying through the air, and down below, all of these brightly colored rides and roller coasters rise to meet us. Then out in the distance, right past all the rides and stuff, there's the ocean.

I look over at Rani, who seems just as amazed as me. And as I stare at her—I think that's something I'm allowed to do now—I can't stop my face from smiling.

"This is Coney Island–Stillwell Ave," the automated announcer says. But then a real person comes over the loudspeaker and says, "Last stop, folks. Have a *fan*tastic day at Coney Island!"

And with that, we get off the subway.

The five of us head straight to the boardwalk, which is teeming with people. It feels completely different from every other amusement park we've been to. For one thing, you don't need a ticket to get in, just for the rides you want to go on. It's like the whole place is here for anyone who wants to go on some rides or swim in the ocean, which seems like pretty much the entire world. There are kids running around in bathing suits, adults who are maybe on dates laughing and eating hot dogs. It's magical.

"Let's get on line for the Cyclone," Alexa says, pointing to the wooden roller coaster off to the edge of the park.

"I think we're actually waiting for one more person," Dhruv says, looking down at his phone. He scans the crowds, and I follow his eyes.

No. Way.

"What?" Alexa turns to him. "No we're not. Who—"

"Hey!" Sara comes up from behind Alexa and wraps her arms around her.

Alexa's eyes go super wide, but then she must realize who it is, because she turns around and hugs Sara so, so tightly.

"Did you do this?" Alexa asks Dhruv when she's done squeezing the air out of Sara.

He smiles mischievously at me and Rani. "I thought it might be fun to have a Dorney reunion."

Alexa laughs and hugs Dhruv almost as tightly as she hugged Sara. "All right, *now* let's go on the Cyclone," she says, her arm around Sara's waist.

We all walk through a turnstile to get on line, and now that we're all together, I feel an intense need to tell them some Cyclone facts. "Did you know—"

"Here we go," Alexa interrupts, rolling her eyes. But she's also grinning at me.

I make a big show of clearing my throat, and then I continue. "Did you know that the Cyclone wasn't the first roller coaster built on this spot? It was actually this thing called the Switchback Railway, which was built in 1884. It was the very first roller coaster ever made in the U.S., and there's, like, real video of the railway, which is kind of wild because I didn't even know there were videos in 1884. And like it looks kinda silly because it's all these fancy 1800s people dressed in their going-out clothes and they're riding on this really gentle thing that's more of a train than a roller coaster." I take a huge breath. "And it was so slow that someone had to actually stand at the top and push the train down the track, because it wouldn't go by itself. Like imagine if roller coasters *now* did that. It would be so freaky. And, I mean, the Switchback Railway thingy was probably pretty boring to ride, but I guess if it hadn't been built, then we wouldn't have any roller coasters at all. It's like the roller coaster ancestor." I'm a little out of breath, and there's a pause where no one says anything. They all just sort of stare at me like I have four heads and each of those heads has four more heads sticking out of them.

But then Rani says, "That's so cool," and my cheeks get hot. But this time, I don't even try to hide it.

With all of us here, talking and laughing, the line goes super fast. And soon it's our turn to board.

We almost fill up the entire roller coaster train, which makes me weirdly happy. I like the feeling of all six of us together—Alexa and Rani and Dhruv and Sara and David and me—like we're this huge fun group that everyone else at Coney Island wishes they were a part of.

Rani scrambles into the car and I get in next to her. The ride attendant pushes everyone's lap bars down, and then we start moving.

"Here we go," I say, looking over at Rani. But she's not looking at me. She's staring down at our lap bar, and I'm worried I imagined everything on the subway and we're still not talking and Rani hates me.

Then she grabs onto my hand, even though we're not even close to the drop yet. And my hand starts to get all clammy and wet, but I don't want to move it. I don't want to scare her away now that we just made up.

But she doesn't let go for the whole ride, so I guess I don't really have to worry about that now.

After the Cyclone, we go on a few more rides, but it's ridiculously hot, so we all decide to change into our bathing suits and head down to the beach. It's super crowded, and everyone is playing Frisbee or building sand castles or just sitting out in the sun.

We make our way down to the shore, past huge umbrellas in every color of the rainbow, past people blasting music from speakers and dancing together. The music is so loud that it's vibrating in my chest.

When we get down to the ocean, I dig my feet into the sand and watch as the imprints of my toes fill up with water.

"Well, I'm just gonna run in," Dhruv says. "The water looks amazing."

Then David's like, "I'll race you," and they sprint into the water, splashing and falling over each other.

The rest of us stand on the shore, laughing.

"I'll watch your stuff if you three want to go in too," Sara says to me and Alexa and Rani.

"You don't wanna come?" I ask her.

Alexa rolls her eyes. "Sara's afraid of sharks."

Sara shakes her head and splashes a bit of water up at

Alexa with her foot, and some of it gets on me and Rani too and it's freezing and we all scream. Alexa waits for the next wave to come in and then she bends down and fills her hands with water and pours it over Sara's head.

Sara shakes her short hair out, spraying all of us with cold, salty drops of ocean water, then she pulls Alexa close. They kiss a little, out here, on the beach, in front of all of Brooklyn.

I look away, but Rani catches my eye and she's smiling and so then of course I'm smiling too. Grinning, really.

"You didn't wanna run in with Dhruv and David?" I ask Rani.

"I'm actually, um . . . I'm kind of scared of the ocean."

"*You're* scared of the ocean?"

I can't believe it. She's the first one in the pool at swim practice. The first one to duck her head under and start her laps. It's hard to imagine Rani being scared of anything.

She looks down at the sand that's being pushed and pulled by the waves. "But I'll go in if you go."

My eyes get wide.

Because, okay. It's not like I'm scared of the ocean. I'm not. I love going in the water. But usually I walk in slowly, letting each part of my body get used to the freezing cold, until I'm up to my shoulders and it's not that hard to just dive in.

But now I have a chance to be the one to help Rani be brave. She was the one who pulled my hand up on the roller coasters. She was the one who touched my foot first that night in the motel room.

I want to be the brave one now.

"You going in?" Alexa asks.

I nod, but then a big wave crashes on the shore, and the water splashes up my whole leg. It's freezing, and I shriek and run away from the ocean.

So much for being brave.

"It's! So! Cold!" I jump up and down and wrap my arms around myself.

Alexa walks toward me, but Rani and Sara stay where they are, feet in the water, watching Dhruv and David floating over the mellow waves.

"I can't do it," I tell her.

Alexa thinks about this for a moment. "You know," she says, out of earshot of Rani and Sara, "it doesn't get warmer the longer you wait."

She raises her eyebrows at me, and before I can respond, she runs all the way into the water, no hesitation.

I almost feel proud, watching her run in. I think about how she's a Long Islander, just like me. About how it makes sense that she likes the ocean too because we, like, live on an island.

I guess that's just another thing we have in common. And we have a lot in common, when you think about it. Me and my stepsister.

I walk back over to where Rani's standing.

I know that Alexa's right. That the water's going to be cold no matter what. That it's not going to magically warm up if I stand awkwardly on the shore. That sometimes you just have to run in.

"You ready?" I ask Rani.

"No," she says, laughing and jumping up and down in the shallow water.

I reach down, and my fingers brush against hers. And then I hold on.

She looks up at me, grinning, and squeezes my hand back.

"On the count of three," I say.

She screams as the water crashes on the shore and runs a few steps back, but I hold her hand steady.

"You have to count," she says. "I'm gonna chicken out."

"All right." I take a deep breath. "One . . ."

I always feel braver around Rani.

"Two . . ."

Maybe running into the ocean is just like going down the first drop on a roller coaster. Once you start running in, that's it—you're there. And in those moments, there's nothing else in the whole world.

"Three!"

I tug on her hand and we both run in, screaming, our legs carrying us past the breaking waves until all we can do is swim.

The water is so cold, it makes my head hurt, but it's exhilarating.

Going from a pool to an ocean is like going from POV videos to roller coasters. It's wilder, and it's messy and loud and sort of, like, I don't know . . . happier, maybe. More real, at least.

I dip underwater, the current loud as it rushes past my ears.

After this trip, I want everything to be different. And now that I'm underwater, beneath the freezing ocean, it feels like a real promise. Like I'm making a commitment to caring about other people with every part of me, with every inch of my body that's submerged. With my hair, my neck, even the tiny space under my fingernails.

When I emerge, I feel different, somehow. I don't know how to explain it, but I do. The ocean made it real, like how my whole world changed when I first went on Kingda Ka.

I reorient myself and spot Rani stretching out her long arms to swim, and I try my best to keep up with her.

And we swim together toward the people who, somehow, in one short week have gone from strangers to something like a family. One I'm excited to choose. Now they're calling us over to them, lifting their hands to welcome us into the gentle ocean waves.

CHAPTER TWENTY-NINE

"WHERE are you taking us?" I ask Alexa. We've been walking down the boardwalk for like ten minutes, and my whole body's sweaty and tired. We got out of the water and changed a little while ago, and I thought we were heading to some more rides or something.

Alexa turns to face me and Rani, then puts a palm to her forehead. "Don't be mad."

Oh no. "Um, okay?"

She slides her hand down her face. "I tried to ignore them when they asked to come today, but they didn't listen."

"Who?" I ask.

Then I see two people walking toward us. Two people who look a lot like my dad and Vanessa.

My eyes go wide, and Alexa gives me a guilty look.

"Dalia!" my dad shouts, and then he's running over to us. Which is completely weird, because my dad never runs.

He opens his arms like he wants me to hug him, but I take a few steps back. I don't even mean to, but I do. I accidentally bump into Dhruv, who puts a hand on my shoulder.

My dad scrunches his eyebrows.

I've been avoiding thinking about this moment, and now I have no idea what to say. I thought I'd have more time to figure it out.

My dad is here, standing in front of me. And I want to tell him how mad I am, but I can't find the words.

"Can't your old man have a hug?" he asks. "I've missed you so much!"

"You've got to be kidding me!"

"Alexa," Vanessa says, in the same warning tone she had at the pizza place and the bowling alley.

And that's when Alexa starts screaming.

"No. I'm sorry, but no." Now Alexa turns on her mom. "Did you know your fiancé didn't even tell Dalia about you until a few *weeks* ago? *Weeks.* She had to deal with all of this, every part of it—her dad dating someone, her dad *getting married,* having a stepsister—in less than a month. How is that fair?"

Dhruv squeezes my shoulder even tighter, and Rani moves closer to me.

"And you." She rounds on my dad. "Did you think you could just show up here and hug your daughter like nothing happened?"

Vanessa doesn't say anything, and my dad's eyes get

wide, but he tries to laugh it off. "Dalia's tough," he says. "She can get used to anything."

"Of course she's tough," Alexa screams, and my heart feels warm and sad and a million other things at once. "But she shouldn't *have* to get used to all of this, and especially not so fast!"

"Alexa, you do *not* need to raise your voice," Vanessa says.

"But if I don't, who will? You two literally just dropped all this information on us and then you were like, 'Go deal with it somewhere else!'"

Vanessa lowers her voice and says, "We can talk about this later."

"No, actually, we can talk about this right now," Alexa says, and Sara walks closer to her and grabs her hand. "You think *Sara's* the reason I've been so angry this summer?" Alexa says to her mom, but in a slightly quieter voice than before. "She's the only one keeping me calm." Sara rubs her thumb over Alexa's hand, like they're having their own silent conversation while this one's happening. "I can't take hearing 'Paula Weinstein did this,' and 'Oh, did I tell you Steve did that?' I didn't change this summer. I just know better. Sometimes I need you to be my mom. To treat me like your daughter, and not some random friend."

And then, something terrible happens: Alexa starts crying.

Vanessa doesn't say anything, and neither does my dad,

but they look at each other. Sara rubs Alexa's back, and no one's talking, and there's still so much that needs to be said.

So now it must be my turn.

Because Alexa defended me, and she told her mom what was bothering her. She actually *told* her mom about how she doesn't feel like she's always a mom to her.

And now I need to do the same with my dad. I need him to know how I feel. Because I can't keep holding it in.

"How do *you* feel, Dalia?" my dad asks, and there's an edge to his voice now.

Well. That's an opening if I've ever heard one.

It's now or never.

Alexa wipes her face and looks over at me, eyebrows raised. I can tell she's ready to keep yelling at him, but I shake my head.

And then, so quietly that even I can barely hear it, I say, "I'm kind of mad."

"What?" my dad asks.

So then I say it louder. "I'm mad at you!"

And now that the floodgates are open, I need to say everything.

"After Mom left, you *promised* you'd be there for me. You said we were a team." Tears prickle at the corners of my eyes, and I can feel my voice getting thick, but I need to keep going. "But how can we be a team if you don't tell me anything? If you just expect me to go along with your plan? You didn't even give me a chance to get used to any of this! You didn't even give me a chance to see how I would've reacted. Like, maybe I *could've* gotten used to it, but it all happened so fast. I had to figure everything out on my own."

I take a breath. And even though my throat is scratchy and my face is wet, I feel lighter.

I glance up at my dad, and his face looks like someone who just stepped on the world's sharpest Lego.

"Dalia." His voice cracks. "Why didn't you tell me all of this before?"

I look down at the sunbaked boardwalk. All I can manage is: "I didn't want you to be mad."

"Sweetheart, I wouldn't have been mad," he says quickly. "I want to know what you're feeling, even if you're mad at me." He takes a step forward, but doesn't reach out. I look back up at him. "I should've made that clearer. You can tell me anything, *any*time. We're a team."

I sniffle and rub my nose on my arm. "But *you* didn't tell *me* about Vanessa."

"That was wrong of me." He sighs. "Dalia, I'm so sorry. I should've told you about her the moment I knew she would be an important part of my life."

"Yeah," I say, scuffing my shoes on the boardwalk, "you should've."

"From now on, we need to be honest with each other. You have to tell me when you're mad, and I'll tell you about all the important things in my life. I promise."

I don't respond right away. Because you know what? Maybe I don't even want to be on a team with my dad, or with anyone else for that matter. I'd rather just have people in my life who I care about, and who care about me. I don't want to feel like I have to pick sides anymore.

I look up at where Alexa and Vanessa and Sara are standing. It seems like they've been talking too. Vanessa's saying something to Sara, and they're laughing a little. Alexa looks hesitant but calm, with her arm around Sara. She even smiles a bit.

Maybe we all need to be more honest with each other. Especially my dad and Vanessa. Like, they need to be more honest with us. But, yeah.

I mean, we're going to be a family.

And a family's different from a team. Like Alexa told me, it's the people you choose.

So I take a breath and say, "Yeah, that sounds good."

My dad beams at me. I give him a small smile back.

Vanessa and Alexa and Sara come back over to where the rest of us are standing.

My dad and Vanessa hold on to each other's hands, and Vanessa says to me, "I was just talking to Alexa and Sara, and I feel terrible."

Alexa moves to stand next to me. The others—Rani and Dhruv and David—have been watching all of this unfold, which is kind of awkward, but I'm still glad they're here.

"We didn't realize how hard this would be for the two

of you," Vanessa says to me and Alexa, "but we should've. We've been selfish." She looks into my dad's eyes all romantically (blech.) "But sometimes, falling in love makes you selfish."

Then they kiss (ew).

I look over at Rani, who seems super concerned, so I give her a little thumbs-up.

Because maybe things are on their way to being okay. I feel lighter, at least. And, I mean, maybe I'm still a little mad at my dad. Okay, more than a little. And I probably will be for a while.

But I told him how I feel. I got *mad*. And it . . . helped? Like, telling him all that stuff didn't make him mad at me. It didn't chase him away.

"Group hug?" my dad asks.

Alexa rolls her eyes, and Vanessa gives her a look. I don't know how much a group hug is going to solve, but my dad thinks they're, like, the cure for everything. So somehow, a moment later, the four of us are wrapped in an awkward mess of a hug.

Then my dad's like, "Come on, everyone in," and Rani and Dhruv and Sara and David join in, and we're a weird circle of arms and heads and long fish legs on the Coney Island boardwalk.

We let go after, like, two seconds, but then my dad holds out his arm again. I put my arm up too, and we kind of loosely side-hug. He's trying, I guess. And I like that *he's* the one who's going to have to work to regain my trust. Not the other way around.

When we let go, Alexa walks up to me and whispers, "If you want me to yell at them again, I can do that at any time."

She smiles at me, and I smile back.

"You two seem to be getting along pretty well," my dad says, eyebrows raised.

Alexa and I look at each other, then she puts her arm around my shoulder. "We're practically sisters."

I roll my eyes a little and try to duck out of her grasp, but secretly I'm super happy. Because I know it's true.

After that, my dad and Vanessa leave us to get some food, which is fine by me. I'm glad we got a chance to talk (or, yell), but right now I'd rather just be with everyone else.

"Maybe we should go on a ride?" I say once they're gone.

"How about the Wonder Wheel?" Sara asks, pointing to this giant Ferris wheel, which is the tallest thing in the entire park. I don't know as much about non–roller coaster rides, but it looks awesome.

When we get to the Wonder Wheel, there are two lines, one for swinging cars and one for non-swinging.

"I wanna go in one of the swinging cars," I say.

"I don't think I can handle that," Dhruv says, looking at the ride.

And Sara's like, "Me neither."

So, Alexa says, "What if me, Dalia, and Rani go on a swinging car, and the rest of you go on a non-swinging one?"

Sara high-fives Dhruv and David. "Go Team Non-Swinging Cars!"

The three of them enter the non-swinging car line, and Alexa, Rani, and I enter the swinging car line. We wave to each other from across the fence.

"Team Non-Swinging Cars is the best!" Dhruv shouts to us.

"Um, hello, have you even *seen* Team Swinging Cars?" Alexa asks. "We're clearly better."

Rani and I giggle at this. Maybe teams are okay some-times, especially when they're for swinging cars on the Wonder Wheel.

I can't believe how lucky I am, to be at Coney Island with all these people. I think back to the beginning of the week, when it was just me and Alexa and Dhruv and Rani. Back before I knew that Dhruv has a boyfriend and Alexa has a girlfriend and that family is something you can sometimes choose for yourself. And really, I don't think I could've chosen a better group of people.

Team Non-Swinging Cars boards the Wonder Wheel first, and then there's a swinging car ready for us right after. There are two rows of benches, so Alexa sits in the back, and Rani and I sit up front.

We start going up, creaking slowly along the steel beams. It's a calm ride, nothing like the Cyclone.

"This is nice," Alexa says. "I needed a little relax—"

And then she screams. Because we're being launched forward, swinging. It feels like a mistake. Like a screw came loose and we're going to plummet to our deaths.

We're all grabbing onto the wire on the side of the cage, but after a minute, it's back to a nice, gentle swing.

"Well," Alexa says. "Never mind."

The three of us laugh, and then it's pretty quiet, just the sound of the Ferris wheel starting and stopping and starting and stopping. Alexa was right—other than the occasional swinging, it's nice to just watch the amusement park below us and the ocean out in front of us.

Then, suddenly, we're at the very top. And there's nothing around us except cage and sky.

One whole side of my body is pressed against Rani, and she leans into me. My heart almost flies out of the Wonder Wheel.

"Remember when we were watching Boulder Dash at my house?" Rani asks so quietly that only I can hear her.

"Yeah," I say. Because of course. I could never forget.

"This is way better," she says. And then Rani leans over and kisses my cheek.

Rani. Kissed. My. Cheek.

I immediately put my hand up to where she kissed me,

and I never want to let go. My whole face is hot. I can't even look at Rani.

"Sorry," she says, "I just really wanted to do that."

"Don't be sorry," I say. And then someone's poking my shoulder. "Ow!"

I turn around, and Alexa's pointing at Rani, mouthing *Kiss her back!*

I roll my eyes, but I turn toward Rani and focus on her cheek. It looks so soft, and I want to kiss it more than anything in the world. So, I do.

Now Rani's the one whose face gets hot, but we're both grinning at each other.

She takes out her phone and opens the camera. "Everyone smile." She holds out her hand to take a picture, like she did the first time we watched the Boulder Dash POV together.

I barely even recognize myself on the screen, that's how big my smile is. Alexa's laughing, and giving me and Rani bunny ears.

"Team Swinging Cars for life!" Rani says, and we cheer.

It's a beautiful day, and the water is a deep, sparkling blue. If I really squinted, I could probably see all the way across the ocean.

I don't know for sure if it's possible for your whole life to change in a week, but I think it might be.

And then I do something I never could've imagined at the beginning of the trip. I grab Rani's hand. She squeezes my palm, and I squeeze back.

I look down at where our fingers are laced together.

All I wanted at the beginning of this summer was to make, like, one new friend.

But that didn't happen.

Instead, I got my dad to actually listen to me. And I got Dhruv and Sara. And a sister. And a girl who I *like* like and who *like* likes me back.

The car swings again, and the three of us scream.

I think I like this feeling best. Being on the swinging cars. Because you couldn't even try to put it in a POV video. No one could capture the feeling of swinging over Brooklyn, my screams mixing with Rani's and Alexa's.

And I think that's okay.

Our screams turn to laughter, and it really is better than any roller coaster POV video I've ever watched. Because I'm not just staring at a screen, alone and under the covers.

I'm living it.

ACKNOWLEDGMENTS

I'M the kind of person who dreamt of writing the acknowledgments for my debut novel when I was a little kid (we love an idiosyncratic child), but now that it's time to actually write them, my brain is empty. It's just cobwebs up there.

Which is partially due to the fact that this book was edited entirely during a pandemic. So of course, the first person I have to thank is my incredible editor, Ellen Cormier, who gave me the most thoughtful feedback imaginable during a time when having any thought at all was a miracle.

Thank you times a million to Jim McCarthy, agent extraordinaire, for truly just about everything. To quote Tina Turner, you're simply the best. I know you've told me not to apologize for all the anxiety-induced emails I've sent you, but I really am sorry, because those will never stop (lol). A huge thanks to Maria Fazio, Cerise Steel, Regina Castillo, Tabitha Dulla, Ashley Spruill, and the whole team at Dial and Penguin Young Readers for making this book beautiful and getting it into the hands of readers. To my cover artist, Marcos Chin: Thank you for bringing Dalia, Alexa, Rani, and Dhruv to life. And thank you to Zareen Johnson for reading this book possibly three times (?) and for giving me the best, most needed notes each time.

Thank you to Lena Kogan and Lylia Li, for proving that bisexuals make the best alpha readers.

So much love to my beta readers Andrea Patella, Cameron Appel, Flannery James, Julia Zeh, Linden from Camp NaNoWriMo, Louisa Melcher (stream New York Summer), Lucien Baskin, Sally Mann Kuan (who came up with Jay Walker and Dame Judi Finch), Sarah Leidich, Sarah Frankie Sigman, Shiraz Johnson, Sophie Brett-Chin, and especially Saskia Baskin.

Thank you to everyone listed for providing such incredible feedback, and for responding to my absolutely feral finsta post that started it all. Thank you to Angelo, for reminding me how much I love POV videos, and thank you to leg goblin Deb Lee for commiserating about publishing and for having powerful legs. Thank you also to Christina Li for even MORE publishing commiserating, and for reassuring me that these acknowledgements aren't too long (I'm still not sure if that's true). A lot of commiserating happening, I guess (we also have fun here).

I owe a life debt to all the YouTube channels that have posted (legal and maybe not as much) roller coaster POV videos. I've definitely watched more POVs than Dalia at this point (but don't tell her that). And thank you to Girl in Red (yes, obviously I listen to Girl in Red) for being the inspiration behind the song that Rani plays for Dalia in the car, and to Louie Zong, for the groovy instrumentals that helped me power through revisions.

To Ellen McLaughlin, thank you for assigning us the inner monologue prompt in playwriting class. That's where the original idea for this book came from, and I took it and ran with it.

I wrote most of the first draft of this book at the Port Washington Public Library, located on stolen Matinecock Land.

I'd like to offer an extra special thanks to the librarians in the children's room at the PWPL who didn't bat an eye when I, an overgrown child, would browse the middle-grade section by myself.

Thank you to Eliza MoHo and Lena D. for always making me feel comfortable, and for being an absolutely powerful queer Jewish couple. You were the people I was thinking of when I wrote the scene in Sara and Alexa's motel room.

Thank you to Rabbi Schacter for getting me thinking about water as a holy and restorative space during a Zoom discussion. And thank you to Vanessa Zoltan, along with Casper Ter Kuile, whose words have calmed me on many occasions, but especially while I wrote this book. When

Alexa tells Dalia that the water doesn't get warmer the longer you wait, that came from something Vanessa said on a podcast that really stuck with me. Thank you, thank you, thank you.

Thank you to my school-sanctioned social worker. I would not have been able to write this book if I hadn't processed things with you every Friday for the entirety of my senior spring.

Obviously, this acknowledgment is entirely anonymous on both ends, but I still remember what you said to me about knowing I could move on, knowing I could do great things, about seeing my name in a newspaper one day and just nodding to yourself, saying, "There's Jake . . . that makes sense." It meant more than you could know when you told me that you were proud of me.

To the teachers who have altered the course of my life: Ms. Leonard, who encouraged my love of writing; Ms. Zarkh, who tolerated my high-school self (and who told me that I write like I'm from the seventeenth century before there were standardized rules for capitalization—trust me, it hasn't Gotten Better); Dr. Alexandra Horowitz, who helped me realize that I'm better suited to sitting in front of a laptop than a lab bench; and Weike Wang, who helped me realize I could write fiction.

Thank you to Adrianne (and Ollie, of course)!

Thank you to my grandparents, and grandparent-adjacent people who I love so dearly.

Thank you to Zaidie, for being endlessly proud of me. Thank you to my Auntie Sally and Auntie Lucy for many, many book discussions, and for always giving me books for my birthday. Thank you to my Grandma Carol and of course my Nana Jae, who have loved (and did love) me unconditionally for my whole life. Your little Jakey Wakey wrote a book! Thank you to my Grandma Phyl, for letting me stay with you, for the Trader Joe's biscotti, and for regaling me with stories of the Feminist Press (along with Grandma Carol).

To my Popsie, who died while I was working on this book. He never got to know me as a queer adult, but based on how much he loved Rachel Maddow, I have to imagine that he would've loved me no matter what.

To my dad, for showing me how to spot a good bagel and a great book cover, and for teaching me the importance of kerning.

To my mom, my first editor, who's always willing to read a draft. Thank you for loving me unconditionally from when I was but a small bebe to now, when I am a large bebe (as Moira Rose would say).

To Zachy: my reading buddy, the most stylish kid I know, and the best baby brother a girl could ask for. I'm so glad you're in the target age range for this book—which means you BETTER LIKE IT AND MAKE YOUR CLASSMATES READ IT OK LOVE YOU FACETIME ME.

And, most importantly, thank you to the people who I've chosen to love, and who have chosen to love me in return.

To Daniela, thank you for keeping me company during all the late nights I spent revising on the googie hangout. Thank you for picking up my computer from the University District and for making me coffee and oatmeal and pancakes and for loving me as much as I love you. You are the person I couldn't even let myself dream about when I was Dalia's age. ¡EsTOY enamorada de ti! (This better make you cry or else!)

And to my best friends, my chosen family, the only people I would ever want to start a commune with—Ana Espinoza, Andrew Ross Gruber, Lena Vlada Kogan, Sabina Sethi Unni, Sally Mann Kuan (along with Coco and Tux Kuan), Sameer, Zareen Johnson—you are the best people I know, and I can't wait for eleganzas for years to come.

Finally, to the queer and questioning kids reading this, just know that there are people out there who will love you exactly as you are, and who will love whoever you grow up to be. I'm proud of you!!!! Also, yes, that weird feeling you have about your English teacher is definitely a crush.